RAVE REVIEWS FOR
ELAINE BARBIERI!

"A powerful story that evokes every human emotion possible . . . pure reading pleasure . . . a must read."
—*Rendezvous,* on *Tattered Silk*

"Ms. Barbieri's wonderful writing is a marvelous mingling of sensuality, passion, and adventure, combined with authentic historical detail."
—*Romantic Times,* on *Defiant Mistress*

"Uniquely different . . . Elaine Barbieri delves into the depths of the human soul and comes up with a winning novel."
—*Romantic Times,* on *More Precious than Gold*

"Elaine Barbieri shines with a story that brings tears to the eyes and enchantment to the soul."
—*Ann's World,* on *Wings of a Dove*

INFLAMED DESIRE

The sweet scent of her skin . . . the heat of her naked flesh pressed intimately close . . .

Gold Eagle covered her lips with his, drinking deeply. He savored the taste of her, finding it unmatched by any he had known. The shadows of the darkened room could not conceal the beauty of eyes the color of new spring. The semi-light could not dim the glory of tresses streaked with the color of sunset. It could not dull the gleam of flawless, white skin that inflamed his desire.

She was his enemy.

Gold Eagle's kiss deepened.

She would despise him if she knew.

His hunger grew.

The arms now clutching him close would repulse him when his secret was revealed.

Gold Eagle was seared by need.

Allowing her long moments to memorize his face, Gold Eagle adjusted his weight against her. She would look back on this moment and she would remember. . . .

EAGLE

Elaine Barbieri

LEISURE BOOKS   NEW YORK CITY

To my loyal fans, this one's for you.

A LEISURE BOOK®

January 1999

Published by

Dorchester Publishing Co., Inc.
276 Fifth Avenue
New York, NY 10001

ISBN 0-8439-4469-2

The name "Leisure Books" and the stylized "L" with design are trademarks of Dorchester Publishing Co., Inc.

Printed in the United States of America.

EAGLE

Chapter One

Mallory Tompkins was still fuming.

Turning her head toward the window, she attempted to dismiss the uncomfortable clatter of the rails and the bump and sway of the train as it rattled along the tracks. Beyond the soot-streaked pane lay a prairie white with snow although spring had almost arrived, a prairie that seemed to stretch on for endless miles without appreciable variation.

Where were the great herds of buffalo described as "darkening the plains with their incredible number"?

Where were the "painted Indians galloping across the land with an eye to every white man's scalp"?

Strangely, amidst all the protests, warnings,

and silent worry that had beset her before she had undertaken her journey, the thought had never occurred to her that she might become *bored*.

The train whistle blasted shrilly, contributing yet another cloud of grainy smoke to the icy drafts that penetrated the car, depositing sooty residue on all within. Mallory groaned and flicked a sharp particle of grit from her cheek. She had not bothered to make the acquaintance of the other passengers, a scurvy lot of bearded, booted, buckskin-bearing bumpkins whose interest in her did not go beyond a first, appreciative glance to assess the size and sway of her female portions.

Other thoughts occupied her mind.

Angry memory returned again to haunt her. She was still incredulous at her father's statements. She had always thought he understood that she wasn't like the other women of their set, that her days didn't begin and end with giddy chatter and the hope of making a good marriage. She had made no secret of her suspicion that her appeal to the eligible men of the social register was partially based on her father's position as one of the most influential and wealthy newspaper publishers in the country.

Mallory considered that thought. Not that she hadn't felt a strong attraction to a few of those fellows. There was Barry Lake, who was more handsome than any man had a right to be, and there was William Donnelly, whose sense of humor had amused her. She had been disappointed to discover, however, that they were no different than their peers—men who were either vain, pompous, or held their male gender in such superior regard that their interpretation of "a woman's place" nauseated her.

The sting of a greater disappointment returned. She had always told herself that her father wasn't like that. She was certain she had not mistaken his pride in her, a pride not based solely on her beauty, on which so many seemed to lay undue importance, but on her keen mind and quick grasp of current events, which set her apart from other women her age. She had thought he shared her loathing for the oppression of women, and that he understood and accepted her driving desire to prove she had as much to offer as any man.

How could she have been so wrong?

Incredulity still lingered in Mallory's mind. She would never forget the day she was faced with the truth, or the angry exchange that followed.

"You're not going!"

"I am!"

"You're not!"

The battle lines suddenly clearly drawn, Mallory remained stiffly silent as her father rounded his desk and approached her. Bearded and balding, Willis Tompkins was of medium height and slender build, but his common appearance did not negate the quiet authority evinced in a steely stare and uncompromising stance that were more intimidating than she dared acknowledge. He halted a few feet from her, his jaw so firmly set that it appeared to be made of stone.

"Don't look at me like that, young lady." Her father's voice rebounded against the mahogany walls of his office, although he spoke in a tone barely above a whisper. "It's out of the question. You are *not* going to the Western frontier—for any reason. I forbid it, and that's the end of it."

"You forbid it?" The words rankled. "I'm twenty-one years old, Father. I'm a woman, capable of making my own decisions about the direction of my future. You've always told me you're proud of my intellect. I want to make a contribution with that intellect."

"You can make a contribution here. In Chicago. The *Chicago Examiner* is a highly respected newspaper, and your weekly column has been very well received."

Mallory barely withheld a sneer. "Oh, yes . . . it's eminently successful. Fashion tips and social gossip have endeared me to every English-speaking woman in the country."

"You should be grateful for the strides you've made!"

"Limited success, with limited satisfaction!" Her expression suddenly ardent. Mallory continued, "The war's over, Father. Reconstruction continues in the South but the Western frontier is aflame. Treaties with the Indians have been made and broken. I've studied the reports coming out of the area, but they're so conflicting and the situation is so unclear. I'm sure the whole story isn't being told."

"I've assigned coverage of the frontier to some of the best men I have."

"Yes, reporters based hundreds of miles from any real Indian activity. They rely on military reports that even Washington can't seem to sort out. I want to go there and see what's going on for myself, so I'll be able to report the truth!"

"I already have reporters as close to the area as possible. It's winter. Travel to the extreme frontier isn't feasible. Besides, the military is against it. The tribes surrounding the outlying forts are rumored to be gearing up for an attack as soon as the grass is up in the spring. There's talk that a strong government force will soon be moving into the area. The situation is critical, and nothing is certain. The tribes are totally unpredictable. Savage depredations are an everyday occurrence." Willis paused. When he spoke again his tone was adamant. "I won't let you go. It isn't safe."

"You were a war correspondent. It wasn't safe when you reported from the thick of battle."

"That was different."

"Why was it different?"

"That was war."

"And this isn't?"

"Not yet, it isn't!"

"But you intend to send Harry Reese out there."

Willis Tompkins stiffened. "How did you know that?"

"So, you *are* sending him."

"Eventually."

"He's making plans to go as soon as the weather breaks."

"Harry Reese is an experienced reporter."

"I'm as good a journalist as he is!"

"But he's a man and you're a—"

Her father's hesitation was telling. Mallory finished the sentence for him.

"—and I'm a woman."

Willis Tompkins's face flushed. "That's right, you're a woman."

Mallory allowed that last thought to trail into a pained silence. She then forced a smile. "So . . . sadly, I'm only a woman. Then why did you encourage me to further my education?"

"Maybe that was my first mistake."

"Father!"

"Does it surprise you to know that I've wondered about that more times than have made me comfortable in the last few years? Most other young women your age have already married, settled down, and provided their fathers with grandchildren."

Mallory's forced smile twitched. "Grand*sons*, of course."

Willis continued with a warning squint. "You've turned down every eligible man within a radius of three hundred miles."

"Every one of those eligible males was so interested in looking down the neckline of my gown that he didn't listen to a word I said! If I was plain and stick-thin like Marguerite Waller, poor girl, not a one of them would have come panting at my door."

"My dear, it may come as a surprise to you, but there's much to be said for that panting. Without it, you never would have been born."

"Father!"

"All that aside, yes, I've done my best to encourage you. I enjoyed watching your natural intelligence blossom. I was proud that you never undertook a project without working as diligently as a man to make it a success."

"But I'm not a man."

"No, you're not, Mallory." Willis struggled with obvious frustration. "Somehow I suppose I've seen this moment coming for a long time. I thought if I ignored your restlessness, I might be spared stating the uncomfortable truth. I was wrong. My dear, no matter how difficult it is for you to accept it, or how inconsistent it seems for me to say this, the fact is that as a woman, certain opportunities will always be beyond you."

"Nothing I've ever attempted before has been beyond me!"

"I've seen to that, haven't I?" His meaning clear, Willis continued, "But this time you go too far. Mallory, dear, you've achieved so much more in a man's field than any other woman could. You have the ability to achieve even more, right here in Chicago, where it's safe, if that's what you want. Women look up to you. Your column is exceedingly popular."

"Oh, yes, I can take comfort in that, Father.

Reporting the fashion news from Paris is so very challenging."

"Women all over the country are envious of your accomplishments."

"My mind is going to rot!"

Willis stepped closer. He placed a firm hand on her shoulder, his expression unyielding. "You're intelligent and ambitious, Mallory. If you were a man, you'd doubtless already be on your way toward success on the frontier. But, you're *not* a man, and you must accept that there are inherent differences between the sexes which prohibit what you want to do."

"I'm curious. What are those differences, Father?"

"My dear"—Willis's patience was wearing—"as much as you would deny it, women are the weaker sex, perhaps not mentally, but physically. The Western frontier is rough—uncivilized and violent, unlike anything you've ever experienced. You're not equipped to handle yourself in that atmosphere."

"Where am I lacking?"

Dropping his hand to his side, Willis Tompkins showed true signs of exasperation. "At this moment, the track for the Kansas Pacific Railroad ends somewhere between Salina and Spring Creek. In order to reach the reported location of Indian activity, you'd have to travel through wilderness territory. You know nothing about survival under those conditions, and your riding skills are limited at best. How would you expect to get there?"

"Is that all?"

"No, it isn't." Mallory's persistence darkened her father's expression. "You have no experience with firearms—another skill that's necessary on the frontier if you expect to protect yourself. Also, because of your sex, you'd be a burden and a distraction to military personnel who already have more than they can handle in the area."

"Anything else?"

"Countless other subtleties too numerous to list!"

Mallory held her father's gaze for long moments. When she responded at last, her voice was level and emotionless. "Thank you, Father."

She turned resolutely toward the door as her father spoke his final words without equivocation.

"Mallory . . . I'm sorry."

Those words were still as clear in her mind as the moment her father had spoken them. Mallory reached for her reticule. Her expression firmed as she touched the bulge of the derringer within. She consoled herself with the knowledge that a more adequate firearm lay amongst her dainties in the suitcase above her head— and with the fact that she was now more accomplished than the average male in the use of both.

Also enclosed in her suitcase beside that firearm were copies of the most recent and reliable maps of Indian territory available to the public. She had memorized them.

As for her riding skills—Mallory suppressed a groan. She might have developed calluses in places she cared not to specify, but an intense course of instruction had left her confident that she was equal to any equestrian endeavor that might face her.

She had left a letter of explanation to her father behind her, and she was determined enough to promise herself she would not return until her reports from the Western frontier had been published under her own byline.

A screeching blast of the train whistle returned Mallory to the present with a start as a settlement appeared in the distance. She looked up as the conductor strode past.

"Salina! Next stop, Salina!"

A tremor of excitement turned Mallory back toward the window, where her gaze halted abruptly at the sight of a lone, mounted Indian standing motionless on a rise in the distance. Struck suddenly breathless at the sight, Mallory felt her heartbeat quicken. The supreme dignity and power of the image held in dark relief against the late afternoon sun was unexpected.

The Indian held his mount immobile without visible effort, appearing to scrutinize the progress of the train with a gaze as engrossed as her own. Strangely, she could almost feel his intensity. Her sense of loss was acute when the train traveled behind a rise and the Indian disappeared from sight.

Mallory struggled to calm the wild racing of her heart in a moment of sudden realization. Angry disagreements, protests, and uncertainties were now immaterial.

She had arrived at her destination.

Her adventure had begun.

Chapter Two

Brilliant sunlight glistened against the snow-covered terrain as Gold Eagle observed the progress of the train in the distance. He frowned when the engine whistle screeched, shattering the silence with a belch of angry black smoke that momentarily darkened the clear blue of the sky. Halting his mount's startled prancing with a gruff command, he watched, his scowl tightening as the train slipped momentarily out of sight behind a rise. Its resemblance to a large, black snake slithering rapidly into the safety of its den did not escape him.

The import of that thought lingered.

Icy gusts battered his face while warm rays of afternoon sun glinted on Gold Eagle's fair hair. Gold Eagle ignored those who likened its gold wash of color and his powerful expanse of shoulder to those of the fierce bird of prey whose name he bore. He knew his mastery in hunting and his ability to evade pursuit invited similar comparisons.

Gold Eagle was keenly aware, however, that it was the specter he posed in battle—blond hair flowing, pale eyes burning, and white skin painted with the colors of death—that had earned his name true notoriety. The pony soldiers wagered which of them would be the first to bring him down, but he had no fear. Secure in the greater destiny revealed to him in the sunlight of a sacred hilltop, he knew himself to be impervious to the white man's bullets—just as he knew he would one day lead his people to ultimate victory.

The train moved again into view, and Gold Eagle felt the resurgence of a strangely unidentifiable emotion. The image that had filled his dreams the previous night returned—a black snake attempting to elude him as it moved swiftly across the snow-covered ground. He recalled the intensity with which he'd pursued it, the inevitable capture, and the moment of pure elation he'd experienced when he held the serpent in his hands. He was not certain how it suddenly escaped him. His frantic search to recapture it went unrewarded, and as the dream faded, he knew a sense of loss that was with him still.

The passion of that dream tightened again within Gold Eagle. The resultant pounding of his heart puzzled him as the train approached the station on the horizon.

His clear eyes straining, Gold Eagle sought to see beyond the metal walls of the train. The track below him, gradually creeping deeper into Indian land, was the greatest threat his people had yet faced. His skin was white, but he did not think as a white man, and he felt the lack. He had heard rumors of a great general's proposed advance into the land of the Cheyenne, but he was familiar with the deceptions practiced upon his people. He could not be certain if that word had been meant to reach their ears.

The pony soldiers would know. Rumors would be buzzing behind the walls of the forts if such a force was awaited, but he was not privy to their talk—and those who were, were not to be trusted.

His quandary still on his mind, Gold Eagle turned at the sound of a familiar summons to see Spotted Elk riding rapidly toward him. He recognized the urgency in the warrior's approach. Something was wrong.

Gold Eagle wheeled his mount and spurred him into a leap toward the approaching rider.

Mallory paused on the step of the train. She had pictured her arrival in Salina, the last completed stop on the Kansas Pacific, in many ways. But never, in all her fanciful imaginings, had she expected to be greeted with a smile, a helping hand, and the words, "Miss Tompkins, ma'am, it's my pleasure to welcome you to Salina."

Incredulous, Mallory looked at the handsome soldier who guided her down onto the platform.

"Ma'am? You are Miss Tompkins, aren't you?"

Mallory responded cautiously, "I'm Miss Tompkins."

Touching the brim of his hat in a brief salute, the soldier continued with a broadening smile, "My name is Lieutenant Charles Moore. Your father wired Major Bullen that you'd be arriving, and he asked the major to see to it that you were met at the station."

Deftly retrieving her suitcase, the lieutenant took her arm.

Annoyance flared. Major Bullen was an old friend of her father's, and her father had obviously arranged for her to remain under his protective care. She should have expected it. She was surprised her father hadn't arranged to have her taken into custody and shipped back East on the next train.

Realizing that she just might have struck on the next step in her father's plan, Mallory scrutinized the smiling officer. He had a nice, honest face. It was probably absurd, but she couldn't help wondering if her father had requested that Major Bullen hand-pick the fellow for the job. The lieutenant couldn't be more well suited to distract her from her purpose—if she were the type to be distracted. She was sure his even features and athletic physique had turned many a young woman's head. He was also obviously well-spoken and polite, with a hint of mischief in eyes the exact shade of the dark hair partially concealed by the rakish tilt of his hat. And there was no doubt the lieutenant also liked what he saw when he looked at her. Of course, if she were to judge from her surroundings, *any* civilized woman would look good to him at this point.

The young lieutenant urged her gently forward, and Mallory brought her speculation to a halt with a final, determined thought. She saw no deception lurking behind the lieutenant's dark eyes—and, yes, he was a handsome fellow—but neither this appealing young lieutenant nor the whole of Major Bullen's army was going to succeed in sending her back to Chicago before she accomplished what she had set out to do.

Mallory began cautiously, "I didn't realize my father had contacted Major Bullen. I suppose he was worried about me. He didn't want me to come."

Lieutenant Moore nodded. "I can certainly understand that. The Indian situation here is unstable, to say the least."

"Really?"

"Yes, ma'am. So much so that the major has restricted civilian travel to the outlying forts, except in cases of extreme emergency."

Mallory ventured with casual deliberation, "Does that include reporters for major newspapers?"

"The presence of reporters and all other unnecessary civilian personnel is discouraged right now."

"Oh. I wasn't aware of that." Mallory's smile flickered. "I'm sorry my father put Major Bullen and you to so much trouble. I fully expected to make my own way."

Lieutenant Moore shook his head. "Ma'am, with all due respect, that wouldn't be wise. It isn't exactly safe in this country right now. I don't expect the Indians will act up until the weather turns warm, but there's no way to really figure them out."

They had crossed the street. They were standing in front of a poorly constructed two-story frame building, and they were looking down a narrow, unpaved thoroughfare that appeared to be the main street. She had never seen a more primitive site.

"This is the hotel, ma'am."

The hotel.

Lieutenant Moore looked apologetic. "It isn't up to Eastern standards. I suppose you're glad you won't be needing it. If you'll tell me whom you are visiting in Salina, I will be happy to escort you."

It was now or never.

"I'm not visiting anyone in Salina, Lieutenant."

Mallory did not miss the young officer's almost imperceptible stiffening, or the tone of his reply.

"You're not?"

25

"I'm looking for someone, you see." Improvising as she went along, Mallory continued with as earnest an expression as she could muster, "His name is Joshua Barnes . . . you wouldn't happen to be familiar with the name, would you? He's a young man, four years older than I am, which would make him twenty-five. He's not too tall, with brown hair and eyes and a friendly smile."

The lieutenant's demeanor did not change. "No, ma'am, I don't know him."

"He came out here last summer, determined to strike gold and make his fortune. I received a few letters from him, and then nothing at all. Father told Joshua that he was a fool to go into Indian territory, but Joshua was adamant. I'm afraid something's happened to him. I couldn't wait any longer, not knowing. Father didn't approve, of course, so I came out to find Joshua without his consent." Mallory took a breath, adding with fervor, "And I tell you now, Lieutenant, I don't intend to go back East again until I've accomplished what I came out here to do."

"Where exactly did you expect to find him, ma'am?"

"The last letter I received from him came from the area of Fort Larned."

"Fort Larned!" The lieutenant's expression grew grave. "I'd say that's about the most dangerous area in this part of the country right now."

"Why?"

"The Cheyenne have their winter camp not

26

far from Fort Larned. If there's going to be trouble in the spring, it'll probably start there."

"I suppose that means I'll have to get to Fort Larned and find him before the trouble begins, doesn't it?"

"No, ma'am, it doesn't." His manner suddenly formal, the lieutenant studied her from the top of her feathered hat to the tips of the delicate leather boots protruding from the hem of her fashionable winter coat. "That would take some hard riding into dangerous territory. It's not safe. And even if it were, you're not suitably attired. You wouldn't last an hour in the clothes you're wearing."

"I'll purchase whatever I need for the journey."

"I can't allow it, ma'am."

"I'm going."

"Ma'am . . ."

"I'm determined, Lieutenant." Mallory looked directly into the young man's eyes, speaking truthfully for the first time. "If you don't take me, I'll find a way to get there alone."

"I'll have to report this to the major."

"Do what you must."

"He won't stand for it."

"Short of putting me in irons, there's no way he's going to stop me."

"He might do just that."

Mallory managed a smile. "He might *try*, Lieutenant."

"Ma'am . . ."

"I'm going."

"Ma'am . . ."

Mallory raised her chin.

The lieutenant's silent groan was almost audible. "I'll see what I can do."

Healing smoke, blue and sharply scented, greeted Gold Eagle's nostrils as he entered Walking Buffalo's lodge. The low monotone of the aged shaman's chanting, the rhythmic hiss of the buffalo-hide rattle he shook in time with the ritual pattern of his dance, were both familiar to Gold Eagle. He had witnessed the power of the old Indian's healing ways in the past, and he did not question them.

The shaman turned slowly toward Gold Eagle. His bared chest was heaving from exertion, his gray hair limp with perspiration despite the frigid temperature beyond the walls of his shelter. He stared at Gold Eagle. He pointed a knobby finger abruptly toward a still figure lying in the shadows of the fire.

Gold Eagle looked at the man who lay covered from chest to foot, seeing the bearded, frost-bitten face of a white man. He addressed Walking Buffalo sharply.

"Why did you summon me? I have no place here."

Halting his dance, Walking Buffalo waved his hand across the fire with a practiced flourish, casting a handful of spirit powder into the flames.

Clouds of aromatic smoke filled the air between them, momentarily obscuring the sick man from view. Gold Eagle spoke irritably. "You waste your healing powers on a white man. You would save his life so he may return to the fort and repay your favor by shedding the blood of our people!"

"The eye of the eagle . . ." Walking Buffalo shook his buffalo-hide rattle with new vigor, his wrinkled face creasing into disapproval. ". . . The eye of the eagle is blind if he will not see. Close your eyes to the hatred within you, Gold Eagle. Come closer. Look harder. Gaze deeply, and you will see why you have been summoned here."

Resentment flared within Gold Eagle. He did not need to look at the man lying across from him. He recognized the kind of man the stranger was. He had seen the horse tied up outside. It was not a prospector's mount. Nor was it the mount of a soldier, or that of a settler. Carefully tied among several neatly bound bundles on the saddle were books—black books that were gold-edged—and he knew what that meant. This man was like the one who had come to the Cheyenne camp many years earlier, like the preacher who had come to reclaim the white boy said to be living with the Indians.

The taut planes of Gold Eagle's face sharpened. Eyes as gray as summer mist looked back to his youth, to the day he first saw the preacher. He remembered the enmity in the preacher's eyes and the hatred in his voice when he shouted that he would bring the wrath of the pony soldiers down on the village if the white boy was not returned to his own kind. He recalled the heat of the council that followed—his father's protests, his mother's tears, then his own anguished cries when the council was over and the preacher dragged him from his mother's arms.

And he knew that even if he should live to see one hundred winters, he would never forget the moment when the Cheyenne village disappeared into the distance behind him.

The memory of all that followed was seared into his mind.

The white man's world was more cruel than he could have imagined. "Young savage" that he was, he had not understood the preacher's use of a whip against his bared back when a word would have sufficed. He had not comprehended the preacher's tirades against youthful skills he had patiently learned, against a code of conduct he'd been carefully taught.

His two years with the preacher taught him new things. His fair hair crudely cut, his buckskins burned into ash, he learned to look and dress "as a white boy should." His hands beaten with a switch until they ran red with blood, he learned to eat and drink the way the white man did. Deprived of nourishment when he spoke the Cheyenne tongue, deprived of sleep if his lessons lapsed, he learned to speak and read and write the white man's words.

He was nine years old when he decided he would rather sacrifice his life than live one more hour in the white man's world.

Yes, he recognized the kind of man the stranger was.

Gold Eagle turned away from the motionless figure beside the fire. He halted as Walking Buffalo called out harshly, "You look, but you see only your own pain. Come back! Look again! This man whose life is almost spent brings you a gift that once escaped you. Come back, Gold Eagle, and see!"

Respect turned Gold Eagle toward the shaman as he crouched beside the fire. The old man's skin glistened with sweat as he waved his hand again across the billowing flames, urging as he did, "Look into the smoke with me, Gold Eagle. Come. See."

The ardor of Walking Buffalo's plea brought Gold Eagle to his knees beside the flames as the old man rasped, "The black snake that escaped you . . ."

Gold Eagle looked up sharply at Walking Buffalo, only to be reprimanded. "The answer does not lie in my eyes. It lies waiting to be revealed to you." Directing him again to the smoke, Walking Buffalo whispered, "See how you searched while the snake evaded you. Recall how you yearned to feel its skin against your palms. And see . . . see who will restore that joy to you once more."

It was there, in the smoke as Walking Buffalo said, the shadows of his dream unfolding. He experienced again the excitement of the chase, the joy of capture, then the despair of loss and the frenzy of his frantic search. But another shadow was appearing. It was the man by the fire. His hands were outstretched as he approached, and in them lay the object of Gold Eagle's desire.

The smoke faded from the darkened lodge. Gold Eagle's opposition dispersed with it.

He assumed a position beside the fire and waited.

She was a fool. Mallory berated herself. She had made such careful preparations for this journey. She had read, studied, memorized, learned skills she had never expected to possess . . . but she had failed to take into account the sheer, frigid desolation of the country into which she was to make her way.

A chill slid down Mallory's spine as she turned to look out the window toward the snow-swept prairie clearly illuminated by the silver rays of the moon. Primal, untamed . . . and so cold. The protective walls of the train had left her unprepared for the chill that had descended on Salina with the setting of the sun. She had recognized the accuracy of Lieutenant Moore's judgment when that icy dampness penetrated her fashionable coat as if it were made of paper. Her dainty boots were equally impotent to protect her against the dropping temperature, and when she looked into the young lieutenant's eyes, she had felt almost humbled by her inadequate clothing.

Almost humbled.

Experiencing that uncharacteristic emotion

only briefly, Mallory had waited until the lieutenant situated her in the best hotel room available and then went to wire his report to Major Bullen. Knowing she could not afford to wait for the major's response, she had found her way to the nearest store and purchased the crude garments now stretched out before her.

Mallory scrutinized the common clothes with a critical eye. Mallory Tompkins, the renowned authority on Paris fashions, was now contemplating conventional pioneer clothing in the form of shapeless woolen trousers and an oversized shirt, heavy boots and outerwear, a hat knitted in a style too horrendous to deserve a name, and *long johns*. The last garment's crude "trap door" had startled her at first, but it now amused her. Necessity was truly the mother of invention.

Mallory consoled herself with the thought that however dreadful an appearance she might make, she would be warm. It had taken her only a few minutes in Salina's cold to recognize the value of practicality.

Mallory withdrew her maps from her bag and spread them out atop her recent purchases. She didn't have much time. Lieutenant Moore was most likely awaiting a response to his wire at this very moment. She needed to make her plans.

Mallory followed the dotted lines that indicated the route of the Smoky Hill Stage Line. She could travel on the stage from Salina to Walker's Creek, where she would then head south to Fort Larned. She would find someone to—

Mallory jumped when a heavy knock on the door shattered her silent contemplation. She turned toward it, frowning when Lieutenant Moore answered her response. Silently cursing at his unexpectedly swift return, she pulled the coverlet up over the revealing pile she had amassed and replied, "Come in."

"Ma'am . . ." Lieutenant Moore advanced hesitantly into the room. He smiled and Mallory noticed the faint dimple that winked in his cheek. She frowned when he glanced at the rumpled coverlet. His gaze halted on the corner of the map protruding from it.

"You won't be needing any maps, ma'am."

Mallory's jaw tightened. "Won't I?"

"No, ma'am. I wired a brief report to Major Bullen. His reply was quicker than I expected."

"I'm sure it was." Mallory's smile was almost a grimace. "Let me preface what you're about to say with a statement of my own, Lieutenant. I don't care what Major Bullen has to say. I'm going to Fort Larned!"

"Yes, ma'am, you are."

"I am?"

"With the escort of the U.S. Army in the person of Lieutenant Charles Moore and detachment." Lieutenant Moore shook his head. "I don't know what your father said to Major Bullen, but my orders are to get you to Fort Larned as soon as possible, to help you conduct your business there, and to escort you back to Salina

34

before the weather turns so you may board the train back to Chicago."

Stunned, Mallory managed, "Those are your orders?"

"Yes, ma'am." Lieutenant Moore's smile broadened. "And I might add that I'll be honored to carry them out."

Mallory struggled to regain her composure. "That's kind of you, lieutenant. I suppose it's kind of Major Bullen as well to guarantee my safety, but I want you to know that I don't intend to repay those kindnesses by compromising my mission in any way."

"I don't expect that you would."

"Nor do I intend to leave before the weather turns if I'm not ready."

"I suppose we can cross that bridge when we come to it."

Discomfort nudged at Mallory. This was too easy. She pressed, "I want to leave soon."

"Yes, ma'am."

"Tomorrow morning."

"That's fine." Lieutenant Moore glanced again at the ungainly pile under the coverlet. "I see you've already bought more suitable attire."

Damn! He didn't miss a trick.

Mallory raised her chin defensively.

The lieutenant continued, "An early start is preferable. My men and I will be ready at six A.M., if that's not too early for you."

"I'll be ready."

"In the meantime, it would be my pleasure if

35

you'd join me for supper." He added, "It would be my *great* pleasure."

Too easy . . .

Mallory reached for her reticule. "I *am* hungry."

She placed her hand on the lieutenant's arm as he drew the door closed behind them. Mallory looked up at him to see a familiar sparkle in his dark eyes as he said, "If you don't mind my saying so, you're a very beautiful woman, Miss Tompkins. I'm going to be the envy of Salina tonight."

And if she were plain and stick-thin, like poor Marguerite Waller, he'd probably be cursing his luck.

So, all men were alike, after all.

She supposed it didn't matter. Whatever he was thinking, he'd change his mind when he found out that almost everything she'd told him was a lie.

The stranger's breathing was labored.

Many hours had passed, long hours while Walking Buffalo continued his healing ways, but the stranger was not responding. The camp was now silent beyond the hide walls of the lodge, and a glance up through the smoke hole overhead revealed a glimpse of night sky where the stars shone brightly. Gold Eagle had waited impatiently through the long hours for revelations that had not yet come.

The stranger stirred.

Gold Eagle's heart thudded unexpectedly

when the stranger's eyelids fluttered, then lifted at last. He saw the confusion in the man's eyes, the pain and the weakness, and he saw the shadow of death.

Responding to instinct, Gold Eagle moved closer to the stranger. When he spoke at last, his words were unplanned and unexpectedly sincere. "You need not fear. You are among friends."

The stranger's gaze met his. His hands fluttered weakly, but he made no attempt to reply.

"Who are you? Why are you in the country of the Cheyenne?"

The stranger's hands moved again, but he did not speak.

Gold Eagle pressed, "Why do you come to this camp?"

The stranger formed a cup with his hands. He raised it shakily to his lips.

Recognizing an Indian sign commonly used, Gold Eagle poured water from a pouch nearby and put the cup to the stranger's lips. The man sipped breathlessly, then responded with a weak downward sweep of his palms.

The Indian sign for thank you.

With sudden comprehension, Gold Eagle responded, "You cannot speak."

The stranger nodded his right index finger beside his head in affirmation.

"What are you doing on Cheyenne land?"

The stranger signed again.

"You were lost?"

The stranger's signs grew weaker, his

breathing more ragged. Gold Eagle glanced up as Walking Buffalo moved to his side from his position across the fire. The shaman's expression confirmed Gold Eagle's opinion that the stranger would not last much longer.

An unexpected touch on his arm returned Gold Eagle's attention to the dying man as the fellow's hands moved weakly, speaking a desperate plea as clearly as the spoken word.

. . . In pouch . . . name . . . my wife . . . tell her I die . . .

Gold Eagle felt the man's despair.

. . . my children . . .

Gold Eagle could not respond.

. . . tell them I love . . . tell them . . .

The stranger's hands fell silent. His breathing stopped.

Gold Eagle looked down for silent moments into the stranger's motionless face. A man whose name he did not know had come to him with a special purpose. And now he was gone before it was revealed.

Walking Buffalo's ritual chanting continued behind him as Gold Eagle walked out into the clear night. Unmindful of the cold, he approached the place where the stranger's horse was tied. The frigid wind whipped him viciously as he removed one of the black books from the saddle. In the bright, silver rays of moonlight, he opened the first page to read, "Journal of Matthew Bower, Botanist."

Untying Matthew Bower's horse, Gold Eagle walked it the short distance to his lodge and secured it there. Taking the remainder of the black books in his hands, he entered the shelter and closed the hide flap behind him.

The fire burning within illuminated the carefully recorded pages as he started to read.

It was still dark outside.

The rough texture of her new clothing chafed at the delicate skin of Mallory's neck as she made her way down the hotel corridor toward the landing. She knew she was a ridiculous sight in bulky attire that erased every trace of the fashionable woman who had come to Salina the previous day. However, it took only the first icy blast of wind when she reached the street and saw her entourage assembling to assure her that on this occasion, appearance was the least of her concerns.

At her side in a moment, Lieutenant Moore took her bag.

"Good morning, ma'am. You needn't have carried the bag down. I was about to come up for you." His gaze swept her appearance. She thought she saw a flicker of a smile before he continued, "It looks like we're going to have a cold ride before the sun rises, but I don't think you'll suffer from the temperature in those clothes." He tipped his hat. "Ma'am, you look right fine."

Liar.

Mallory couldn't help smiling. In her brief acquaintance with the lieutenant, she had learned that the young fellow was no fool. At dinner the previous evening, he had shown himself to be an intelligent conversationalist, a congenial companion, an accomplished flirt, and a truly appealing man. She liked him.

Mallory responded, "Good morning, Lieutenant. To set the record straight, yes, it's cold and you were right about the clothing; and, to the contrary, you're too generous with your compliments. There was a mirror in my hotel room. I know how I look."

"Ma'am, to set the record straight"—the lieutenant's eyes twinkled—"you're the only woman I know who could look as fine as you do in those clothes."

Mallory's smile broadened. "You give me new respect for the perspicacity of the U.S. Army, sir."

The twinkle brightened. "If you'll follow me, your horse is saddled and waiting."

Proceeding a step behind the lieutenant, Mallory halted abruptly and stared at the monstrous brute awaiting her. Black with a white blaze on his forehead, the animal was by far the largest and most intimidating horse she had ever seen.

"I wouldn't let Tartan's size fool you, ma'am. He's strong and dependable, and he's a gentleman. I don't doubt he's as pleased as we all are to be traveling with you. Isn't that right, men?"

The chorus of assent that came from the four mounted soldiers a short distance away was unexpected.

"Miss Tompkins, I'd like you to meet Corporals Hodge, Bell, Whittier, and Knoll."

Mallory scanned the men assembled. They were a varied group: Bell seemed to be barely out of his teens, while the others appeared to range in age from twenty to thirty-five. Two were mustached, the others clean-shaven. The common denominator among them was the blue uniform they wore and their expressions of homesickness and respect when they looked at her. The lieutenant had doubtless related to them the story she had told him about the fictional Joshua Barnes. They admired her courage and loyalty to a man who did not exist.

Her conscience nagged.

Making a proper response to Lieutenant Moore's introduction, Mallory mounted without assistance, then turned to see true esteem in Lieutenant Moore's eyes.

"You sit a horse well, ma'am." He mounted his own horse and pulled up beside her, suddenly sober. When he spoke again, his earnestness somehow touched her.

"Ma'am, my men and I will do what we can to make the journey comfortable for you."

He was sweet fellow. If she regretted anything since embarking on her quest, it was the necessity for all the lies she had told him.

But this was no time for regrets.

Suddenly annoyed with herself, Mallory spurred her horse into motion.

Chapter Three

A brisk afternoon wind buffeted the wild terrain, bending the denuded branches of trees in a nearby wooded copse, but Matt Bower's steady pace was unaffected. Woolen trousers were tucked into his boots to ward off the chill, his heavy coat was buttoned securely, and a fur hat was placed squarely on his forehead. He reached down unconsciously to touch the rifle sheathed on the saddle as he scanned the trail ahead. He was keenly aware of the gunbelt that rode low on his hips, and the knife also secured there.

Matt Bower was a well-educated, dedicated man—and a man who traveled well armed.

Gold Eagle *was* Matt Bower. His disguise was complete. He wore Matt Bower's clothes. He rode Matt Bower's horse. He knew almost as much about Matt Bower as the man had known himself, thanks to the meticulous botanist's detailed journals. Not a single day's entry was missing from the inception of Bower's journey. Even the long days while he wandered lost on the frozen prairie were included. He had terminated his entries only when his frozen fingers could no longer function.

Gold Eagle was satisfied that the time he had taken to study the journals was well spent. He had come to know Matt Bower, to feel his spirit. As his posthumous acquaintance grew, an unconscious kinship with the man expanded inside him.

Matt Bower had come to the Indians on a mission resulting from a chance encounter. A conversation with an army doctor who had served on the frontier convinced him that Indian healers were able to effect cures with native medicines in cases where the white man was ineffective. Bower became convinced that the herbal remedies those Indian doctors used needed to be defined and recorded for the benefit of all mankind. He had sacrificed his life for that cause.

Gold Eagle's eyes narrowed. Such honorable intentions were in direct contrast with the activities of the white men Gold Eagle knew, men who often put the "savage" to shame with their violence and cruelty. From the first entry in Matt Bower's journal, however, it was evident that he was not one of that breed. He had recorded his open approach to the northern tribes and his request for their help. Gold Eagle was amazed that Bower had been accepted by tribes who distrusted most white men. He could only assume that the botanist was allowed to travel freely on their land because his selfless heart shone in his eyes.

From his writings, Gold Eagle learned that Bower's inability to speak hindered him little. Bower was impressed by the sign language that formed a common means of communication among all tribes. Learning it with uncommon speed, he apparently put it to good use in dealing with the healers of the Blackfoot, Pawnee, Shoshone, and Crow. It seemed to matter little to him whether these tribes were enemies of each other. They were not *his* enemies.

Recorded meticulously in the black books were the results of Bower's findings. Each plant used in healing was skillfully sketched and identified in careful, even columns. Beside the drawings were listed the ailments for which the plant could be used, and the method of treatment. Samples of each herb were carefully packaged and labeled in separate envelopes. In all that Bower had done, Gold Eagle recognized a brilliance that far surpassed the mind of the average man, as well as a steadfast commitment to be revered in whatever world the botanist chose to travel.

But for all his brilliance, Matt Bower had made a fatal error. He had failed to heed the warnings of his Indian hosts. He hesitated too long before beginning his long journey home across the unfamiliar prairie. That mistake, and the snows that followed, cost him his life.

Gold Eagle considered that thought. He did not doubt that destiny had delivered the dying Bower to his camp. His dream vision had clearly announced the import of Bower's arrival. He sensed that the train, following the track that snaked its way into Cheyenne land, had somehow brought him both challenge and solution.

Full comprehension of that challenge was not yet his, but it was clear that the solution was Matt Bower.

Gold Eagle squared his broad shoulders under the uncomfortable white man's clothing he wore. There was little danger in his present disguise. Matt Bower had traveled in the north. He could be known only by reputation in this area. Bower's journal references to Fort Larned had made that point clear.

Gold Eagle almost smiled. Nor would he be recognized by the pony soldiers. Few had succeeded in getting close enough to be able to identify him, and the few who did had not lived to tell the tale. He knew that even were that not so, with his hair carefully confined with a leather thong and his face free of paint, he bore little resemblance to the man most soldiers knew. His identity would not be challenged, and Bower's known handicap and his preference for communicating in Indian sign language eliminated the need for lengthy explanations he might not be able to provide.

His plan was to enter the fort on the pretext of being lost. Then he would listen and learn if the rumors of a military advance against his people were true.

Gold Eagle savored the moment of reparation soon to come. For the first time in his life, his white skin served a purpose. He would take advantage of his white skin; then he would turn his red heart free.

That thought spurring him onward, Gold Eagle increased his pace. His time on the trail was coming to an end. It was not much farther. He would reach the fort by nightfall.

She was finally warm again.

Mallory glanced around the small room she had been assigned after their weary entourage arrived at Fort Larned in mid-morning. Hours had passed since then, but the memory of the torturous trail remained. The frigid temperatures and interminable miles of snow-swept terrain had pointed up the folly of her original plan to attempt the journey alone. It had also impressed her with the extent of the burden she had inflicted on the men ordered to accompany her.

On the positive side, Mallory's heart warmed at the thought of the surprisingly comfortable friendship that had developed between her and Lieutenant Moore. Choosing not to add to the lies that pricked her conscience each time the lieutenant turned a sympathetic glance her way, she avoided the subject of the fictitious Joshua Barnes. She had decided early on that she liked Lieutenant Charles Moore. By the time their journey ended, she had developed a true affection for the man, and a sense of ease with him that belied their short acquaintance.

She had grown comfortable with the men in his detachment as well. She recalled with a smile the young, beardless face of Corporal Robert Bell, who confided that he had left his home in Ohio to fight the Indians as soon as he turned eighteen the previous year. Tall and lanky, he had a quality of youthful exuberance about him that she found endearing. She had been shocked, however, at his offhanded enthusiasm when he spoke of "getting himself his first Indian scalp." The other men's acceptance of his remark had somehow surprised her even more.

"Just talk" had been Lieutenant Moore's excuse for Bell's comment, but a chill had run down Mallory's spine nonetheless.

The other men had been quieter, seeming to prefer to let Corporal Bell do the talking during their limited opportunities to converse. She sensed that they held back for fear of frightening her, but it was clear that they believed her quest was doomed to failure.

Her thoughts wandering, Mallory unconsciously assessed the sparse furnishings in her temporary quarters. She assumed they were better than most at the fort, since one of the lesser officers had been ordered to relinquish the room for her use. Desperate to shed the chill that had worked its way into her bones, she had wrapped herself in the army blanket provided and settled herself into the broad bunk bed in the corner as soon as the door closed behind her. She had been surprised to find the bunk more comfortable than she expected, and despite the lack of the luxury to which she was accustomed, she had slipped into a truly restful few hours of sleep.

The room's other furnishings were adequate, consisting of a wooden washstand, a scarred chest, and a nightstand on which a stained-glass lamp rested. The small, pot-bellied stove in the center of the room, however, was *divine*.

It had not taken Mallory long to settle in, but it had taken her even less time to realize that she had underestimated the vastness of the Western frontier. When Fort Larned finally appeared in the distance, she had comprehended for the first time the meaning of the phrase, "an outpost at the end of nowhere."

Nor had she realized that women were so scarce in this wilderness that the only females she would see in Fort Larned would be those openly referred to as "half-breeds."

Mallory had frowned her disappointment upon learning that the fort commander had been called away temporarily. Her disappointment had been compounded when she met Captain Arthur Tierney, who had been left in charge in the commander's absence. A good-

looking fellow, Tierney had dark hair, light
eyes, a compact muscular frame, and a high
opinion of himself, which she suspected was severely over-inflated. His references to the Indians were denigrating and imperiously
expressed, and the blood lust in his tone had left
her speechless. She didn't like him.

It hadn't taken Mallory long to discern something else, as well. Captain Tierney wanted to
impress her. He had invited her to sit at his table in the dining hall that evening "if she were
rested enough to attend." She had received the
invitation while she was still exhausted and de-
sirous of nothing more than a warm bath and
a comfortable few hours' sleep, but she had
known she wouldn't miss the opportunity for
the world.

Mallory gazed out the rear window of her
room as she awaited her escort to dinner. Her
first day at Fort Larned was coming to an end
with a breathtaking display of a glorious red
and gold sunset reflected against the snow's
shimmering surface. Looking beyond the fort
walls, she saw an endless sweep of sky the likes
of which no Chicagoan could ever imagine.
Beautiful. It was hard to believe at that particular moment that so much blood had been shed
under that sky, and that such a deadly battle
raged for the land below it.

Turning back to the washstand mirror, Mallory scrutinized her appearance. Instead of the
warm bath for which she had longed, she had
made do with kettles of hot water delivered to

her washstand by a shy "half-breed" woman named Penelope. With the cinders of her journey washed from her hair, the fiery strands glowed in the limited light. Her skin was clear and unmarked from the cold, except for the strip of irritated skin at her neck where her rough traveling coat had rubbed the flesh raw. She noted that her delicate features showed little sign of the strain of her journey, and that the green gown, which matched the color of her eyes, lay surprisingly unwrinkled against her slender curves. She looked good. It amused her momentarily that although she had so ardently disdained the importance placed on her beauty in the past, she was now poised to employ it to full advantage.

Turning at a knock on the door, Mallory responded. She smiled at the sound of Lieutenant Moore's reply. She snatched up her coat and, slipping it on, opened the door. Placing her hand on the lieutenant's arm, she walked out into the yard.

The long trail had come to an end.

Gold Eagle drew his mount to a halt before the gates of Fort Larned, anticipation causing his heart to pound. Fearless, he studied the sturdy enclosure, noting that torches flickered from within although the sun had not yet set. He looked up as a sentry called out to him from atop the wall.

"Identify yourself, stranger."

Gold Eagle's eyes narrowed. He resisted the

tight smile that played at his lips as he removed his unfamiliar woolen mittens. His mind silently replied, *Look closer and see who I am! Your rifle is in your hand. Shoot! This is your chance, for if you do not shed my blood now, I am certain to shed yours.*

His gaze intent on the sentry's rifle, Gold Eagle signed a very different response.

His wordless reply going unnoted, the sentry demanded more harshly, "Identify yourself, I said!" The rifle tilted toward him as the command reverberated in the twilight air, "Identify yourself now!"

Contempt knotted tight inside Gold Eagle. He could almost see the fellow quaking.

"I'm warnin' you one last time!"

Another head appeared beside the sentry's. Signing again, Gold Eagle touched his thumb to his chest; then, holding his hands diagonally in front of him, he passed the right under the left.

Gold Eagle repeated the motions as the second sentry frowned, then muttered, "Hide . . ." Then speaking more loudly, the fellow declared, "No, he's not sayin' 'hide'. He's sayin' he's lost!"

Gold Eagle felt satisfaction surge as the first sentry demanded impatiently, "What are you talkin' about, Nevins?"

"That fella's usin' Injun sign language."

"Hell, why would he do that? He ain't no Injun!" The first sentry looked back at Gold Eagle suspiciously. "Why don't he just answer?"

Gold Eagle placed his hand over his mouth,

then cupping his palm, motioned as if to push out words that would not come.

"He's sayin' somethin' about talk."

Gold Eagle signed the word, "no," then signed "talk" again.

"No. . . . talk . . . He says he can't talk!"

An authoritative voice from behind the gates entered the exchange, demanding, "What's going on out there, Private?"

The first sentry turned back to respond, "There's a big fella outside the gates, sir. Corporal Nevins here says he's speakin' with Injun signs, sayin' he can't talk. He wants to come in."

"Is he an Indian?"

"No, he's white."

"Is he alone?"

"Yes, sir."

The silence was brief. "Let him in."

The gates slowly opened. Gold Eagle rode inside, noting as he dismounted that soldiers were beginning to gather in the yard. He heard the scattered whispers.

"Hell, he's a big fella, ain't he?"

"Makes up in size for not bein' able to talk, I expect."

"Wonder if it's his brain or his tongue that don't work."

Snickers sounded as an officer stepped forward and addressed him.

"My name is Captain Tierney. I'm in command of this fort. Who are you and what are you doing here?"

Gold Eagle removed Bower's leather purse

from his pocket. He withdrew a card and approached the officer.

"Stay where you are!"

Gold Eagle halted.

"Get that card, Corporal Walker."

A heavily freckled soldier standing nearby took the card from Gold Eagle's hand and handed it to the officer. Captain Tierney read it and looked up. "This card says you're a botanist, and that you're mute. Is that right?"

Gold Eagle nodded his index finger beside his head.

"What's he saying? Who else understands him?"

"I do." The soldier called Walker spoke up. "He said yes."

"What's a botanist doing out here?"

Gold Eagle extended his hands edgewise in front of him, right hand higher than the left as he raised and lowered them with rapid twists of his wrists.

"What's he saying, Corporal?"

"He says he's working."

Enjoying the officer's frustration, Gold Eagle signaled with a tremulous motion of hands and arms, then with sharp, cutting movements. The officer demanded irritably, "What's he saying now?"

"He says he's cold and he's hungry. He wants somethin' to eat, Captain."

"Too stupid to talk, but not too stupid to beg for food . . ."

"I don't think you're being quite fair, Captain!"

The unexpected interjection of a female voice turned Gold Eagle toward the woman who emerged from the shadows of the yard. She advanced toward them, another officer walking behind her as she continued with an unmistakable air of disapproval, "This gentleman is mute, but that doesn't mean he's stupid. His card identifies him as a botanist. That's a respectable occupation. I would think it wise for you to treat him with the courtesy he deserves."

The woman stepped fully into the light and Gold Eagle's eyes narrowed. The glow of lamplight danced on hair no less brilliant in hue than the flames reflected in the startling green of her eyes. She looked directly at him, smiling as she added, "You can see by his demeanor that he's a civilized, educated man who's far from ignorant." Gold Eagle sensed that the intent of the woman's smile was to chastise the captain for his harsh remarks, but that knowledge did not lessen the unexpected heat it raised inside him as she continued, "But even an intelligent, educated man who can't speak is able to feel hunger and cold. My suggestion would be that Mr.—" The woman hesitated and turned back toward Tierney. "You have his card, Captain. I would appreciate it if you would introduce him to us."

The captain's jaw was tight. "His name is Bower, Matthew Bower . . . Botanist *extraordinary*."

The woman laughed unexpectedly, "Well, if

that's what the card says, I guess he is extraordinary! But you were just being facetious, weren't you, Captain Tierney?"

Gold Eagle remained motionless as the woman walked closer to him. At close range, it was clear to see that she was beautiful in the way that white women sometimes were. Her pale skin was smooth and unlined, and her features fine. Her lips were soft and full. They quivered almost imperceptibly when she extended her hand toward him.

"My name is Mallory Tompkins, Mr. Bower. I'm pleased to meet you. I was just as hungry and cold as you are when I walked through those gates this morning, so I suppose we have something in common."

Gold Eagle realized something else at close range, as well. The quivering of her lips and the sparks that glowed so clearly in her direct gaze were reflections of her barely controlled fury. With surprise, he realized that she was incensed at the officer's treatment of him. This slight, white woman was attempting to protect him! He almost laughed.

Awaiting his response, the woman held his gaze.

The spontaneous heat within Gold Eagle expanded as he reached out to accept the hand she offered him.

He enclosed her hand in his, and the heat surged to flame.

*　　*　　*

Matt Bower's hand closed around hers, dwarfing it with its size, and Mallory barely restrained a gasp. She sensed in that instant a supreme energy held forcefully in check, and a strength that could easily crush the hand he then relinquished with a nod of his head.

Uncharacteristically silent, Mallory struggled against a sudden inner quaking. There was something about this man. She was certain it wasn't his proportions, although the height and breadth of him were almost overwhelming at close range. Nor was it his chiseled features, so emotionless that they could have been carved of stone. She had certainly known more handsome men than he.

Mallory studied the stranger a moment longer. It was his eyes. They were a clear gray, and as cold as ice. Yet, when he looked at her, his eyes seemed to—

Mallory's throat tightened, and she took an instinctive step back. Immediately regretting her impulse, she raised her chin, smiling once more. She turned toward Captain Tierney to see that his face was unnaturally flushed, and she cursed her impulsive behavior. She despised Captain Tierney's ignorance and intolerance, but she couldn't afford to turn him against her.

Looking back at the silent botanist to see that his gaze had not left her, Mallory attempted to dismiss the annoying fluttering within her. She suddenly wondered what had possessed her to leap to his defense. It was obvious that the man

56

was more than capable of taking care of himself.

Mallory addressed Captain Tierney with a cajoling smile. "Mr. Bower would probably like to freshen up before eating. I don't think he'll mind if we don't wait for him."

Suddenly realizing she had all but forgotten Lieutenant Moore's presence behind her, Mallory turned back to take his arm. Ignoring his frown, she drew him along beside her. She slipped her other arm through Captain Tierney's in a conciliatory gesture when she reached his side, but the captain did not respond.

Mallory silently cursed. Despising the sickening sweetness of her tone, she added, "I've been looking forward to a chance to get to know you, Captain. You're an expert on this area of the country. I know you'll be able to help me find Joshua."

Still no response.

Mallory gritted her teeth. She had made a mistake, all right. In the heat of the moment, she had cut the obnoxious captain down to size, and he was determined to make her pay for it.

Captain Tierney addressed her formally, "Miss Tompkins—"

Mallory interrupted, "I'd prefer that you call me Mallory . . . if I may call you Arthur."

Silence.

Mallory forced herself to add, "I suppose Major Bullen's interest in my visit is due to his *close* friendship with my father. Their acquaintance goes back to the war, long before my father's newspaper chain became one of the largest in the country. The major was concerned for my safety and wanted me to conclude my mission quickly so I would be able to return home as soon as possible. I regret the unfortunate burden that places on you, but I know Major Bullen will be pleased to hear that you've been generous with your help."

"Miss Tompkins . . ."

"Please call me Mallory."

The captain's stony expression twitched. He turned abruptly toward the freckled soldier nearby. "See to it that Mr. . . . Bower gets a place to stay and something to eat, Corporal Walker. I'll talk to him later."

Taking the lead, Captain Tierney drew Mallory along with him toward the dining hall.

Straining to concentrate on the stiff conversation that followed, Mallory felt the heat of Matt Bower's gaze following her. The quaking within her started anew.

She had never met a man who affected her so . . . so . . .

Who was this Matthew Bower?

She had to know.

"Follow me."

Gold Eagle ignored the young corporal's command, choosing instead to watch the woman's progress across the fort yard. He had felt the heat of her, and she had felt his. She had defended him, and she had then sensed a need to defend herself *against* him. Her instincts were keen. She was also bold, courageous, and clever. It was clear to see that she had regretted her defense of him when Captain Tierney revealed his anger. He could not believe she cared for the man. She had seen the distaste she barely concealed when she spoke to him.

Gold Eagle scrutinized the captain's arrogant stride. The captain had made no effort to conceal his contempt for his visitor's disability. But the captain was a fool and Gold Eagle felt little threat from him. The other officer was the one to watch, the one who had stood silent behind the woman and to whose arm she first turned before leaving. He had seen the way that officer looked at Mallory Tompkins, and then at him.

"Follow me, Mr. Bower."

Ignoring the young corporal's request, Gold Eagle allowed his gaze to linger on the three departing figures. A deep voice spoke mockingly from the group of soldiers gathered nearby.

"Maybe you'd better talk a little louder, Walker. This botanist can't talk. Maybe he can't hear, neither."

"You ain't funny, Hayes!"

"Maybe you're right, Hayes!" another soldier added with a sneer. "A botanist. Hell! I wonder if that fella even knows what the word means!"

The freckles on his youthful face standing out against his sudden flush, Walker stepped aggressively toward the heckler. "Maybe it's you who don't know what the word means, Archer!"

Archer's bulky frame stiffened. "We was only

havin' a little fun. There ain't no need to get hot under the collar." His jaw jutted out belligerently. "But if you want to make somethin' of it, I'm ready whenever you are."

Unwilling to surrender his view of Mallory Tompkins until she disappeared through the dining hall door, Gold Eagle turned back toward the heated conversation in progress. He had not missed a word. Nor would he forget it. He looked squarely into Archer's face.

"What're *you* lookin' at?"

Responding in Gold Eagle's stead, Walker spat, "I'd say he ain't lookin' at nothin' much."

"You little—"

Taking a step between them, Gold Eagle planted himself in front of Archer. Frowning, he signed a harsh comment.

"What did the bastard say, Walker?" Archer's face flamed. "I ain't afraid of no *botanist*. Tell me what he said!"

"You don't want to know." Turning toward Gold Eagle, Walker barely restrained a smile. "Let's go, Mr. Bower. These fellas have had enough fun for the night."

Leading his mount behind him, Gold Eagle followed Walker toward the stable. When they turned out of sight of the others, the young corporal halted abruptly and faced him with a grin. "What did you call him?"

Gold Eagle signed again.

Walker laughed aloud. "I wasn't sure. I ain't never seen nobody sign 'jackass' before."

Walker took a few steps more, then turned

toward Gold Eagle again. When he spoke this time, his voice was a whisper.

"What in hell *is* a botanist, anyhow?"

Her breath rising in frosty puffs into the night, Mallory left the dining hall and strode stiffly across the fort yard toward her quarters. For a moment she fancied that it wasn't really her breath visibly freezing on the chill air, that it was, instead, steam from the anger boiling inside her.

Turning to Lieutenant Moore, who walked silently beside her, she blurted, "Charles, I ask you honestly, did you ever meet a more perfect ass in your life?"

"Mallory . . ." Lieutenant Moore's smile flashed even as he glanced back toward the doorway through which Captain Tierney had just disappeared. "He could've heard you."

"I don't think I care." She paused. "You didn't answer my question."

"No."

"No what?"

"I never met a more perfect ass in my life. But I think Captain Tierney was telling the truth when he said he'd never heard of Joshua Barnes."

"Of course he was telling the truth!" Catching herself, Mallory added, "He . . . he would've gotten himself into trouble if he had lied. But he went out of his way to make sure he volunteered no other information at all!"

"He was angry. You made a fool out of him

in the fort yard when you defended that stranger."

"The poor man needed defending!"

"I doubt that."

Mallory's eyes widened. "Don't tell me you approved of the way Captain Tierney spoke to Mr. Bower—or the way he allowed his men to speak to him!"

"Of course I didn't!" The lieutenant's tone grew suddenly intense. "The men behaved badly and Captain Tierney's attitude encouraged them. There was no excuse for their behavior—but that didn't mean that you should have stepped in."

"No one else did!"

Charles paused, his eyes searching hers. "Tell me something, Mallory. Did Bower look disturbed by the way the men were talking?"

"No, but he—"

"He can't talk, but he can hear, so why do you suppose he had so little reaction?"

"He was a gentleman. He didn't want to contribute to such boorish behavior."

"Really?"

"He was too humiliated to reply."

"Did he look humiliated?"

"No, but—"

"He didn't *care*, Mallory."

"Of course he cared! They were ridiculing him because of his handicap! The man couldn't reply. He was defenseless against them."

Charles's expression tightened. "That man never had a defenseless day in his life."

"What are you saying?"

"Listen to me, Mallory." Gripping her arms, Charles held her immobile. "Bower wasn't embarrassed and he wasn't upset."

Mallory felt herself flush. "Are you trying to say he was too cowardly to resent what was said?"

"No."

"Well?"

"Did you take the time to look at him? He didn't care what those men said. It was as if they were speaking about someone else, not him. I'd say the only emotion he felt was contempt."

"I'd say his contempt for them was well deserved."

"You're missing my point."

"Am I?"

"You put yourself in a difficult position with the captain for no reason."

"I had a very good reason."

"You're wrong!"

Mallory's flush deepened. "I don't usually like being told I'm wrong."

"Even when you are?"

"I wasn't! It was a matter of principle. The poor man is mute. He couldn't respond, and they were ridiculing him!"

"You said that already."

"Charles, are you trying to make me angry?"

"No, Mallory, I'm trying to remind you of the reason you came here."

Mallory stiffened. "I don't need reminding."

"I think you do, especially if you expect to get

anyone here to cooperate with you so you'll be able to find out what happened to your friend."

"I don't see how one thing relates to the other."

"Yes, you do."

"Charles . . ." His hands were biting into her arms, and Mallory had suddenly had enough of the conflict between them. "I don't want to talk about Mr. Bower anymore."

"You're going to have to if you want to straighten out the situation you've gotten yourself into." Charles moved closer. She could feel his warm breath on her cheek. When he spoke again, his voice was a husky rasp. "Your first priority is still to find out what happened to Joshua Barnes, right?"

Conscience stabbed her.

"Mallory?"

"Yes."

"*I* want you to find out what happened to him, too."

Mallory could not reply. She could see the sudden zeal in Charles's dark eyes. His face was so close to hers that she could taste his sweet breath. She felt his restraint as he whispered, "I want you to find out what happened to Joshua Barnes so you can put your concerns about him behind you. Until that's done, I won't feel free to speak openly about the way I feel about you."

Mallory swallowed. She hadn't expected this. Charles was a friend. She shook her head unconsciously. "You hardly know me, Charles."

"I know you better than you realize."

"No, you don't."

"I know you're intelligent, brave, and one of the most determined women I've ever met."

Mallory's smile was weak.

"You're honest . . ."

Mallory's smile disappeared.

"And in case you aren't aware of it, you're beautiful."

"Not that again."

Charles smiled. He had a wonderful smile. She couldn't deceive him any longer. "Charles, I want to tell you about Joshua Barnes."

"I don't want to hear it."

"I want you to know, Charles!"

"It doesn't make any difference what you tell me about him." Charles was so close that his lips were almost brushing hers. "I want your business here to be finished and forgotten. I just want to make sure that you don't forget me, too."

"I couldn't forget you, Charles! You're my—"

"Don't say it!"

"Don't say what?"

"Don't say I'm your *friend*."

Mallory stared at him.

"I don't want to be your friend. I want to be to you what Joshua Barnes was to you."

Trapped, Mallory said, "No, you don't."

Charles whispered, "I'm not going to ask you what you mean by that. I don't want to know."

"Charles . . ." Mallory avoided his gaze. "You told me yourself that you've been on the frontier for almost a year. You probably haven't spoken to a civilized woman since you came here. I expect you'd feel the way same about the first one you saw."

"I'm not homesick."

Flushing, Mallory forced herself to say, "I'm not ignorant of the ways of men. You need a woman. If there were any available, you wouldn't feel so intensely."

"There are always available women, Mallory."

Mallory's gaze jerked up to meet his as Charles continued, "I'm twenty-eight years old. I've known a lot of women, but I've never met another one who made me feel the way you do." His endearing smile flashed again. "All that, and I haven't as much as kissed you."

Mallory offered weakly, "You'd probably be disappointed. I'm not all that proficient."

"I don't believe it."

Mallory almost smiled. "A challenge isn't going to work, you know."

But Charles wasn't smiling. "What *will* work, Mallory?"

"Oh, Charles . . ."

How could she fight the appeal of such a dear man? Hardly realizing her intent, Mallory offered her mouth to his.

Accepting her lips with unexpected passion, Charles drew her into the shadows as he crushed her close. He tasted good—so male and hungry for her. He smelled good—of the outdoors and faintly of men's cologne. His arms were warm and familiar around her, and the swell of his arousal raised a responsive warmth

66

inside her. She felt his hands in her hair. She allowed him to draw her closer, only to be stunned when he suddenly drew back from her.

Holding her a measured distance from him, Charles whispered, "I'm sorry. I took advantage of you."

"No, you didn't."

"Yes, I did. You're alone in unfamiliar territory. Whether you'll admit it or not, you were beginning to be overwhelmed. I was the first friendly face you saw. You rely on me. You trust me." He frowned. "But you came here to find another man. You're going to be angry with yourself in the morning."

"No."

"Then you're going to be angry with me."

"Charles"—Mallory tried to smile—"I'm not going to be angry with anybody—except Captain Tierney."

Charles stroked her cheek. His touch was gentle. "I'm not comfortable trying to edge out a man behind his back."

Joshua Barnes.

"I want you to finish what you started so we can go on from here," he continued.

"The situation is more complicated than you realize, Charles."

"Maybe, but everything starts with the first step. We'll take that step tomorrow. I'll help you."

Mallory sighed. "I suppose you're right."

"All right. It's settled, then."

Charles drew back from her with obvious reluctance, and she realized she was reluctant as well.

She liked him. She liked him very much.

But Charles was suddenly frowning. "There's only one thing I ask, Mallory."

"What's that?"

"I want you to stay away from Bower."

The sound of Matthew Bower's name tightened inside her. Mallory's protest was instinctive. "Why?"

"He doesn't need you to look out for him. He can take care of himself. There's something about him. I don't trust him."

"He's mute."

"He can take care of himself."

"I know he can, but—"

"Promise me."

She couldn't make that promise.

"I wouldn't ask if I didn't think it was important."

"Don't ask me for promises, Charles."

His expression suddenly more sober than she had ever seen it, Charles nodded, "All right, I won't. Not yet, anyway."

She saw the effort it took for him to take another step back and extend his hand formally toward her. "I'll escort you to breakfast in the morning. Good night, Mallory."

Mallory hesitated after their brief handshake. She wished she could express the way she felt, that he was one of the nicest men she had ever known, that she—

"Go inside, Mallory."

"I never liked taking orders, Charles." She softened her objection with a smile.

Charles's wonderful grin flashed. "All right. *Please* go inside, because I won't leave until you do, and I don't know how much longer I can remain a gentleman."

Mallory flushed, then opened the door to her room.

"And lock the door." Charles caught himself. "*Please* lock the door."

She really, *really* liked him.

Mallory closed the door, then locked it. She waited for Charles's footsteps to fade before turning toward her bed.

Charles turned away from Mallory's door. His footsteps echoed hollowly in the silence of the yard as he strode toward the barracks, his shoulders rigidly erect.

Cloaked by the darkness of his room, Captain Arthur Tierney drew back as Charles passed the window where he had covertly watched all that transpired.

So, that was the way it was.

The humiliation Mallory Tompkins had served him earlier stung anew and Captain Tierney seethed. Were she another woman, he would have taught her the proper way to respect a man right then and there, but she wasn't just any woman. She had made that point clear.

Tierney sneered. Major Bullen this . . . Major Bullen that . . . The name had slipped off her tongue so many times during the long evening that he was sick at the sound of it! Rich. Spoiled. She had probably never been denied anything in her life. For all he knew, this Joshua Barnes she was looking for had come out West to escape her. Well, he'd teach her a thing or two if it was the last thing he ever did!

Tierney's sneer turned malevolent. Whether the beauteous Mallory realized it or not, he had the upper hand. She had humiliated him in front of his men, but he had served her a frustration that night at dinner that she wouldn't forget for a while—and he had enjoyed every minute of it! His commanding officer wasn't due to return for two weeks, and even though the rumors about Major General Cotter's approach were true, he had plenty of time to teach her the lesson she deserved.

Joshua Barnes wasn't a problem. Whoever he was, his scalp was probably already hanging on a pole in a Cheyenne village somewhere. He didn't intend wasting a moment's thought on him. He suspected Mallory Tompkins wasn't as concerned as she claimed to be, either. He had seen the way she responded to Lieutenant Moore.

As for Lieutenant Moore—the man was a fool! All he had needed to do when the hot witch was in his arms a few minutes earlier was to move her a few forceful steps backward, and he would have been in her room. Women were all the same. They might put up a fight at first, but once they were satisfied well enough, they never complained.

Perhaps Moore was not man enough to satisfy her, Tierney thought. He reached down to grip his swelling crotch. Well, *he* was.

Tierney suddenly laughed. The rich witch, Mallory Tompkins, didn't know it yet, but she had a treat in store for her!

All trace of amusement abruptly disappeared from Tierney's expression. He had just a few loose ends to take care of first.

The shadows of the dark fort yard shifted, gradually taking on human form as Gold Eagle stirred in his place of concealment.

Agitation again knotted inside him as Gold Eagle recalled the shadowed image of Mallory Tompkins held tightly in Lieutenant Moore's arms. He recalled the lieutenant's crushing embrace and his ardor when he took her lips. He remembered the caress of the lieutenant's hands as they tightened in her hair.

Gold Eagle's eyes narrowed and his breathing grew strained. For too brief a brief moment, it had been *he* who tasted her mouth with that kiss. It had been *he* who held her softness tight against his strength. It had been *he* who wound his fingers in the fiery strands and felt the warm silk against his palms. The rage that assaulted him when reality returned was with him still.

The lieutenant had left, but all was not yet finished between the woman and him.

The captain had watched, but all was not finished between Mallory and the captain, either.

His step silent, Gold Eagle slipped through

Elaine Barbieri

the shadows and paused before the woman's door. The lamp within flickered and went dark as the image of the flame-haired woman flared brightly in his mind.

She was not of his people. She was a stranger to the land of the Cheyenne. But she had raised a hunger within him that could not be denied.

Gold Eagle saw the danger there.

He knew what he must do.

Chapter Four

Bright shafts of morning sunlight slanted through the window of the office, drawing broad, geometric patterns on the scarred desk over which the two officers faced each other stiffly.

Enjoying the tense silence, Captain Tierney allowed it to drag on. He had spent the previous night in restless sleep while the humiliation of the red-headed witch's outspoken reprimand in the fort yard raised his fury anew. But those sleepless hours had produced a plan and a determination so keen that he had sent for Lieutenant Moore immediately upon reaching his office that morning.

Captain Tierney observed Lieutenant Moore with cool satisfaction. He knew what the lieutenant was thinking. He saw anger waging bitter war with better judgment before the lieutenant replied with obvious restraint, "I don't understand, Captain. My men and I were ordered by Major Bullen himself to accompany Miss Tompkins to Fort Larned. His specific instructions were to remain with her until she could be escorted safely back to Salina."

"And I'm telling you now that I'm countermanding those orders."

"On what grounds, sir?"

Captain Tierney felt irritation resurfacing. "I don't see any need to explain myself to you, Lieutenant. Suffice it to say that I feel we have adequate personnel at this fort to help Miss Tompkins conduct her inquiries." He forced a deliberate smile. "In fact, I intend to see to it personally that Miss Tompkins is satisfied in *every* way."

The flush that colored Lieutenant Moore's face restored Captain Tierney's spirits, as did the tight twist of the lieutenant's lips when he replied, "There's no need to take you from your duties, sir, when my men and I have already been assigned to Miss Tompkins."

"I can understand your feelings, Lieutenant. Losing the company of such an *accommodating* young woman is discomfiting."

"Accommodating, sir?" Lieutenant Moore's jaw was tight. "I don't think I understand what you mean."

"Oh, I think you do. She's a beautiful woman who enjoys a man's company. I think she proved that when you escorted her to her door last night."

"You're mistaken if you think anything unseemly happened."

Captain Tierney assessed the darkening of the lieutenant's flush, the rigid set of his shoulders, and the unconscious clenching of his fists. Damned if the dupe wasn't ready to do battle over the woman!

He hoped he would.

Captain Tierney continued in a deliberately provoking tone, "You know what I mean, all right. You weren't very circumspect last night."

"I didn't realize I needed to be."

"Well, you were wrong, weren't you, Lieutenant?" Tierney added, "I admit I'm looking forward to assuming your duties with Miss Tompkins. Professionally, I guarantee that she won't be neglected after you leave. Personally, I assure you she'll enjoy every minute of my company."

Lieutenant Moore's fists tightened. "I would be derelict in my duty if I didn't follow Major Bullen's orders, sir."

"And if you don't follow mine, you and your men will spend your time at Fort Larned in the stockade!" Allowing the lieutenant a moment to digest his threat, Captain Tierney continued, "Any explanations that become necessary will be made directly to Major General Cotter when he arrives here. He and *my* father are old acquaintances, you know."

"Major General Cotter?" The lieutenant appeared confused.

"He's on his way here. I thought everybody had heard the rumors."

"There are always rumors."

"These rumors are true. Major General Cotter is conducting a march in this direction with over fourteen hundred men—cavalry, artillery, infantry—even a pontoon train! He's going to settle the Indian problem once and for all. He should arrive here soon, and I anticipate that he'll expect me to play a major role in any confrontation that results."

"I wasn't aware that the Indians in this area were a problem. Chief Two Bears has made his intentions clear. He wants peace for the Cheyenne. I understood that he has his people under control."

"An Indian's an Indian, Lieutenant! They're all alike, and there's not a damned one of them to be trusted! Major General Cotter knows that as well as I do."

"But he—"

"I don't intend to discuss the matter any further. I expect you and your men to be ready to start back to Fort Riley by mid-morning."

"Today?" Charles frowned. "Sir, our horses aren't ready to travel that distance yet."

"Requisition yourselves other mounts."

"Sir—"

"That's all, Lieutenant, except that I expect you to keep the particulars of the information I've told you confidential."

"Yes, sir."

"You can tell Major Bullen when you see him that Major General Cotter will respond to any questions he might have about the orders I'm now issuing."

"Yes, sir."

"Good-bye, Lieutenant."

The door closed behind Lieutenant Moore and Captain Tierney smiled.

"*Good riddance,* Lieutenant."

He was feeling good. It wouldn't be long now.

"The bastard!"

Charles turned toward Mallory's quarters. His mind was still reeling. It had taken only one look at Captain Tierney after Mallory had spoken up the previous day to see that he wasn't the type to let her get away with rebuking him, but Charles hadn't expected such extreme measures. Whether Tierney really knew Major General Cotter as well as he claimed didn't matter at the moment. The arrogant bastard was prepared to jail him and his men if they didn't leave Fort Larned as ordered.

There was only one solution.

Charles halted in front of Mallory's door. He knocked.

No response.

He knocked again, a sense of urgency rising in him.

Silence within.

Charles turned to scrutinize the fort yard. Where was she?

*   *   *

"Well, well, if it ain't the *botanist!*"

Gold Eagle entered the dining hall and turned at the sound of the familiar voice to see the burly Corporal Archer seated with a group of soldiers at a table a few feet away. He felt Corporal Walker stiffen beside him as they started in the opposite direction.

"Seems like you're famous, Mr. Bowers!" Corporal Archer's tone was openly caustic. "A few of the boys in the barracks said they heard all about you! You've been livin' with the Injuns up north—sleepin' and eatin' with them, actin' like you was one of them."

Gold Eagle did not acknowledge the man's words as Walker and he sat at a nearby table. Quartered on a cot in a fort supply room, he had slept fitfully the previous night. He had awakened early, irritable and determined to get the information he needed as quickly as possible, so he might leave Fort Larned and the red-haired woman who haunted his thoughts. He was about to step out the door when Walker arrived with a ready smile to assume the unsolicited role of interpreter for another day.

A long-suppressed memory of his friend Running Wolf had stirred at Walker's boyish smile. Running Wolf and he had been children together. Running Wolf, older than he, had made it clear to all that he would stand by the thin, undersized, and pale-haired youth in all battles with boys who doubted that a Cheyenne heart beat within Gold Eagle's white-skinned chest.

But the undersized youth grew rapidly, both in size and in stature within the tribe. He surpassed most in feats of daring and courage—though he never surpassed the kindness in Running Wolf's heart.

Gold Eagle's memory grew sorrowful. Running Wolf was a young man of only twenty-two summers when he was confined in the white man's fort for the crime of stealing cows grazing on Cheyenne land. The crime was no crime at all in the eyes of his people, but that mattered little. Running Wolf's confinement was so harsh that he did not live to face a white man's court.

Corporal Walker spoke up sharply, banishing Gold Eagle's memory as he looked at Archer with no trace of a smile.

"What's your problem, Archer?"

"Me? I ain't got one. It's your friend who's got a problem. He ain't only dumb. He smells bad, too."

"Oh, yeah?"

"Yeah. He smells like an Injun."

Gold Eagle went still at the man's unexpected statement. Then he inched a hand toward the knife at his waist as Walker responded, "You're crazy, you know that, Archer?"

"Am I?" Archer turned abruptly toward Gold Eagle. "The fellas in the barracks was right about you, wasn't they? You're the fella who was livin' with the Injuns up north, talkin' to them Injun medicine men and treatin' them like they was somebody. That's where you learned that heathen sign language, ain't it?"

Gold Eagle directed a deadly glance in Archer's direction.

Reacting hotly, Archer sprang to his feet and took an aggressive step forward. "Don't look at me like that! I ain't like Walker here, makin' excuses for you just 'cause you can't talk. To me an Injun lover's an Injun lover, whether he can say it out loud or he can't!"

Springing to his feet as well, Walker returned, "Mr. Bower don't need to make no explanations to you about where he's been *or* where he's goin', because it's none of your business!"

"What are you, his puppy guard dog?" Archer swaggered a few more steps forward, his eyes intent on Gold Eagle, who regarded him with eyes narrowed into slits. "If there's one thing I hate worse than the stink of a white man who sides with them murderin' Injuns, it's a white man who makes another man fight his battles!"

Still seated, Gold Eagle clenched the handle of the knife at his waist. He had not done what he came to the fort to do, and he struggled for composure. To allow the foul-mouthed soldier to divert him from his purpose now would be to surrender to the man's threat, no matter the outcome of the encounter.

Gold Eagle considered that thought. Silence now. Victory later.

His decision made, Gold Eagle did no more than stare at the man called Archer. His eyes cold with silent promise, he did not bother to stand.

"Get up, you cowardly son of a—!"

Archer advanced rapidly toward him.

Mallory shivered against the morning chill and glanced around the fort yard. She had waited as long as she could for Charles to appear at her quarters. She was hungry and annoyed that after his ardent declarations the night before, he had seemingly chosen to keep her waiting.

The aroma of warm food had drawn her to her destination. Standing in front of the dining hall, Mallory swallowed her annoyance and opened the door. She stepped back in sudden alarm at the scene before her.

The sweating Corporal Archer, his expression livid, stood over the silent Matt Bower. Seated and showing no intention of rising, Bower returned Archer's stare with a look somehow more frightening than the open fury on Archer's face as he hissed, "Get up, you bastard! You're nothin' but an Injun-lovin' coward! Get up and show what you got between your legs, or I'll—"

Mallory's gasp turned all eyes toward her, halting Archer momentarily and providing her an opportunity she knew she must not allow to escape her.

Striding forward, Mallory ignored the heavy hammering of her heart. She forced a smile and addressed Archer in a tone cultivated over years of privilege.

"I don't know what the difficulty is, Corporal, but I do know that this isn't the time or place for this discussion. Mr. Bower, Corporal Walker, and I have an appointment for breakfast, and I'd appreciate it if you'd return to your table and take the matter up another time."

Archer muttered an unintelligible reply that snapped Mallory's chin an angry notch higher. "Excuse me, Corporal. Did you say something?"

Archer did not respond.

"Since you have nothing to say, please go back to your table." Mallory stared hard into the man's angry face, continuing, "I'm sure, when you've had time to think about it, you'll realize it was the best thing to do."

Archer did not move.

In a moment of pure grit, Mallory slipped herself between Corporal Archer and the silent Matt Bower. She then turned to the table and addressed the two men as if Archer did not exist.

"Good morning, gentlemen. I'm sorry I kept you waiting."

Intensely aware that the furious corporal still stood behind her, Mallory breathed a silent sigh of relief when she felt him turn, then heard him walk away. Corporal Walker, his youthful face flushed, stared at her in stunned silence as Matt Bower stood up unexpectedly and drew out her chair. She was startled to see no trace of stress in his expression as he signed with brief, concise gestures. Frustrated, Mallory addressed the youthful corporal, who was still standing.

"Please sit down, Corporal. I'd appreciate it if you'd tell me what Mr. Bower said."

Corporal Walker sat abruptly. He swallowed,

then responded, "Mr. Bower said good morning, ma'am."

"Good morning . . . oh." Mallory felt herself flush. She unconsciously touched the irritated strip of skin at her neck as she addressed Matt Bower, whose gaze had not left her. "I hope you'll teach me to understand your signing."

Matt Bower motioned with the crooked index finger of his right hand.

"He said yes, didn't he, Corporal?"

The corporal nodded.

Extremely pleased that she had recognized the sign used the previous day, Mallory slipped off her coat and looked back at Matt Bower. When she spoke again, her tone was soft and earnest.

"I hope you don't mind my interference. And I hope you'll accept my apologies for the intolerance that's been shown to you. Whatever that corporal's problem is, there's no excuse for his behavior."

Matt Bower signed again, a rapid series of movements that left Mallory bewildered. She looked at Corporal Walker and was surprised to see the young man grin.

"What did he say?"

The corporal's grin widened. "Mr. Bower said Corporal Archer's a jackass."

"Oh!" Mallory suddenly laughed. Strangely, Matt Bower did not smile. Instead, his expression remained sober. She sensed in him an emotion that did not match the indifference of his comment. His gaze refused to surrender hers.

A familiar breathlessness assaulted her, and Mallory was again struck by the silent intensity of the big man across from her. She noted that his hair was paler than she'd realized, a shade lighter than blond, and that he wore it long and tied at the back of his neck with a leather thong. His skin was also light, but tanned by the sun to a soft gold that emphasized the almost translucent quality of his eyes. It occurred to her that he spoke with those light eyes, but it was in a language she was not yet able to understand. She was determined in that moment that she would learn to comprehend that language as clearly as she intended to learn the signing motions he had promised to teach her.

Unconsciously fingering the sore strip on her neck again, Mallory inhaled softly. Matt Bower was indeed handsome, but in a way unlike any man she had ever known. Who was he? She wondered again. A botanist, yes, but that profession did not explain his presence alone in the dead of winter on a frozen prairie that was dangerous to all—most especially a white man. There was a mystery behind his pale eyes. She would solve it, one way or another. She needed to, and then she would—

"Mallory."

Turning at the sound of her name, Mallory was startled to see Charles standing beside her. She saw his spontaneous frown when he glanced at Matt Bower. He was obviously disturbed to see her seated there, but she sensed that wasn't all.

"Is something wrong, Charles?"

"I apologize for being late this morning. It was unavoidable." His expression said he wished she had waited for him.

"I thought you had forgotten me." She paused, uncertain. "In any case, I knew you'd find me. I certainly couldn't go far."

Charles glanced again at the two who sat silent witness to their conversation, then offered, "There's something I have to talk to you about, Mallory. I'm sure Mr. Bower and Corporal Walker will excuse us if we leave."

"No . . . I don't think so, Charles." Mallory glanced furtively toward Corporal Archer, then shook her head. "It's been a difficult morning here."

Matt Bower's eyes caught hers. His expression was unrevealing.

"I don't have much time, Mallory."

The urgency in Charles's tone brought Mallory's head back toward him. She felt the weight of Matt Bower's gaze as Charles continued, "I'll be leaving Fort Larned before noon."

"Leaving!" Her attention wholly his for the first time, Mallory gasped, "Why?"

"Will you excuse us, gentlemen?"

Not waiting for their reply, Charles helped Mallory to her feet and escorted her to the door.

"She's some woman, ain't she?"

Corporal Walker's freckled face reflected his

awe as he stared at the door that closed behind Mallory and the lieutenant. He turned to look at Gold Eagle, suddenly flushed.

"I ain't never seen nothin' like her. I can't believe the way she—"

The young corporal's words continued, barely touching Gold Eagle's mind. Plates of steaming food were placed on the table, and Gold Eagle picked up the fork and knife provided. The utensils felt strange in his hands after years of disuse, but he had not forgotten the skill. Nor had he forgotten his "manners."

Gold Eagle's lips tightened at the memory of Mallory Tompkins's smile when he'd stood to pull out her chair. White man's teachings that had left scars on his body and mind. . . . they would prove useful before he was through.

". . . and did you see the way she took on Archer? Hell, she stood nose to nose with him, and she wasn't backin' down."

Silent, Gold Eagle met Walker's eyes briefly in assent. Yes, he had seen the woman's brave display. Were she a man, and were she Cheyenne, she would be a warrior to be feared. But she was not Cheyenne, and she was only a woman.

Annoyed that the stirring within him belied his thoughts, Gold Eagle looked up again at Walker as the corporal shoved a forkful of food into his mouth and continued almost inaudibly, "Good-lookin', too, ain't she? I ain't never seen no woman better lookin' than she is, neither. Seems to me that Lieutenant Moore's kind of staked her out for himself, even if she came here lookin' for some other man."

Gold Eagle stilled at Walker's unexpected statement.

"You didn't know that? Hell, what am I sayin'? How could you? Seems like she came here lookin' for a fella named Joshua Barnes, who came out prospectin' for gold and never returned. Ain't nobody here who thinks she'll find him, neither, if he was prospectin' in the territory she was talkin' about. I'd say the lieutenant's thinkin' of steppin' right into old Josh's shoes." Walker shrugged. "Can't say as I blame him."

Walker paused in his remarks, then suddenly shifted the topic of conversation. "I gotta ask. How'd you do it? How'd you manage to stay alive wanderin' around up north with them bloodthirsty Blackfeet, Pawnee, and Cree all around? Archer made sure to let everybody know how he thinks you did it."

Gold Eagle signed sharply.

"I'd rather not say what he said, if you don't mind," Walker replied. "I'm thinkin' that might make you mad enough to stand up and fight after all."

Gold Eagle's gaze turned cold.

"I ain't sayin' you're a coward. Hell"—Walker gave a short laugh, his expression wise beyond his years—"there's no way I see any fear in them eyes when you look at Archer. No, I'd say you've got a reason for holdin' back like you are. Whatever it is, it ain't my business. I just want to know how you stayed alive in that Injun territory—if the stories about you livin' there are true."

Gold Eagle signed his response.

"They're true—so, how'd you do it?"

Gold Eagle signed again.

"Hell, that's no answer! If it was so easy just to tell all them Injuns that you came in peace, how come it didn't work for any of the others who tried it?"

Gold Eagle's response was short.

"'Cause you was tellin' the truth?" Walker paused. His youthful face creased into a contemplative frown. "Yeah, maybe you got a point there."

Gold Eagle accidentally scraped his fork against the dish in the silence that followed. He inadvertently winced, recalling youthful years when a painful blow had followed such a lapse in etiquette.

"Well . . ." Breaking his silence at last with a smile that was suddenly shy, Walker continued, "It ain't often that a fella meets a true man of peace in these parts. My mama always said, 'Blessed are the peacemakers, for they shall be called children of God.'" Walker's thin face flushed more darkly as he stretched a hand out toward Gold Eagle unexpectedly. "I'm real pleased to meet you, sir."

Gold Eagle looked at Walker, seeing the face of Running Wolf more clearly than ever before.

About to accept Walker's hand, Gold Eagle was stopped by a snide hiss behind him.

"What're you doin', Walker? Kissin' up to In-jun lovers again?" Gold Eagle turned around as Archer continued, "Yeah, I mean you." Archer leaned closer to Gold Eagle, his face so close that Gold Eagle could see the remnants of breakfast on his teeth as Archer spat, "Don't think you got away with nothin' this mornin' just because that nosy witch got between us. You can't hide forever behind a woman's skirt. But I suppose some fellas are more comfortable hidin' behind a woman's skirt than gettin' them-selves under it."

Gold Eagle's gaze spoke volumes.

"Anytime, Mr. Botanist."

Dismissing him with a sharp laugh, Archer swaggered toward the door. Gold Eagle watched the burly soldier's retreating figure, his heart hammering in unspoken promise.

"Mr. Bower?" Ignoring Walker, Gold Eagle continued watching Archer as he closed the door behind him. "I gotta say that you don't look like no man of peace right now."

Close to losing control, Gold Eagle stood abruptly. He strode toward the door, seeking the relief of solitude and hoping Archer would not be in his line of vision when he reached the fort yard. He breathed deeply when he pulled the dining hall door closed behind him and scanned the yard to see Archer disappear through a door across the way. Grateful to be allowed the time he needed to regain command of his emotions, Gold Eagle turned toward the supply room where he was quartered. He halted at the sight of Mallory and Lieutenant Moore in close and intimate conversation a little distance away.

The bright sunlight turned Mallory Tompkins's hair into a glorious blaze of color as he viewed her delicate profile against the shadowed area beyond them. He noted the concern in her gaze, and he recognized in the lieutenant's expression a hunger and ardent determination that was unmistakable.

No, that man would never have her.

But Gold Eagle suddenly knew, beyond doubt, that *he* would.

Mallory repeated, "Why, Charles?"

Mallory's pained surprise both pleased and distressed Charles as she halted their progress across the fort yard with her impatient question. The bright morning sunlight lit fiery sparks in her hair, and he allowed himself a moment to commit the picture to memory. He had never seen hair its equal, nor had he ever seen skin so clear and fine, or eyes so vivid in color. She was beautiful, but her beauty was of little consequence to her, he knew. She was beginning to care for him, he was sure of it, even if the depth of her feelings did not match his. He cursed the bizarre circumstances that were parting them. Now was the wrong time to leave her, for so many reasons.

Frustrated, Charles responded, "Captain Tierney ordered me back to Fort Riley. He said he'll arrange for you to be able to make the necessary inquiries about your friend."

"That doesn't answer my question, Charles. Why did he order you back?"

"I answered that in our conversation last night. He's angry and he's not the kind to forget an insult. He's going to do his best to find a way to make you regret what you did."

"I'm not afraid of him!"

"You should be!" Sorry to daunt the courage he so much admired in Mallory, Charles continued, "He has the upper hand. He's sending me away because he knows I'm your ally."

"He wouldn't dare try anything untoward!"

"No, maybe not, but he can make things difficult for you if he wants to. I'm hoping that's all he intends."

"What are you trying to tell me, Charles?"

Charles responded cautiously, "I'm telling you that Captain Tierney may enjoy putting obstacles in your path after I leave. Then again, he may try ingratiating himself with you." Charles paused, his expression tightening. "If he does, you may be sure his intentions won't be honorable."

Mallory gave a scoffing laugh. "I've met men like Captain Tierney before. Their good intentions are limited to whatever serves them best. I'm not fool enough to fall into his trap."

"The circumstances you face at this fort are different from any you've ever encountered before, Mallory. The captain has absolute power here until his superior returns."

"Absolute power . . . maybe." The delicate line of Mallory's chin grew stubborn. "But only temporarily."

They resumed their walk toward Mallory's quarters. She turned toward Charles as she reached for the door handle. "We can talk more privately inside."

"No, I think not." At Mallory's wordless surprise, he continued, "It wouldn't be wise. We were watched last night."

Hot color tinted Mallory's ivory cheeks. "Do you mean Captain Tierney? You can't be serious!"

Charles's gaze did not waver.

Mallory's breast began an angry heaving. "I'll see that Major Bullen hears about this!"

"That's in the future, Mallory. What we have to be concerned about now is the present. I don't have much time. I have to get my men ready and be out of here within the next hour."

Charles paused, his emotions in a turmoil. The urge to take Mallory into his arms and reassure her that everything would be all right was so strong that it was all he could do to subdue it. Instead, he took a step back, his jaw tight as he whispered, "I have to follow orders, Mallory, but if things work out my way, I'll be back here within the week."

To her questioning glance, he responded, "The telegraph lines aren't far from here. I can contact Major Bullen then. I intend to request that he send a direct order via wire to Captain Tierney reinstating me and my detachment as your escort. I intend to deliver it personally to Captain Tierney. He won't dare countermand an order placed into his hand—whether Major General Cotter is a personal friend of the family or not."

"Major General Cotter . . ." Mallory was immediately alert. "I thought Cotter was back East, resting on his laurels after Chancellorsville. What does he have to do with this?"

Charles considered his response. He owed no allegiance to Captain Tierney's supposed confidence and Mallory deserved to know. He replied, "Captain Tierney confirmed that Cotter is marching toward Fort Larned with the largest force the Indians in this area of the country have ever seen. His orders are to make direct contact with the Cheyenne."

Startled that the information she sought should come to her in such an unexpected way, Mallory responded, "So, the rumors of an expected Indian uprising are true."

"I don't know if they're true or not, but it looks as if Washington is taking them seriously. Cotter's been given a force of fourteen hundred men and artillery."

Mallory gave a tight laugh. "I suppose it's safe to conclude that with a force of fourteen hundred men, Cotter doesn't expect to conduct extended negotiations."

"Do you want the truth?" At her nod, he said, "I think that there are some officers in this part of the country who are spoiling for a fight with the Indians, even though Two Bears has already made it clear that he wants peace for his people."

"His people . . . the Cheyenne? That's not what I understood from published reports."

"Two Bears and his tribe were at Sand Creek. He doesn't want to see a repetition of that massacre."

Mallory shook her head, confused. "I don't understand what Captain Tierney has to do with all this, most especially with Major General Cotter."

"Nothing, probably, but Tierney claims to know Cotter personally. He took great pleasure in holding that over my head when I questioned his reversal of my orders."

"Do you believe him?"

"I don't know." They were deviating from the problem at hand. Concern a tight knot within him, Charles continued, "But it's now that I'm worried about. I don't like leaving you alone here."

"I can take care of myself, Charles. I'm not helpless."

"You don't know what you're facing. I can't leave with a clear mind if you won't make me some simple promises."

"You know how I feel about promises."

"Mallory . . ."

The anxiety in Charles's expression modified Mallory's response.

"What do you want me to do?"

"I want you to sit tight while I'm gone."

"Sit tight?"

"Make any inquiries you feel necessary here in the fort—but stay within the fort walls."

"I don't know if I can promise to do that, Charles. I came here with a specific purpose in mind. If I get an opportunity, I won't pass it up."

"I'll only be gone a few days—a week at most. When I get back, I'll help you go wherever you want to go to conduct your inquiries. I'm asking you to wait only a few days."

"You don't have to worry about me, Charles. And even if Captain Tierney isn't to be trusted, there are other good men at this fort who—"

"—who're all under Tierney's command!"

"Mr. Bower isn't under Captain Tierney's command."

Charles stiffened. "Stay away from him, Mallory."

Mallory stiffened as well. "Why don't you like him, Charles? He's an educated, courteous man who goes out of his way to avoid trouble."

"I'm just trying to warn you to be cautious."

"I don't want to be warned."

"I'm trying to tell you that there's something about that man. I can't put my finger on it, but I don't trust him."

"I trust him."

"You're being persuaded by compassion for his handicap, but you're forgetting that there's a man behind that handicap. Step back and look at him more clearly. You know nothing about Matthew Bower—nothing at all, yet you've already alienated the man who could've been your most valuable ally because of him."

"I told you, Charles, it's a matter of principle! I couldn't stand by and see Mr. Bower tormented!"

"Is that all it is, Mallory?"

Mallory broke the brief silence that followed Charles's question by responding coolly, "I'd answer that question, Charles, if I thought you had the right to ask it."

Charles's handsome face colored, and Mallory immediately regretted the harshness of her reply. "I'm sorry. I know you mean well, but—"

"It's true. I have no right to ask you that question." Suddenly gripping her arms, Charles drew her close. Mallory felt the heavy pounding of his heart as he rasped, "But I *will* have that right someday, I promise you that."

Suddenly covering her mouth with his, Charles kissed her long and deep. His warmth filled her and she—

Stunned when he again separated himself from her abruptly, Mallory saw the ardent fervor in his gaze when he rasped, "Wait for me, Mallory. Don't take any chances while I'm gone. I'll be back soon, I promise."

His gaze lingering only a moment longer, Charles did not allow Mallory the opportunity of a reply before he turned abruptly on his heel. Within moments, he was out of sight.

Confused by the myriad emotions assaulting her, Mallory pushed open the door of her quarters and walked inside.

Chapter Five

"Captain Tierney say to bring you a pitcher of hot water. He say you will like hot water to refresh yourself before dinner."

The sun was setting, lending breathtaking color to the darkening blue of the sky, but Mallory was immune to the display as she studied the small half-breed woman who stood at the door of her quarters, a steaming jug in her hands.

"Captain Tierney instructed you to bring me fresh water to bathe?" Mallory's expression twitched as she stood back and allowed Penelope to enter. "How thoughtful of him."

The miserable hypocrite that he was.

Mallory had had a difficult day, and she knew that although she could not prove it, the source of every obstacle she had encountered went by the name of Captain Tierney. Charles had departed the fort on schedule that morning, and the day had gone downhill from then on.

Finally admitting to herself that she had come to depend on Charles's smile and the security of his presence, she realized that she'd started missing him the moment he slipped from her sight. He was so sure that he would return within the week . . . but, somehow, she wasn't. There were too many intangibles.

Nonetheless, she had determined to make good use of her time, only to be thwarted again and again when each attempt to strike up a conversation with the men at the fort ended in the same way:

"Sorry, ma'am. I don't know nothin' about that."

"You'll have to ask Captain Tierney. He's in command."

"Captain Tierney don't like us talkin' to civilians about military affairs."

"Captain Tierney would be the man to talk to about that, ma'am."

Captain Tierney . . . of course.

Mallory gave a groan of disgust. It was time for the evening meal. She hadn't received an invitation from Captain Tierney to dine with him, but she expected it would come, sooner or later. She supposed the warm water was a kind of peace offering.

The man was a snake. She would like nothing more than to grind the heel of her shoe into the neck of that snake, but Charles was right. Tierney had the upper hand.

How the thought rankled.

The young half-breed woman walked to the washstand and poured the water carefully into the pitcher there. Mallory was struck by how small Penelope really was. Aside from being delicately boned, she stood almost a head shorter than Mallory. Penelope stepped back from the washstand and turned toward her, and Mallory realized for the first time that the young woman was really quite pretty in her way. But her shy smile was strangely absent.

Mallory attempted to coax her smile as she inquired, "Do you live at the fort?"

"Yes, with my husband, Jay Dolan. He is the blacksmith."

Mallory couldn't help asking, "Do you like it here?"

"I wish to be with my husband and I want my son to learn the ways of his father."

Penelope's reply surprised Mallory. "You have a son?"

Penelope nodded, a brief smile flashing. "He is a year old. He is a handsome boy who looks like his father."

Mallory ventured. "Is it difficult for you here—I mean, with the conflict between the government and the local tribes?"

"No."

Her response, a trifle too quick, raised a silent question in Mallory's gaze that Penelope responded to with unexpected candor. "There are some who turn away from me, but I must be strong if my son is to be strong."

"I admire you for that."

Penelope moved toward the door, then turned back to add, "I have not heard anyone speak of a man named Joshua Barnes. I am sorry."

Mallory responded in the only way she could. "No one else has, either." She took the opportunity to ask, "Are your people Cheyenne?"

"My mother was Arapaho."

Mallory considered her reply, then inquired, "Will it be hard for you if there's an uprising in the spring as the rumors say?"

Penelope's expression went blank. "I must go. My son is not well."

Truly dismayed, Mallory offered, "I'm sorry. I didn't mean to make you uncomfortable."

The door closed behind Penelope, and Mallory felt her frustration soar. It was almost dinnertime and the end of her second day at the fort, yet she had been unable to get a single person to elaborate on the information Charles had given her. The soldiers knew more about the military plans than they would let on, she was sure. She needed to get some of them to talk to her. Without authentic background information, any articles she would write would be too loaded with speculation to overcome the bias against her gender.

The image of a tall, fair-haired man entered Mallory's thoughts as it had numerous times during the long afternoon. She hadn't seen Matthew Bower since Charles had left that morning. She couldn't imagine where he was, but she knew she had unconsciously been hoping to run into him as she made her way around the fort.

The thought of Matthew Bower evoked a familiar fluttering within her, and Mallory gave a snort of disgust. The truth was that Charles was right when he said there was something about that man. . . . But aside from his obvious masculine appeal, she was certain Matt Bower could tell her all she needed to know about what Indians in the area were planning. He was an educated, civilized man who had been accepted by the Indians and who had lived successfully and peacefully with them. He would be the perfect judge as to whether they were truly the savages they were made out to be.

If only he could talk.

Mallory amended that thought. Matt Bower could talk. She just needed to learn the language he used.

She mentally chastised herself for the thrill that chased up her spine at that thought. What was wrong with her?

Mallory made a decision. She would find Matt Bower and she would remind him of his promise to teach her to communicate with Indian signs. They would be able to converse without Corporal Walker's assistance then, and she would be able to get all the information she needed about the Indians.

That determination returned Penelope's

slight image to her mind, and Mallory's discomfort returned. The young woman had seemed unusually tense when she'd appeared at her door, but she'd made an overture of friendship by volunteering information about the fictional Joshua Barnes. Mallory had responded by thoughtlessly pressing Penelope for details that she was not prepared to give and the young woman had beat a fast retreat. She'd make sure that the next time Penelope came to her room, she'd—

A knock on the door sounded as if on cue, and Mallory's smile flashed. Penelope had returned. She would have the opportunity to make up for her thoughtlessness sooner than expected.

Mallory strode to the door and jerked it open. She went stock still at the sight of the person standing there.

A slow trembling beset her.

He was feeling really good.

Captain Tierney turned toward the sight of the setting sun outside his office window. He smiled with satisfaction. The day had gone well. Captain Moore and his detachment had departed the fort on schedule that morning. He had almost hoped Moore would ignore his orders. He would have loved to see that smart young officer looking back at him from behind the stockade bars.

Tierney almost laughed aloud. He wondered what the tight-lipped lieutenant was thinking now. He had put enough bees in that fellow's bonnet to keep his mind buzzing. Moore was probably torturing himself with the thought that he would make his move on Mallory before the night was out.

Well, if that was Moore's thinking—he was right. Tierney had to congratulate himself. He had already sent the half-breed to Mallory's room with some warm water so the spoiled witch might refresh herself. It had amused him to send warm water as a "gift" to a woman who was probably more accustomed to receiving roses. He had made a subtle statement with that gesture—reminding her that she was no longer in the *civilized* world, that her comfort relied on his good will, and that he was prepared to see that everyone in the fort cooperated with her to the best of their abilities. As for the price . . . well, he was certain she would get the message when the time came.

Tierney stood up and strode to the window. Paying no attention to the sun setting in a last blaze of vibrant color in the distance, he paused momentarily to check his reflection in the glass. He was good-looking. Women always told him that. He was in his prime physically, and he was more than ready for the beauteous Mallory.

Tierney rubbed his jaw, then frowned at the stubble beginning to appear there. Normally, he would wait until morning to shave, but he wanted his face to be smooth tonight. He had no desire to leave any marks on Mallory's fine white skin.

When that thought caused a predictable reaction in his groin, Tierney snapped a soft curse. Drawing the office door closed behind him a few moments later, he headed for his quarters. He was hot for the red-haired witch, all right. It would give him great pleasure to bring her down a peg. After he did that, he would enjoy himself even more.

One step at a time . . .

He had never failed with a woman, and Mallory Tompkins was only a woman, after all.

He had waited until the right moment.

The right moment was now.

Gold Eagle stood in the doorway of Mallory Tompkins's room. He had watched Lieutenant Moore's departure that morning. It was not difficult to see that Moore had left under duress and that Mallory was distressed. That thought had remained with him through the day while he wandered around the fort, scrutinizing its defenses with an expression of feigned indifference.

It amused Gold Eagle that Captain Tierney had deliberately removed Corporal Walker from his self-appointed task as interpreter. He knew Tierney had done so in the hope of discomfiting him, while in reality, he had merely given him the chance he needed.

Gold Eagle had made good use of the opportunity. He had listened carefully to whatever conversations he had been able to overhear in passing. He had lingered when possible, but it did not skip his notice that casual talk between the men grew stilted whenever he was near. The words "Injun lover" had been spat in his direction by a few. Archer had done his work well, but he had merely accepted the term as a compliment to the man whose identity he had assumed.

He had done what he needed to do and had then returned to his quarters to search the pages of Matt Bower's journals with another purpose in mind. As evening approached, he had made his way to the doorway in which he now stood, and to the woman who now looked up at him with clear, light eyes.

Mallory Tompkins trembled, but he knew instinctively she was not trembling from fear.

"Hello!" Mallory Tompkins took a short step backward. "I'm surprised to see you." She hesitated. "Won't you come in?"

Gold Eagle entered, his gaze intent. He felt the true weight of his silence for the first time. The desire to speak was never greater, but he knew that, in the end, this woman and he would have no need for words.

"I'm pleased to see you, again."

He knew she was.

"I was hoping to run into you this afternoon."

He had seen her, but he had avoided a meeting until the time was right.

"I was hoping to talk to you. Aside from natural curiosity, I was interested in your experiences with the Indians. I thought you might help me learn some things I'm trying to understand." She smiled, her lips curving in a way that held Gold Eagle's attention. He saw the heat that rose to her cheeks. "Strangely enough, I didn't realize until this moment how difficult it would be to converse with you without Corporal Walker's assistance."

No, the last thing he wanted at that moment was to have Corporal Walker standing beside them.

"I hope you still intend to teach me to speak with Indian signs."

Gold Eagle raised a crooked finger beside his temple.

"Yes." Mallory smiled at the familiar gesture. She turned as if searching for something, then reached up with a spontaneous grimace toward the raw abrasion on her neck when the collar of her gown rubbed against it.

Gold Eagle grasped her hand and held it fast, and Mallory caught her breath.

Her hand was small and warm in his, a captive bird that did not struggle to escape him as the silence between them stretched long.

His touch was strangely familiar.

Silent as Matthew Bower held her hand in his, Mallory looked up at the big man whose pale eyes scrutinized her with an almost palpable touch. His overwhelming size . . . the intensity he radiated . . . his aura of restrained power again assaulted her, leaving her breathless and as mute as he in the few moments before he released her hand and reached into his pocket to produce a small leather pouch.

Struggling to regain her composure, Mallory managed a smile. "What's that?"

Matthew Bower opened the pouch and held it out for her inspection. She looked at the substance within.

"I don't know what that is."

His gaze searched hers for long moments; then Matt Bower took another step that brought him intimately close. The heat of his body bridged the remaining distance between them. The purely male scent of him incited her senses as he brushed a wisp of hair back from her face with a stroke just short of a caress. His touch singed her cheek with heat where his hand brushed it. Watching as if mesmerized, she was unable to move as he dipped his fingertip into the pouch, then slowly, with great deliberation, spread a clear salve on the abrasion on her neck.

Mallory caught her breath at the sensuous warmth of his touch. She shuddered as Matt Bower continued smoothing the substance against her skin. The action sent waves of an intense emotion she could not quite define coursing through her veins, and she closed her eyes briefly. She opened her eyes to see Matt Bower's lips move with an unspoken word, and she was suddenly possessed of a shattering longing to hear the sound. Her heart pounding and her breathing strained, she watched motionlessly as his mouth descended toward hers.

The touch of his lips, the strength of his arms

around her, the unexpected passion of his kiss . . .

Crushed tightly against Matt Bower's muscled length, Mallory surrendered to the heat expanding within her. There was no time beyond the moment. There was no place but within his arms. Lips and bodies melded, and a long-awaited awakening budded within her. The bloom gradually unfurled, its impending brilliance so vibrant that Mallory was powerless to resist it.

Yielding to the wonder, Mallory slid her arms around Matthew Bower's neck. She drew him closer, encouraging his kiss. She separated her lips, allowing him entry to her mouth. She heard the groan that sounded deep inside him. Its echo rumbled within her, stirring the burning heat to an all consuming blaze.

Sudden realization flashed across Mallory's mind as Matt Bower pulled her closer. She had recognized this man the moment she saw him! Though she had never seen his face or heard his voice, he had lived in the shadows of her mind for more years than she could recall. He had implored her patience while she waited for him to appear. He had filled her heart with promise.

Matt Bower's lips left hers. They trailed to her ear to explore the hollows there. They followed the line of her jaw with heated ardor. They settled on her mouth once more and the glory flamed anew.

Mallory was alive with the wonder of his embrace. She had waited for him for so long. She did not need to hear him speak to know he felt the same. He communicated with her in ways that needed no sound, and she responded with an inner voice of her own.

Uncertain of the moment when Matt Bower scooped her up into his arms, Mallory knew only the certainty that his arms were meant to hold her. She uttered no protest when he strode to the wide bunk in the corner and paused briefly there. She met the burning heat of his pale eyes as they devoured her, and she felt his longing to speak the words so clearly written in his gaze. Her lips parted. His hunger was her hunger. His need was her need. She raised her mouth to his and he—

A heavy knock on the door shattered the moment.

Mallory gasped at the almost feral fury that flashed across Matthew's face when the knock sounded again. She closed her eyes briefly, then managed a steady response.

"Who is it?"

"It's Captain Tierney."

Matthew's lips tightened. She felt his silent protest when she replied, "Just a minute."

Matthew released her and Mallory struggled against an almost debilitating sense of loss. Taking a moment to regain control of her emotions, she felt Matthew follow her as she walked toward the door. She sensed his gaze going cold when she drew it open.

*   *   *

Captain Tierney's smile froze as Mallory opened the door. His gaze locked with Matthew Bower's. The fellow stood a few steps behind Mallory, and he mentally cursed.

Damn that mute bastard! What was he doing there?

Managing to subdue his anger, Tierney forced himself to speak calmly.

"I came to escort you to dinner in Lieutenant Moore's absence, but I see that Mr. Bower preceded me. I hope I'm not intruding."

"No, of course not." Mallory glanced back at Bower. The man's bold glare did not change as she raised a hand to indicate the mark on her neck. "Mr. Bower brought me some salve for this annoying abrasion."

Tierney glanced at the pouch on the table. He frowned. "Is that what he brought you?" He looked at Bower accusingly. "What is it? Indian medicine?"

"Yes," Mallory responded in his stead, "I suppose it is. It's quite effective."

"Indian hocus-pocus." Tierney addressed Bower directly. "Did those savages teach you the dances that accompany their cures? That would be amusing to see."

Her displeasure obvious, Mallory replied, "No . . . Matthew didn't attempt any dancing."

Matthew. He didn't like the sound of that.

"But the salve has given me relief."

Tierney looked back at Mallory, barely restraining his annoyance. The arrogant witch was still defying him for the sake of a dumb,

Indian-loving coward who refused to face him down! He'd make her pay.

Mallory forced a smile. He saw the effort she made to alleviate the growing tension. He knew a minor victory had been won when she continued, "I accept your invitation to dinner, Arthur. Of course, I know you're including Matthew in your invitation as well."

Of course . . .

A litany of curses reeled across Tierney's mind as the stiff-faced mute helped Mallory with her coat. But when Mallory paused outside the door, making sure to take each of their arms before they started across the yard, Tierney inwardly snarled. Mallory Tompkins didn't like him or the way he treated the voiceless botanist, but she knew she couldn't afford an outright confrontation—a significant concession for a spoiled witch accustomed to having her way. Well, he'd get rid of Bower just as he'd gotten rid of Lieutenant Moore. The bastard would be gone from the fort by sundown tomorrow. And then he'd put Mallory in her place.

Tierney sneered. *Underneath him . . .* that's where Mallory Tompkins's place was.

And that's where she'd be before the week was out.

A heart that was pure Cheyenne pounded hotly in Gold Eagle's chest as he strode beside Mallory toward the dining hall. It had taken all his restraint to release her when he did. Her touch seared him where her hand now rested lightly on his arm, and his control was so tenuous that he dared not look at Captain Tierney.

Gold Eagle caught Mallory's quick, sideward glance. He saw her face flush, and his agitation increased.

She had almost been his.

But he had also seen the way Tierney looked at Mallory. He knew the reason Tierney had come to her room that night, and he knew the man's need was not fed purely by desire.

Those thoughts raised Gold Eagle's blood to new heat. Recognizing the danger there, he steeled himself against the weakness the woman had created within him. He could not allow himself to bow to an emotion that would corrupt his judgment. He needed to remember that the part he would play in his people's future had been revealed to him in the sunlight of a sacred hilltop, and that the dying Matt Bower had been delivered to him to advance that purpose. The woman was not worth the price his people would pay if he failed.

Those thoughts filling his mind, Gold Eagle did not see the woman who darted out of the stable beside him until it was too late. Her small body struck his larger frame solidly and rebounded backward. Catching her arms, he steadied her, then looked down to see her dark eyes widen with recognition.

"Penelope, are you all right?"

Mallory's concerned inquiry registered in Gold Eagle's mind as he allowed his powerful grip on the woman's arms to linger in silent warning. He recognized her, too. Penelope, who was Owl Woman, daughter of Walking Dawn. She had left her people to honor her white blood. She knew who he was, and she remembered the white man's blood he had shed. Fear was in her eyes.

"Penelope?"

"Idiot half-breeds . . ." Captain Tierney's distaste was obvious. "They're too stupid to watch where they're going."

Mallory turned sharply toward the captain, her tone scathing. "That comment wasn't necessary!"

Grateful for the distraction, Gold Eagle slid his hand covertly to the knife at his waist, and Owl Woman stiffened.

Her lips tight, Mallory asked again, "Are you all right, Penelope?" She frowned. "Is something wrong?"

"It is my son." Owl Woman took a shaky breath. "He is sick. His stomach heaves and a great heat consumes him. My husband is with him now. I come to get the medicine my husband uses for such illness."

Mallory glanced at the bottle the woman clutched with whitened knuckles. "That's horse medicine! Isn't there a doctor at the fort?"

Captain Tierney shifted impatiently. "Her son will be all right. She knows what to do. These people take care of their own."

Mallory turned toward the captain with open disdain. "Why don't you go on to dinner without me, *Arthur.*" Her smile was a grimace. "I've lost my appetite."

A furious glare his only response, Captain Tierney turned abruptly and strode across the yard. His gaze on Owl Woman, Gold Eagle did not spare the man a glance.

"Matthew . . ."

Fear held Owl Woman immobile as Gold Eagle turned toward Mallory. He saw Mallory's concern as she continued, "You mixed some Indian herbs for me. Surely you have something that might help Penelope's child."

Owl Woman flashed Mallory a look close to panic.

"Don't be frightened, Penelope. Mr. Bower is a botanist. He studied herbal medicine with tribes to the north. If you let him look at your son, he might be able to give you something to help him."

"No!"

Appearing surprised at Owl Woman's abrupt response, Mallory glanced at Gold Eagle, then offered, "Please reconsider, Penelope. Mr. Bower can't speak, but if he could, I'm sure he'd tell you that he'll gladly help you."

Gold Eagle took Owl Woman's arm and urged her into motion. Mallory protested his action, but Owl Woman turned abruptly to lead the way.

Daylight was fading. Close to despair, Charles addressed the balding telegraph operator who frowned at him across the scarred office desk.

"What do you mean you can't get the message through?"

"I've been trying to send this telegram for two hours!" The fellow indicated the telegrapher's key in front of him. "It's dead."

"What do you mean, it's dead?"

"There must be somethin' wrong with the wires. Nothin's goin' through, that's what I mean!"

"You aren't going to give up, are you?"

"Look . . ." His jowled face beaded with perspiration despite the chill that came with the setting of the sun, the operator glanced at the encroaching darkness beyond the window. "It's gettin' late. Tomorrow's another day! Somebody's probably already workin' on the wires. If you come back in the mornin', I'll probably be able to get your message right through."

"I can't wait until tomorrow."

"Lieutenant, it don't look like you got much choice!"

The telegrapher stood up abruptly.

"What're you doing?"

"I'm goin' home, that's what I'm doin'." The fellow attempted a smile. "Look around you, Lieutenant. Everybody's gone for the day—except me. I done all I can for you for now. Come back tomorrow."

Charles stared at the man in silence.

"I'm goin' home, Lieutenant."

Charles stared at the fellow a moment longer. "All right. I'm sorry. I appreciate your effort."

Emerging out on the street, Charles watched

115

the telegrapher stride away and disappear from sight. He stared motionlessly at the evening traffic passing on the rutted main thoroughfare.

"Couldn't get through, huh, Lieutenant?"

Charles turned toward the sound of Corporal Bell's voice. The young fellow smiled at him sympathetically. "Me and the other fellas were talkin'. We figure you're tryin' to reach Major Bullen. Hell, we're agreed that's what we'd do if we was in your place, what with being responsible for Miss Tompkins and all." His smile faded into a frown. "I heard the fellas at the fort talkin' about that Captain Tierney. He thinks he's a real big man with the ladies. There's not a one of them fellas that likes him, but there's not a one of them who'd go up against him, neither."

"You don't miss much, do you, Bell?"

The young soldier shrugged. "I just thought you'd like to know that me and the fellas don't like it any more than you do that Captain Tierney threw us out of the fort like that. We all like Miss Tompkins. She's a real nice lady, and . . . well . . . we all want you to know that we're ready to start back for Fort Larned as soon as you give the word." Bell added after a pause, "As a matter of fact, me and the others are ready to start back right now. All you have to do is give the command."

Charles stiffened "I wish I could go back right now, but I think you know as well as I do what'll happen if I do that without a direct order from Major Bullen."

His mouth firming at the young corporal's crestfallen expression, Charles continued flatly, "We'll wait, but you can tell the men I intend to return to Fort Larned as soon as I get Major Bullen's response."

"Yes, sir."

Watching as Corporal Bell walked slowly back down the street, Charles then turned to look at the darkened telegraph office behind him. He didn't like this delay. Mallory's face haunted him. He had a feeling things were moving too fast back at Fort Larned. Mallory was too impetuous, too quick to take on another man's battles. She had made a dangerous enemy in Captain Tierney, and he had the feeling she had made an even more dangerous "friend" in the silent Matthew Bower.

A familiar sense of unrest returned at the thought of the mute botanist. The way the man sat his horse, controlling it with effortless skill . . . the way he carried himself, with a silent confidence that bespoke hard challenges met . . . the way he walked, his stride as smooth and silent as a cat's . . . He hadn't learned any of that in the pages of a botany book. He hadn't earned that powerful stretch of shoulder using a paper and pencil, either. As for those damned, cold eyes, Charles had the feeling that they had seen more than any Eastern botanist would see in a lifetime, and that they hid more than anyone realized.

Mallory's inexplicable need to defend the man baffled him.

Or perhaps it did not.

Mallory's face again flashed before him, and the knot inside Charles clenched tightly. He had never met a woman like Mallory. She was unique—bold, courageous, beautiful . . . and daring. Too daring for her own good!

But he'd be damned before he'd let her get away from him!

His sense of urgency growing, Charles scanned the street. His gaze came to rest on a well-lit saloon midway down. Somebody had to know more about Matthew Bower than vague stories if Bower had been in the territory as long as he claimed.

The lively sounds from within the saloon beckoned. There was no better place to begin.

The small room was warm and brightly lit as they entered.

Gold Eagle looked at the baby, who lay limply in a wooden crib nearby. He was dressed in the clothing of a white man's child and he was covered with a white man's blanket, but the raven black of his hair and the russet tint of his skin declared his heritage boldly. Only his eyes, round in shape and light blue in color, betrayed his father's blood. But the light eyes were unfocused, and the russet skin burned hot and dry.

Gold Eagle frowned at the gagging sound that gurgled within the child the moment before he retched weakly, then lay motionless as Owl Woman wiped the sputum from his face.

"Joseph . . ." Owl Woman's whisper did not

rouse the child. Gold Eagle watched as she turned anxiously to her husband. He saw her whisper to him, and he saw the man's head jerk in his direction.

Gold Eagle slid his hand under his jacket to the knife at his waist. He saw fear flash in Owl Woman's eyes the moment before her husband spoke.

"My name is Jay Dolan. Penelope tells me you have medicine that might help my son."

Gold Eagle searched the white man's face. He saw uncertainty but no suspicion as Mallory stepped up beside him to respond in his stead.

"Mr. Bower can't talk, you know."

"Oh, yeah . . ." Dolan's bearded face creased into lines of concern. "I forgot. That don't make no difference. I understand Injun sign language." He continued, "I heard about you. You was livin' up north with the Injuns. Some of the men here have a lot to say about that, but I don't see as how I got any room to talk." He paused. "Well, can you help my boy or not?"

Gold Eagle held the side of his right hand against his heart. With two fingers pointing left, he rolled his wrist back and forth.

"Maybe?" Dolan cursed and turned angrily to Owl Woman. "Seems like this fella ain't sure of nothin'! Why did you bring him here?"

Gold Eagle signed again.

"You're goin' to try." Dolan took a deep breath, his concern mounting as the baby shuddered almost convulsively. "Well, we ain't got no medicine at all. There ain't a doctor within

119

miles, and Joseph's gettin' worse. Penelope says you know Injun medicine. I don't know how good it might be, but my boy's real sick. I got to do somethin'."

Owl Woman looked at Gold Eagle for a silent moment before she whispered, "I will go with you to your quarters. I will help you get what you need to treat my son."

Gold Eagle turned toward the door. Mallory started to follow him, and he signaled sharply.

"He says he wants you to wait here," Dolan explained at her confused glance. He continued as Gold Eagle signaled again. "He says he'll be right back."

Mallory glanced at Owl Woman, then surrendered her place at his side to the concerned mother, and Gold Eagle's respect for her grew.

Out in the yard, Gold Eagle waited only until they had turned out of sight before he rounded on Owl Woman sharply. He saw her shudder as he addressed her in a harsh whisper.

"You know who I am."

The small woman's face tightened. "Yes, I know. The Arapaho speak of the great courage of the Cheyenne brave, Gold Eagle. They say his skin is white, but his heart is Cheyenne. They say he is the bravest of warriors, that when his face is painted with the colors of battle, death for the white man rides at his side."

She paused. "They say Gold Eagle's eyes are light and clear, so clear that all who look into them may see his Cheyenne heart. I have looked into your eyes, and I have seen. I know you are

Gold Eagle, that you come in disguise to this fort. But I do not know why you risk death to wear another man's clothes and assume another man's life."

"You do not need to know these things."

"I must know you will not bring other Cheyenne here to slaughter all in the night. I must know that my husband's and my child's blood will not be spilled."

"I do not come here to spill blood."

Owl Woman's dark eyes searched his face. "This man whose clothes and name you assume . . ."

"He is dead, but not at my hand."

Owl Woman nodded. "The white woman does not know the mask you wear. She believes you are the man you claim to be. I do not concern myself with that deception, except to ask if it is true that you carry Matthew Bower's medicine and can help my son."

Gold Eagle studied Owl Woman's sober expression. He had seen the look she wore many times in his village, on the faces of desperate women who came to Walking Buffalo to seek help for their sick children. He responded, "I have medicine."

Owl Woman released a shuddering breath. "I ask that you help my son. I will not betray you."

Gold Eagle looked deep into the woman's eyes. Satisfied to see the truth there, he turned to his quarters.

*   *   *

The heat was intense. The acrid scent of herbs filled the room. Leaning over the crib, Matthew looked down on the motionless child.

Standing a few feet away, Mallory watched in silence, as she had for the past few hours since Matthew had returned with Penelope from his quarters.

Mallory glanced at the open journal on the table. She moved closer, noting the detailed drawings of plants and flowers, each carefully labeled in Latin and English. She marveled at the precise descriptions of usage, the detailed methods of treatment, the notations made as to the effect to be expected at every stage of the cure. She noted Matthew's concentration when he reviewed the words written there. She saw the intensity with which he worked to pulverize the labeled herbs carefully matched to the names on the gold-edged pages, before adding them to bath water into which Owl Woman lowered the child. She observed as Matthew turned again to the pages to select new herbs to be used. She watched with particular fascination as Matthew's strong hands worked with the dried blossoms, reducing them to a fine dust which he added to a sweet syrup later fed to the child.

Awed that hands so strong could work so delicately, Mallory recalled the wonder she had felt at their touch. She remembered those strong fingers in her hair, the callused palms against her cheeks. She recalled the subdued strength of those hands as they caressed her back, then curved around her to cup her breasts. She remembered that she had never felt so inflamed by a touch, and so imbued with longing.

Allowing her gaze full range while his attention was elsewhere, Mallory studied Matthew more closely. His hair was longer than she had realized. It had been bleached by the summer sun so that the strands still glowed with its light. His profile was strong and sharply chiseled. His shoulders were broad and straight. She remembered the strength of his arms, the way he carried her as easily as if she were a child. She remembered *being* in his arms, and her heart thudded heavily in her breast.

As if sensing her thoughts, Matthew looked up at her abruptly. His pale eyes locked with hers, and she was swept into the sudden maelstrom of passion reflected there. Her breathing grew ragged.

"Joseph is better."

Penelope's soft statement snapped Mallory back to the reality of the moment. She saw Matthew look back at the child and touch his cheek, then the flicker of satisfaction that crossed his expression before he stepped back.

"You did it." Dolan's thin Irish face relaxed into a tired smile. "You got his fever down and you stopped the retching."

Matthew signed and Jay nodded. "Tell Penelope what to do, and she'll take over from here." The relieved father shook his head. "Thank you. Joseph is—"

His voice failed him as he viewed his son's

comfortable slumber, and Dolan was forced to pause. He took a breath, then continued, "Joseph is goin' to be fine now, I know he is. I wasn't sure about that, for a while." He glanced at the small woman beside him. "Me and Penelope already lost one son the way Joseph was goin', you know."

Mallory looked at Penelope with surprise, in time to see the small woman wipe a tear from her cheek. She looked back at the relieved Irishman to see his eyes fill as he continued determinedly, "I want to thank you for what you did. And I want you to remember—it's here for the askin' if there's anythin' you ever need."

Mallory noted with surprise that Matthew did not respond. Instead, selecting a few herbs from the marked packages, he placed them on the table and turned away. She did not speak when he took her arm and ushered her outside, then closed the door firmly behind them.

They had gone only a short distance when Matthew turned abruptly toward her and pulled her into the shadows. She caught her breath when he looked down at her with eyes of molten silver. His mouth descended toward hers, and her lips separated to welcome his. But he stiffened unexpectedly and drew back. The heat within his gaze froze when a figure stepped into view beside them.

The music was raucous, the shouts of laughter shrill and piercing as Charles tilted his head back to empty his glass with practiced skill. He shivered as the warm red-eye hit his stomach. He frowned at the light touch on his shoulder and the sultry voice that purred into his ear, "Ain't you tired of leanin' up against that bar all alone, soldier boy?"

"Lieutenant, ma'am." Charles turned toward the heavily painted young woman who had tucked herself against his side. "I'm a lieutenant in the U.S. Army."

"Yeah, an officer." She inched closer. "Leanin' up against that bar ain't half as much fun as leanin' up against me, though." She batted her eyes. "I can guarantee that."

It occurred to Charles that the young saloon girl was pretty—somewhere underneath all the paint on her youthful face. Her features were small and her teeth were straight. When she talked, a dimple winked in and out at the corner of her mouth. But her hair was dark, not a fiery color that startled the eye. And her eyes were brown, not a shade of green that was unlike any he had ever seen.

"My name's Jewel."

And her name wasn't Mallory.

"What's yours?"

Charles struggled to clear his head. He glanced up at the clock on the wall. He had been standing at that bar for two hours. He scanned the room. He had approached every man in the place with an inquiry about Matthew Bower. He had raised a few eyebrows and gotten a few general responses, but the responses had all run the same way.

"Yeah, seems to me I heard somethin' about a fella livin' with the Injuns up north—some kind of doctor or somethin'."

"That ain't possible. There ain't no white man who'd get out alive if he went up north alone into Pawnee country. Hell, them bloodthirsty heathens don't give a white man no chance at all."

"You say the fella can't talk? Poor fella."

"What did you say that fella's name was—Matthew what?"

Hell, it was useless. . . .

"What did you say your name was, Lieutenant?"

Charles drew himself erect, then cursed when he discovered the room was swaying. He looked at the empty glass in front of him. Two hours and how many glasses of red-eye? He knew the answer to that question. However many glasses he had emptied, it had been *too* many.

Charles glanced at the table in the corner of the room where Corporals Hodge, Bell, Whittier, and Knoll sat with ladies who looked unnaturally alike with their heavily painted faces and low-cut gowns. He blinked to clear his eyes, realizing that there was not an unsteady smile among the four soldiers.

Good men.

It was time for him to leave.

"What's your name, Lieutenant?"

"You're wasting your time, Jewel." The persistent slurring of his speech annoyed him as Charles continued, "I came in here lookin' for somebody who might know a man called Matthew Bower who—"

"—who lived with the Injuns up north for a while. Yeah, I know."

He smiled. She deserved an answer.

"My name's Lieutenant Charles Moore. But what you don't know is that my body's standing here, but my mind's back at Fort Larned with a special lady."

"Lieutenant, honey . . ." Jewel's purr became a seductive growl, "It ain't your mind I'm after. Your body'll do just fine."

Charles laughed aloud.

"You're a clever woman."

"That's right : . . clever enough to know that you're a special fella who's too good to let get away."

Jewel brushed his lips with hers, and Charles's smile faded. "My lady's back in Fort Larned." He amended that statement. "She doesn't know it yet, but she's my lady. I'm set on her, and there's nobody else who'll do. Sorry, Jewel."

Reaching into his pocket, Charles took out his pouch and pressed a gold coin into her hand. "Here, buy yourself a drink." He took a stabilizing breath. "Never thought I'd see the day . . . but I'm sayin' good night."

Struggling to steady the unnatural sway of the floor underneath him, Charles emerged onto the street with relief. He shook his head, then cursed softly when the street spun briefly around him.

A waste of time . . . the whole night.

He'd be at that telegraph office first thing in the morning, come hell or high water.

Mallory's image flashed in front of him, and Charles felt his frustration anew.

"What are you doing here?"

Mallory stepped out of Gold Eagle's arms as Captain Tierney emerged from the shadows a few feet away.

"I was taking a walk." Tierney's expression was obscured by darkness, but the stiffness of his posture was revealing. Gradually closing the distance between them, he continued, "I noticed that there was a lot of activity in Dolan's quarters. The child is sick again?"

Mallory raised her chin. "He's feeling better. Matthew helped him with some—"

"—some Indian medicine. Of course." Tierney shrugged. "The boy's sickly. It's only a matter of time before he goes the way of his brother. It's that mixed blood—it's weak."

Mallory gasped aloud at his callousness, but Gold Eagle was unaffected. Tierney's strategy was obvious. He wanted to infuriate Mallory, to destroy as thoroughly as possible the passionate moment he had interrupted. Gold Eagle would not let that happen.

Gold Eagle took Mallory's arm and urged her gently forward, but Mallory would not permit Tierney's statement to stand.

"Yes, of course, Arthur. Since you are an

expert on the subject of mixed blood, you would know that to be a fact."

"It doesn't take a genius to know that to mix something is to dilute its full potency."

"Hybrids are often better than the original."

"Half-breeds aren't."

Mallory had had enough. "Good night, Arthur."

Tierney stepped into their path, his taut smile illuminated by the lantern nearby. "I don't mean to offend you, Mallory. I'm just stating a fact. If you had more time to spend out here, you'd realize that what I'm telling you is true."

"I doubt that."

"It is."

His enforced silence almost more than he could bear, Gold Eagle drew Mallory alongside him as he attempted to move past the man planted firmly in their path.

Pointedly ignoring Gold Eagle, Tierney addressed Mallory again. "You didn't come to the dining hall for dinner, so I had one of my men leave you something to eat in your quarters."

Her reply spoken through clenched teeth, Mallory muttered, "Thank you."

"I'll accompany you to your door."

Mallory glanced up at Gold Eagle. Her anger growing more obvious by the moment, she replied, "That isn't necessary. Matthew will see that I'm delivered there safely."

"Yes . . . I'm sure."

Tierney fell in beside Mallory as Gold Eagle maintained a noncommittal facade. He reminded himself that the day of retribution was not far away. When it arrived, it would be sweet indeed.

At Mallory's door, Gold Eagle waited as Mallory turned back to Tierney in curt dismissal.

"Good night, Arthur."

Tierney did not move.

Obviously frustrated, Mallory looked up at Gold Eagle. She whispered, "Good night, Matthew. It . . . it was a wonderfully educational evening. When I go back home, you can be sure that I'll do my best to see that the native cures coming out of this part of the country are taken seriously."

Ignoring Tierney, who stood rigidly silent, Gold Eagle signed a response.

Tierney sneered. "I guess that's supposed to mean good night."

No, that was not what it meant.

Mallory turned and slipped into her room.

It did not mean good night at all.

About to leave, Gold Eagle was stopped by Tierney's low hiss.

"You're wasting your time. You'll never have her!"

Hesitating only long enough for the reply in his gaze to register clearly, Gold Eagle left Captain Tierney seething behind him.

Mallory twisted restlessly on the broad bunk bed. She couldn't sleep. The room was too warm. She was uncomfortable. She pushed the coverlet to her waist, only to feel the nip of the chill air, and she mumbled under her breath. No, she wasn't warm. Nor was she cold. She just couldn't sleep.

Matthew's image returned as it had countless times since she had bid him good night at the door, and her restlessness increased. The memory of the intensity in his clear-eyed gaze again set her heart to pounding, and an aching longing rose inside her. She had never heard him speak. She had never exchanged thoughts with him in any accepted language, yet the communication between them was profound. He had worked laboriously over Penelope's sick child, and she had felt his concern. She had suffered his anger at Captain Tierney's calculated insults and she had admired his obvious restraint. She had shared his hunger when he touched her, and when his lips met hers the communication between them had become a singing joy.

It occurred to Mallory that her arrival on the frontier had been fraught with surprises. She had not anticipated that she would be forced into subterfuge in order to be allowed into Fort Larned, or that she would experience such opposition in obtaining the information she had come to get. She had not expected that she would meet a handsome lieutenant whose friendship and guidance she would grow to value. Nor had she anticipated that she would meet a fort commander whose intolerance and lack of character would leave her frustrated beyond all measure. Confounding her above all, however, was the realization that those frustrations faded into obscurity in the face of the emotions presently running rampant within her.

She hadn't wanted Matthew to leave her . . . not yet. She had wanted time to talk to him, to explore the feelings that came to life each time their glances met. She knew Matthew wanted that time as much as she—time that had been stolen from them by Captain Tierney's appearance.

Strangely, she somehow sensed that their time was preciously short. That sensation lent a compelling urgency to her feelings that she could not clearly explain.

Captain Tierney had been furious at her dismissal of him. He was a man who would not accept—

Mallory's thoughts jerked to a halt at a flicker of movement outside her window. Unable to move, she watched as if mesmerized as the sash was silently raised, and a shadowy figure slipped into the room.

The broad outline approached, visible in relief against the moonlight streaming through the pane behind it. Light hair, left unbound against powerful masculine shoulders, was transformed into a silvery cascade by the pale shafts of light. Shoulders, stripped bare with one smooth motion, stretched to immense proportions as the figure stood over her bed. Clear eyes, warmed again into molten silver, gazed down into hers . . .

. . . and she was his.

Matthew made no sound as he lay beside her and drew her into his arms. His lips touched hers, and she knew no words could describe the myriad feelings that blazed to life inside her.

Hardly aware of the moment when her arms slipped around him in return, Mallory drew Matthew close. She parted her lips under his kiss, surrendering as he plundered her mouth in loving assault. She clutched him closer as he abandoned her lips intermittently to brush her fluttering lids, to explore the line of her cheek, to taste the delicate skin of her neck.

She felt the hunger building as Matthew's kiss slipped lower. She gasped aloud as he found the waiting crests of her breasts and worshipped them with loving ardor. She spoke his name in gasping breaths as the hard, male length of him slid downward upon her heated flesh. Her labored breathing caught in her throat as his lips found the warm delta between her thighs. Her heart seemed to stop when his kiss tasted the sweet moistness within.

Uncertain, her heart pounding so heavily that she feared it would burst, Mallory looked down at Matthew to see his gaze meet hers. His clear eyes spoke of his hunger. They declared his need. They pleaded for her understanding of a longing so great that it could not be restrained. They expressed words of love so clearly that the sound became a throbbing echo within her.

The reverberation lingered as Matthew lowered his mouth in loving intimacy once more.

Devoured by his kiss, Mallory gasped with responsive ardor. Consumed by the wonder, she called his name aloud. Inflamed by the ferocious heat Matthew had kindled to life, Mallory was left breathless by the sweet ecstasy that erupted in sudden, shuddering tumult within her.

Accepting her body's passionate tribute, Matthew slid himself up on her once more.

Mallory strove to catch her breath as Matthew's muscled length lay hard upon her. He waited, the broad expanse of his body silently overwhelming as he loomed above her. The ragged, unbound length of his pale hair streamed against his bare shoulders, emphasizing their sheer, raw power, giving him a savage quality that Mallory had not recognized before. It set her heart to a new pounding as he slowly lowered his mouth to hers.

The sweet scent of her skin . . . the heat of her naked flesh pressed intimately close . . .

Gold Eagle covered Mallory's lips with his, drinking deeply once more. He savored the taste of her, finding it unmatched by any he had known. The shadows of the darkened room did not conceal the beauty of eyes the color of new spring. The semi-light did not dim the glory of tresses streaked with the color of sunset. It did not dull the gleam of flawless white skin that inflamed his desire.

She was his enemy.

Gold Eagle's kiss deepened.

She would despise him if she knew.

His hunger grew.

The arms now clutching him closely would repulse him when his secret was revealed.

Gold Eagle was seared by need.

Allowing Mallory long moments to memorize his face, Gold Eagle adjusted his weight against her. She would look back on this moment, and she would remember. Burned into her mind would be the trembling heat as their bodies met. Etched into her memory would be the mutual hunger they shared. She would not be able to disavow the truth that their passion this night would not be denied.

Gold Eagle thrust himself deep inside her. Mallory gasped as her female flesh closed around him. He read the wonder in her eyes. He saw the joy and need.

Exultation pounded through Gold Eagle. He would sate Mallory's need, and he would sate his own. Together they would bring this moment to full fruition and revel in its glory.

She was his enemy.

She would hate him when she learned the truth.

But for now, she was *his*.

Restless, unable to sleep, Captain Tierney threw back the coverlet and stood up abruptly. The room was cold. He cursed aloud as he walked to the pot-bellied stove in the center of the room and jerked the door open. He cursed again as he threw fuel on the smoldering flames, then slammed the door shut with sudden rage.

This was not the way he had planned to spend the night! The witch had dismissed him—as imperiously as if she were a queen!

His fury of that dismissal flushed Tierney with a scorching heat. Frustrated by the perverse hardening in his groin that followed, Tierney was forced into a silent admission. However harsh his feelings toward Mallory Tompkins, the red-haired witch provoked an excitement that he had not felt in years. She prompted mental fantasies that even now hardened him to the point of pain. Uncertain if his feelings were stirred by revenge or simple animal lust, he was sure of only one thing. He would have her.

Pacing, Tierney considered that thought. He would not suffer this frustration much longer. His only consolation was knowing that the silent bastard who assaulted him with those damned cold eyes suffered the same frustrations as he.

Tierney's pacing halted. There was one difference between him and the mute. That difference lay in the fact that Bower would never have Mallory Tompkins.

But *he* would.

Yes.

Returning to his bunk, Tierney lay down and pulled the coverlet back over himself.

It was just a matter of time.

Passion had faded to sleep. Looking down at Mallory, Gold Eagle felt the heady joy of possession sweep his senses. He had claimed this woman as no man ever had before.

Mallory was sleeping soundly. She had given herself to him wholly, and exhaustion had taken over now. Her slender white body was replete.

Gold Eagle stroked her fiery hair. He caressed her cheek. He drew her closer. She could not hear him.

"Mallory . . ."

The name was sweet on his lips. He savored it.

"Mallory . . ."

It raised a warmth within him reserved for this night alone.

"Mallory . . ."

Her name, softly whispered.

Mallory stirred in her sleep. A strange warmth cradled her, holding her tight.

"Mallory . . ."

She shifted again, unwilling to leave the reassuring heat that held her so comfortingly close.

"Mallory . . ."

Mallory awoke slowly. Reality returned. She lay in Matthew's arms. He looked silently down at her, his eyes unreadable.

Mallory searched the strong, sober planes of Matthew's face, confusion causing her to frown. "I . . . I thought I heard you say my name."

Matthew made no response.

Mallory strained to see past the shadows that

137

shaded his features. She pressed, "It was your voice. I recognized it."

Matthew stroked a strand of hair back from her face. He drew her closer, his hard, muscled body moving to bring her slender curves more intimately close, but she would not be deterred.

"Matthew . . ." Mallory paused. She forced herself to continue, "I heard you speak my name."

Matthew responded at last, a quick decisive gesture that allowed no further argument, and she was suddenly ashamed. "No . . . of course you didn't say my name. I'm sorry." She pressed her hand against his cheek, her smile uncertain. "I was dreaming, I suppose. It was just so real."

Mallory pressed her mouth to Matthew's. She allowed her lips to linger before she drew back. "I know I'll never hear you speak, but I don't need to, now. I've heard you say my name, even if it's only in my dreams, and I—"

Matthew cut her words short with his kiss, and Mallory was lost in the renewed wonder it stirred. His kiss deepened. She felt his body harden, and she surrendered wholly to the responsive heat it raised.

Mallory gasped as Matthew shifted subtly and slipped himself inside her. Her last, remaining thought was fleeting.

She had been so sure he spoke her name.

Chapter Six

The sun was too bright. The sounds of early morning traffic on the street were deafening. His breakfast coffee had been as bitter as poison. It had turned his stomach, and he was truly uncertain if he'd be able to hold down the meager meal he had eaten.

But he'd be damned before he'd let that stop him.

Charles walked stiffly up the street toward the telegraph office. He'd had a difficult night, with nightmares of every shape, size, and variety visiting him during his fitful sleep. Most overwhelming of all had been the fleeting visions of Mallory that had haunted him, awake and sleeping. He had never been more grateful to see the light of morning than he had been that day, and he had already determined that however many more inquiries he had to make before he found someone who could give him information about Matthew Bower, he would *not* make them with a glass of red-eye in his hand.

Charles took a shaky breath as he walked the last steps to the telegraph office. The telegrapher looked up with a smile when he closed the door behind him.

"Good morning, Lieutenant!"

The fellow's voice boomed like thunder, causing Charles to wince as he responded, "Good morning."

"Looks like you had a hard night."

Charles did not bother to reply.

"Well, the only thing I can say about that is, things can only get better from here." The fellow's jowled face moved into a grin. "Looks like whatever happened to the telegraph line might've been fixed."

"What?" Charles blinked, uncertain. "You'll be able to get a wire through to Fort Riley?"

The telegrapher's smile dimmed. "No, I didn't say that."

Charles's patience was in short supply. "Well, what did you say?"

"All I said was that it looks like the line was fixed."

"Which means?"

"I think I can get your wire as far as Salina."

"That's not good enough. I have to reach Fort Riley."

The fellow's smile faded. "I ain't guaranteein' that. All's I can do is try."

Charles took a firm hold on his forbearance. "You have a copy of the wire. Send it. I'll wait."

And wait . . . and wait . . . and wait.

The sounds of morning nudged at Mallory's sleep as she slowly awakened. Her body ached, but a sweet languor she could not quite identify warmed her veins, and she—

Mallory forced her eyes open, moving her hand simultaneously to the bunk beside her. He was gone.

Images of the long night past slipped across her mind in heady progression, and Mallory took a shuddering breath. Raising her hand to her forehead, she felt the heat that flushed her skin, and she gave an embarrassed laugh. Had that really been she—that woman who came alive in Matthew's arms?

Mallory pushed a strand of hair back from her cheek, and she remembered Matthew's touch. She uncovered her naked body to stand, and she recalled Matthew's ardent worship of her flesh. She forced herself to her feet, and she remembered that Matthew had held her tightly in his arms through the night, refusing to relinquish her.

Bright sunlight shone through the window, indicating that morning had fully dawned. Matthew had obviously left in order to protect her from the gossip that would ensue if he was found in her quarters. She knew she should be grateful for that, but she wished it had been otherwise. She missed feeling the warmth of his arms around her.

Halting the advance of her thoughts abruptly, Mallory shook her head. What was wrong with her? She was acting like a lovesick adolescent while she couldn't be certain what Matthew was feeling now.

Mallory faced her nakedness in the washstand mirror. She grimaced. Blazing hair in wild disarray, eyes shadowed from her sleep-deprived night, lips bruised from ardent kisses, an unclothed expanse of white flesh still sensitized from Matthew's fervent lovemaking . . .

The beauty of that lovemaking claimed her mind suddenly. Matthew's taut skin had been smooth and warm under her palms as she returned caress for caress. She had wound her fingers tightly in his pale hair, glorying in that familiarity. She had accommodated his great, muscular length with loving ease as he lay upon her, and he had fitted himself to her slim proportions with a tenderness that set her heart to pounding. Then when they began the slow, sensuous rhythm of love . . .

Mallory amended her previous thought. No, she knew what Matthew was feeling now.

Lifting the pitcher with a shaking hand, Mallory filled the washbasin and snatched up the washcloth. She worked up a lather with the soap provided, then gasped when the cold water touched her skin. She laughed aloud, wondering where Matthew was at that moment.

* * *

"I called you to my office this morning for a specific purpose," Captain Tierney addressed Gold Eagle coldly, continuing, "Corporal Walker is present to interpret your responses. I want to make sure we understand each other completely."

Tierney walked around his desk. Halting a few feet away, he waited for a response that did not come.

Gold Eagle glanced at Walker. The corporal was distinctly ill at ease. It had occurred to Gold Eagle when the young soldier knocked on his door, only minutes after he'd covertly returned from Mallory's room, that the timing had been close indeed. He had awakened later than he'd intended. The warmth of Mallory's sweet flesh had been difficult to abandon, but he had seen the danger in lingering.

"You heard me, didn't you, Bower?"

Gold Eagle did not respond.

Captain Tierney's smoothly shaved face twitched with irritation. "You can hear me, so don't pretend you can't! I expect an answer when I speak, even if it comes from a person who can only talk with his hands!"

Waiting a moment longer, Gold Eagle forced himself to respond.

"He says he heard you, Captain."

"I gathered that. The man's not deaf. He's only dumb." Tierney addressed Gold Eagle directly. "But even a mute can understand what I'm about to say." Squaring his shoulders, Tierney continued, "As temporary commandant of this fort, it's my duty to protect the safety of this post and everyone in it. In my judgment, the time you spent living with savage Indian tribes who have refused to sign peace treaties with the U.S. government makes you a security risk. For that reason, I'm ordering you out of this fort by sundown." Pausing for a moment of pure self-gratification, Tierney continued, "Do you comprehend what I said?"

Gold Eagle restrained the swift rise of his anger. He had not expected this. He would not accept it.

"Do you understand!"

Gold Eagle leveled his stare. Looking directly into Tierney's eyes so that Walker's translation would have the impact of his own spoken words, he signed a response.

"He hears what you say, but he doesn't understand. He thought the military was brought here to protect citizens, not to throw them out into a wilderness that you claim is filled with savages."

Tierney did not evade Gold Eagle's stare. "Savages with whom he has proven friendships. He's in no danger from them."

Gold Eagle signed again.

"He says that's true. He's in no danger from the Indians, but his horse is exhausted and nearly starved because of the time he spent lost and wanderin' on a frozen plain where there was little grass for his mount to eat. He says the animal's too weak to make it to the next out-

post. He says, without his horse, he won't make
it, either."

"Dolan will provide him with a horse in
trade."

"He doesn't want another horse. He wants to
keep his own."

"That isn't an option!" Tierney's eyes narrowed. "And it isn't an excuse. I want him out
of the fort by sundown."

"He says he can't be ready by then."

"He'll have to be!"

Gold Eagle's hands moved in a lengthy response.

"He says he'll compose an official letter of
complaint to your superior, chargin' that he
was expelled from the fort without good reason,
and sayin' that you should be held responsible
if anythin' should happen to him before he
reaches the next outpost. He says he has important friends back East who are waitin' for
him to deliver the work he did, and that if anythin' happens to him because of you, you'll pay
a heavy price."

"Is he threatening me?"

Gold Eagle's response was concise.

"Yes."

Gold Eagle saw the slow rage that suffused
Tierney's face. He watched as that rage warred
with better judgment. He knew the battle was
won when Tierney stepped back and responded
coolly, "I'll give you three days."

Gold Eagle's response was immediate.

"He says that's not enough."

"It's going to have to be, because that's all he's going to get!" Tierney glared as he hissed, "Get out of here . . . now, Bower. Get yourself ready to leave. If you're not out of this fort in three days, you'll spend the rest of your time here behind bars. And I'm warning you, once you're in my stockade, that's where you'll stay until I'm ready to deal with you again. Do you understand?"

Gold Eagle's eyes flashed a heated reply.

"Get out of here!" Turning toward Walker, Tierney added, "You, too!"

Gold Eagle turned away. He felt the man's fury follow them as Walker accompanied him outside and pulled the door closed behind them. They had only gone a few steps when Gold Eagle turned toward Walker and signed an extended speech.

Walker flushed, then glanced cautiously behind him. "I figured you didn't know nothin' about military procedure when you out and out challenged Captain Tierney by sayin' you was goin' to stay at the fort as long as you wanted to. Hell, I knew he'd do somethin' crazy, then! So, I figured tellin' him you'd write an official protest would put a scare into him. That fella's got big ambitions. I didn't figure he'd take a chance of sacrificin' them just because he don't like you and wants you out of his way."

Gold Eagle signed a response.

"Are you sayin' I'm smart? That's real nice!"

Gold Eagle signed again.

Walker's freckled face sobered. "I appreciate

that. I consider you a friend, too. You don't really need to feel you're in my debt."

Gold Eagle extended his hand, and Walker accepted it with a smile. His smile became a grin. "For a man of peace, you sure get yourself into a lot of trouble, Mr. Bower."

A raised brow his only reply, Gold Eagle continued toward the yard.

"No answer yet, Bill?"

The telegrapher and he had long since gotten past formalities as Charles waited hour after hour in the small office, listening to the click of the telegraph key. Corporal Bell had reported to him and had then left to deliver the orders of the day to the rest of his detachment. He had consumed another poisonous cup of coffee, which only gave him a monstrous headache. He felt damned bad, and Bill's reply didn't make him feel any better.

"No, I ain't gettin' nothin' no further than Salina."

"Damn it all!"

Charles stood up abruptly. Whatever the reason for the telegrapher's inability to get his message through, he couldn't take the chance of waiting any longer.

Turning toward the door, Charles halted abruptly as the telegrapher called out behind him, "Hey, where're you goin'? Do you want me to keep tryin' to send this message or not?"

"Keep trying. I'll be back."

Out on the street, Charles took a stabilizing

147

breath that ended in a cough. His stomach queasy, he headed back toward his room. He had ordered his men to wait for him in the restaurant next door to the hotel. He'd give the telegrapher two more hours to get that message through, two hours while he'd sleep off his present physical discomfort. If the message hadn't gotten through by then, he'd have no choice but to start for Fort Riley.

Charles frowned. He had promised Mallory he'd be back within the week. He'd never make it if he was forced to deliver his report to Major Bullen in person. His only remaining hope would be that the lines would clear and he'd be able to get his message through to the major from a station along the way.

Lost in anxious thought, Charles did not notice the two figures approaching him. The young woman addressed him cheerfully.

"Good mornin', Lieutenant!"

Charles turned sharply toward her, regretting the quick movement when his head throbbed worse than ever.

"You don't look so good." The young woman grinned. "Guess you didn't get out of the Maverick early enough last night."

"Jewel . . ." Charles's smile was little more than a grimace. "Some lessons are hard to learn, no matter how many times they're taught."

"I don't know . . ." Jewel looked closer, then raised her hand to his forehead. "You look like you might have a fever."

"If I do, I earned it by forgetting what my limit is."

Jewel shrugged. "There ain't too many of us who realize what our limits are until it's too late." She forced a smile. "Anyways, I thought about you this mornin' when I heard two fellas talkin' outside the saloon. One of them said he knew that fella you was askin' about last night, that he met him when he was up north durin' the summer."

Charles's attention was suddenly acute.

Indicating the small man beside her, Jewel continued, "This here's the fella. His name's Sam Clover."

The small man nodded. "Pleased to meet you, Lieutenant. Jewel says you was real curious about Matt Bower, and that you was hopin' to meet somebody who could tell you somethin' more about him." He smiled. "Well, I'm your man. I ran into him when a tradin' party I was with went to a Pawnee village up north. I don't suppose I'll ever forget him."

Forcing himself to concentrate, Charles extended his hand. "Lieutenant Charles Moore, sir. I appreciate your taking the time to come and talk to me." He proceeded cautiously, "I ran into Matthew Bower back at Fort Larned. I was curious about him, all right. There was something strange about him that I couldn't quite put my finger on."

"Strange . . . I suppose that's so. I never met a fella like him before. Can't talk, you know."

"Yes, I know."

"But he learned Injun sign language just as quick as a snap. Hell, it took me a lot longer to make myself understood when I first started tradin' in Injun country. He didn't have no trouble though. Them Injuns up north took a real likin' to him, them Crows, Pawnee, and Crees."

"Why's that, do you think?"

"Because he treated them real nice, I figure, them medicine men especially. Kind of like they was somethin' special, like real doctors and all. He was always writin' what they told him in them books of his, and payin' such close attention to them cures they did, that you'd think he was studyin' to become a medicine man himself."

"What did you think of him personally?"

"Never met a nicer fella—or a smarter fella, neither. He made you feel kind of peaceful, like you knew you didn't need to worry about nothin' you was tellin' him, 'cause he could be trusted."

Charles was getting uneasy. "He made you feel peaceful, you say, like you didn't have to worry about anything when he was near. Was that because he was such a big man?"

"He was big, I guess. I didn't pay much attention to it. There was somethin' else about him—like it was as if he talked with them eyes of his."

Charles's head was throbbing so painfully that he could hardly think, but the sick feeling growing in his stomach had nothing to do with physical distress. It looked as if he had been wrong about Matt Bower, that he had been influenced by jealousy because Mallory had stood up for the man.

"Them eyes of his was so black that when he looked at you—"

Charles stiffened, suddenly alert. "Black? You said his eyes were black?"

"Black as coal—just like his hair. He'd never pass for an Injun, though, not with a beard that thick."

The sudden pounding of Charles's heart increased the pain in his head as he pressed, "You're sure of that. You're talking about Matthew Bower . . . the botanist who was living with the Indians up north."

"What's that you say? A bot—botanist? I don't know nothin' about that. He was always drawin' pictures of flowers in them books of his, if that helps you any."

Charles took a breath. "When was the last time you saw him?"

"Durin' the summer. He said he was hopin' to leave before the bad weather set in. He wanted to get back home to his wife and kids."

"His wife . . ."

"And kids. He had three, I think he said."

"Black hair and eyes . . ."

"Black as a crow's wing, they was."

Charles extended his hand again toward Sam Clover. "Thank you, Mr. Clover."

"Sam's the name."

"Thank you, Sam. I can't tell you how much I appreciate the information you've given me."

"Say hello to Matt for me if you see him, will you? Real nice fella."

"I will . . . if I ever see him."

But he knew he never would. The real Matthew Bower was gone, and another man, whoever he was, had taken his place. He didn't like this. He had to get back to Fort Larned. There was no need to wait for Major Bullen's orders now. Captain Tierney, bastard that he was, needed to know that a man had entered his fort under false pretenses. And Mallory—most especially Mallory—needed to know that Matthew Bower wasn't the man he claimed to be.

Charles took an unsteady step forward. His head was spinning.

"Somethin' wrong, Lieutenant?" Jewel's surprisingly strong hand gripped his arm.

Yes, something was wrong.

Charles took another step, then another. He was not prepared when the world went black around him.

"How's Joseph?"

Mallory stood at Penelope's door in bright sunlight that did little to alter the morning chill. She had left her room minutes earlier, heavily bundled and finally admitting to herself that she could think of little else but seeing Matthew. Somehow, a need for reassurance had slipped gradually into her consciousness. She had acted like a wanton the previous night. It had occurred to her belatedly that Matthew was an educated man with years of formal schooling; and that in the cold light of day he might view her response to him in a negative way.

She had immediately berated herself for such thinking. She had reminded herself that she was Mallory Winifred Tompkins, that she was intelligent, educated, and talented, that she had fought all her life to attain a personal independence denied to most of her gender, and that she would not subject herself to any man's judgment!

Then had come the moment of truth. It had come in the form of an old adage her father often used: *"There's always a first time . . ."*

How she hated old adages!

But she didn't hate Matthew Bower.

As a matter of fact, she . . .

Refusing to complete that thought, she had been walking across the yard when she came in sight of Penelope's door and thought of little Joseph. The poor babe had been so sick. She recalled the tear in Penelope's eye the previous night, and she was struck again with the depth of the woman's concealed distress. To lose a child, and to then see her new babe stricken the same way . . .

She had been unable to pass Penelope's door without inquiring about the little boy, yet the young woman's expression betrayed no emotion as Mallory continued, "I hope Joseph had a good night."

Penelope stepped back into the room to allow her entrance. She walked to the cradle, where she stood looking down at her sleeping child.

Elaine Barbieri

Her shy smile flashed briefly when she looked up at Mallory. "Joseph is much improved. Heat returned to his body during the night, but it left again soon after I gave him more medicine." She paused. "I have much to thank you for."

"No, not me!" Mallory gave a short laugh. "Matthew's the one responsible for finding the right herbs to help him."

Penelope averted her eyes. "Yes."

Mallory sensed an awkwardness between them. Attempting to alleviate it, she continued, "I hope you won't hesitate to call Matthew if Joseph should feel ill again. I know it gave him great satisfaction to be able to help you."

"Yes."

Mallory turned back toward the door. She paused there, searching for words that would restore the woman's smile. "I'm pleased to see Joseph looking so well, Penelope. He's a lovely child." Suddenly aware that the words she was about to speak came from the heart, she offered, "You're a very fortunate woman to have such a beautiful son."

But Penelope wasn't listening. She was staring out toward the fort yard. Something about her expression turned Mallory to follow the line of her gaze.

Gold Eagle walked briskly across the yard. His anger barely contained, he struggled to subdue the warrior instincts that had come fiercely to life during his confrontation with Captain Tierney. It was clear that his people would have

154

much to fear if this man were put in charge of military affairs, but it had not been hatred of his people that had glared at him in the captain's eyes. It was hatred of the man Tierney believed him to be—a mute, a lesser man whom Mallory preferred over him.

He had responded to the captain with outright challenge, but Corporal Walker had saved him from himself. He knew that if Walker had not altered his reply, he would have lost any chance of achieving his purpose in coming to the fort.

As it was, he had only three days.

Tierney wanted him out of the fort. Tierney had said that he was a danger to the security of everyone there. Yes, he was . . . but in ways Tierney had never dreamed.

The faces of his people passed before him in a blurred rush, and Gold Eagle felt his determination return. He could not allow the captain's jealousy to defeat him. He would make good use of the time remaining to him. The fate of his people was in his hands.

As for Mallory . . . Gold Eagle steeled himself against the warmth the name evoked. The night they had spent together meant little beyond the passion of the moment. She had come to Fort Larned to learn another man's fate. She would soon leave, and she would forget him as quickly as she had forgotten the man for whom she had traveled so many miles. Such were the ways of white women.

Gold Eagle's thoughts halted abruptly as he

rounded the corner of the yard and the blazing color of Mallory's hair caught his eye. She was standing at Owl Woman's door. She did not see him, but Owl Woman did. Her gaze was wary, uncertain in the light of the new day.

Mallory turned toward him. Her smile flashed, but he hardened his heart to her as he approached.

"What's wrong with him?"

Charles heard Jewel's concerned inquiry as if from a distance, although Jewel and a portly fellow he could not identify stood wavering beside his bed. He looked around him. He was in his room at the hotel and Corporal Bell was standing near the door. And he was hot . . . so hot. . . .

"Looks like he picked up some kind of fever." The unnamed fellow turned and glanced down at him. "If it was a different season, I'd say he got bit by a tick of some sort. Otherwise, I can't rightly say what's wrong with him. It doesn't look like it's anythin' serious, though."

"How do you know it's not serious if you don't know what's wrong with him?" Jewel was frowning. "Seems to me you should know what's wrong with him if you was any kind of a doctor at all."

"Young lady"—the fellow's small eyes narrowed—"I know you're upset, but it won't do any good to take your agitation out on me. I'm doin' the best I can for this man."

Turning, the doctor leaned down toward

Charles. He smiled. "Well, it looks like you're conscious. My name's Doctor Stanley, Lieutenant. You passed out on the street, you know. This young lady saw to it that you were carried up here, and then she called me. As you probably heard, she's not too pleased with what I've done for you so far, but I figure that's because she's worried about you." He leaned closer. "You understand what I'm saying, don't you, Lieutenant?"

Annoyed that he could not seem to focus his vision, Charles nodded. He raised a hand to his throbbing head. The weak rasp of his voice surprised him when he spoke.

"I have to get up. I need to leave here. I have to go back to Fort Larned."

"You aren't goin' anywhere for a couple of days, Lieutenant."

"What?"

"Like I told Jewel, I can't say I know exactly what's wrong with you, except that you've got a fever and a powerful headache, if I'm to judge by the way you're holdin' your head. But there doesn't seem to be anythin' serious the matter. Your heart's beatin' just fine, you don't seem to have any stiffness anywheres, and when I looked in your eyes, I didn't see anythin' there that worried me. I've been seein' a bit of this fever goin' around, and it doesn't usually amount to anythin'. It's my guess that you'll be right as rain in a few days."

"I can't wait." When his attempt to pull himself to a seated position failed, Charles closed

157

his eyes against the throbbing in his head. He muttered, "That damned red-eye. It poisoned me."

"Well, if it was the red-eye, you're the only one it poisoned." Stepping into his line of vision, Jewel smiled. "You can't order yourself back into good health, Lieutenant, sir, so you might as well just lie back and give up tryin'."

"I have to get back to Fort Larned. There's an imposter there. I have to tell Captain Tierney. I have to warn Mallory."

Jewel's smile wavered. "Mallory. She's the lady you was talkin' about last night."

Charles tried to clear his head.

"Who's the imposter?"

Charles closed his eyes. "I don't know." He shook his head. "Matthew Bower."

"Matthew Bower's the imposter?"

"Yes."

"The fella that can't talk."

"Yes . . . but he *can* talk, I think . . . talk as well as I can."

"Sam said he couldn't."

"Sam's wrong. I have to go. I have to tell them."

The pounding in his head was almost beyond bearing.

"I think his fever's goin' up, Doc."

Charles felt a rough palm against his forehead. "Yes, I'd say it is. Get me some of those powders in my bag, will you, Jewel?"

Charles felt a cup against his lips. He heard Jewel's voice. "Drink this like a good fella, Lieutenant. Come on. You want to get back to that lady of yours, don't you?"

Charles swallowed. He mumbled, "Matt Bower . . . he's an imposter. . . ." He turned toward the door, where Corporal Bell's thin figure wavered uncertainly. "Corporal . . . take the men. Go back to Fort Larned. Tell them I sent you back because of Bower. He . . . he . . ."

Charles faltered. He was losing his train of thought. Turning back toward the doctor, he grated, "What did you give me?"

"A mild sedative, that's all. You need to rest, Lieutenant."

Charles's mind was drifting. He muttered a slurred curse, then murmured, "Go back . . . to Fort Larned, Corporal. Tell them . . . tell them . . ."

His thoughts clouded again.

"He's delirious, Corporal, but I wouldn't worry about it. I've seen a lot of this in the past few weeks, just like I said. It only lasts a few days."

"I'm not delirious. I'm not—" Charles took a breath to steady himself, but the room went dark.

"What's wrong, Matthew?"

Matthew strode to a halt beside Mallory. His dark expression dispelled her joy and she glanced back in the direction from which he had come. "You aren't coming from your quarters."

Matthew signed a long statement that she

could not comprehend, and Mallory turned toward Penelope anxiously. "What did he say?"

"He say he came from the captain's office. He say the captain told him he is a danger to the fort."

"That's ridiculous!"

Penelope's small face twitched.

Her frustration mounting, Mallory watched as Matthew continued signing.

"He say the captain told him he must leave the fort in three days."

"Leave . . ."

"He say he told the captain he cannot be ready in three days, but the captain say he must go."

"No." Mallory shook her head. "It's too soon."

"He say he must go or captain will put him behind bars."

"He wouldn't dare!"

A rapid panic building within her, Mallory looked at Matthew. She saw confirmation of Penelope's words in the hard set of his jaw, but she was chilled by the coldness in his clear eyes—eyes where only hours earlier a loving heat had burned. She longed to see that warmth return. She *needed* to see it return.

Taking Matthew's arm, Mallory turned back briefly toward Penelope. "Thank you for translating, Penelope, but I don't think Matthew and I will need any help from here. I hope Joseph is soon well."

Grasping Matthew's arm more tightly, Mallory tugged him along beside her. She sensed his reticence, and her heart began a nervous pounding. Matthew had changed. He was hard and angry, not the tender lover who had held her in his arms through the night. She wanted that man to return, and she knew what to say to make that happen.

Waiting only until she had drawn Matthew out of general view, Mallory moved closer. She glanced around them, then whispered, "Don't worry, Matthew. Arthur won't get away with this. He doesn't know it yet, but Charles will be back here by the end of the week. He's only going as far as the first telegraph station so he can wire a report about Arthur's conduct to Major Bullen. He's going to request that Major Bullen issue direct orders by wire that will countermand the actions Arthur took and censure him for his abuse of authority. After Arthur gets that reprimand from Major Bullen, he'll think twice about ordering you out of the fort, and it won't make any difference if Major General Cotter is a friend of Arthur's family or not!"

Matthew's expression flickered at the mention of Cotter's name, and Mallory replied to his unspoken question, "Arthur claims Major General Cotter is a friend of his family. He thought that would impress Charles because Cotter's on his way here with a sizable force to confront the Indians."

Matthew stiffened. He grasped her arms, startling her with the intensity of his reaction to her words. She responded with confusion, "Surely you heard the rumors about Cotter's approach? I thought they were general knowledge. Only, they aren't rumors. Arthur told Charles that Cotter is traveling with the largest force this part of the country has ever seen . . . and artillery. Arthur said Cotter is going to give him an important position during the conflict." She grimaced. "I don't really believe that, of course."

Matthew's hands tightened painfully on her arms, but Mallory saw only the question that still remained in his eyes. She responded, "I don't know when Cotter's supposed to get here, if that's what you're wondering. Arthur might. I suppose some of the other officers might, too, but I don't think they're about to say. None of that really matters anyway, Matthew. Whatever Cotter does, it'll only affect the Indians—not us."

Matthew dropped his hands from her arms and stepped back from her, his gaze frigid. The chill seemed to seep into her bones.

"I'm sorry. That was thoughtless of me. I forgot that you've made friends among the Indians."

Matthew's expression remained frozen.

"It's just that it's difficult for me to think of the Indians as your friends, or even as people like you and me. I've read so much about the terrible, inhumane things they've done. I mean . . ."

She was somehow making matters worse with every word she uttered.

She whispered, "I'm revealing my ignorance, I know. I'm sorry."

Her apology went unheeded.

Overwhelmed by a feeling of helplessness, Mallory reached out to Matthew, but he avoided her hand.

In a moment, he was gone.

"I did it!"

Bill Thayer's satisfaction lit his jowled face as he turned toward Willie Carpenter. Carpenter, a fellow employee and the only other occupant of the telegraph office, looked back at him with a quizzical expression.

"I finally got that damned telegram through to Fort Riley for Lieutenant Moore!" Thayer laughed aloud when Carpenter's expression revealed that he couldn't care less.

"Maybe that don't mean much to you, Willie, but you didn't have that young fella leanin' on you for two days with a look in his eye like his life hung in the balance." Thayer's smile gradually faded. "Where do you suppose that lieutenant is, anyways? He said he'd be back, but I ain't seen him for hours."

"Maybe he got tired of waitin' for the line to clear. Maybe he left town."

"Never happen. Not him." Thayer shook his balding head. "He was wirin' his commandin' officer for permission to return to Fort Larned. He couldn't go back without it, and that's the only direction he was about to travel in, if I read him right."

"You said that from the look of him when he came in this mornin', he spent last night leanin' on the bar. Maybe he went back to the saloon to wait."

"Hell, no! He was feelin' mighty bad. That was a man who had sworn off liquor for some time to come, if I ever saw one. No . . ." Thayer paused in contemplation, "He was more likely to go back to the hotel to sleep it off. Well, I suppose there's no rush. He needs to wait for a response from Major Bullen anyhow."

"Good luck . . ." Willie Carpenter's lined face drew into a sneer. "You know as well as I do that there's big things goin' on with them fellas in the military right now, what with Cotter comin' this way."

"Damn it, Willie! That wire was confidential. Nobody's supposed to know that!"

"Everybody knows it!"

"Not for sure! You'd best forget you read that wire when it came through, or you're likely to get us both into big trouble."

Willie shrugged his bony shoulders. "I already forgot it."

"Yeah . . ."

Turning back to the key in front of him, Bill Thayer stared at it, then laughed uncomfortably. "I don't know how it happened, but that young fella's got me just as anxious as he is to get Major Bullen's reply."

"Good luck. What with things the way they are, that lieutenant's lucky if he ever gets an answer to his wire."

"If I was a bettin' man . . ."

"Save your money."

Thayer grunted. Despite himself, he turned back to stare at the key.

The bright sunlight of morning had faded to an overcast afternoon haze. Gold Eagle breathed the air testily. He allowed his tongue to taste the chill breeze, and his eyes narrowed. More snow to come. A snowfall could be in his favor if he wasn't able to confirm the information Mallory had given him within three days. It would give him the excuse he needed to delay his departure. If Cotter was truly marching toward them with as great a force as Mallory claimed, the snow would delay them also.

If . . .

Gold Eagle leaned against the stable in a deceivingly casual posture. Mallory's face appeared before his mind's eye as it had countless times during the day. Her words resounded again in his ears, each one widening the great chasm that lay between them.

"It's difficult for me to think of the Indians as people like you and me . . ."

Gold Eagle's eyes narrowed.

"I've read so much about the terrible, inhumane things the Indians have done."

Inhumane things not unlike those done to them.

If Mallory knew that the arms that had held her a loving captive the previous night had been those of a "savage" . . . if she knew that the lips that had claimed her mouth, and the body that had filled her were those of an "inhumane beast" . . .

But she did not know. Instead, the verdant color of her eyes had darkened with pain when he avoided her hand, and the slender form which he had held intimately close had trembled when he turned away from her.

Gold Eagle struggled to maintain a casual facade, steeling himself against the emotions assaulting him. If she knew, she would despise herself for wanting him. If she knew, she would feel tainted by his touch.

She was a white woman. She thought as a white woman and spoke as a white woman. So it would always be.

He was Cheyenne. His heart beat as a Cheyenne and for the Cheyenne. And so it would always be.

That difference now clear, he did not want Mallory. He did not need her. He cast all thought of her aside to contemplate the hours just past.

He had had a difficult day. Word of his angry encounter with Captain Tierney had spread rapidly through the fort. Easy conversation ceased when he neared and whispering began. The chance of his learning more of Cotter's approach grew dimmer with each passing hour. He had considered approaching Tierney in the night, but he sensed that his knife pressed to Tierney's throat would gain him little, so great was that man's hatred.

Gold Eagle glanced at two soldiers as they passed him. There were few in the fort who would dare Tierney's displeasure to speak to him. Archer spoke, but only *at* him, not *to* him, with words of ridicule and bias that turned the others more firmly against him. Only Walker remained constant, a friend who suffered for his defense of him.

Gold Eagle's lips tightened. All would be resolved when the time came.

A small figure emerged from the stable, and Gold Eagle drew himself erect. Drawing back, he waited until Owl Woman was abreast of him before stepping out into her view. Her gasp revealed her fear.

Gold Eagle inwardly smiled. She was wise to fear him.

Gold Eagle took Owl Woman's arm and pulled her back into the shadows of the stable. When he spoke, his voice was harsh.

"Did you tell your husband who I am?"

"No . . . I could not."

He knew it was the truth.

Gold Eagle pressed, "You know of Cotter's approach?"

Owl Woman's dark eyes widened, her anxiety apparent.

"Answer me."

"Yes."

"What do you know?"

Owl Woman's small frame shuddered. "I know only what I heard spoken to my husband, that the great general approaches with many men. It is said he comes to talk to the tribes."

"Yet he comes with more soldiers than have ever come before."

"Yes."

"And with artillery."

"Yes."

"When does this great general come?"

Owl Woman shook her head. "I do not know."

Gold Eagle's hand tightened on her arm. He drew her so close that his image was reflected in her eyes as he rasped, "You will get this information for me."

"I cannot!"

"You will . . . for the sake of your people." Gold Eagle added more softly, "And for the sake of your child."

Owl Woman's short intake of breath was his only response. Gold Eagle whispered, "I leave in three days."

After several long moments, Owl Woman nodded.

Releasing her, Gold Eagle walked away without another word.

Night was falling.

"How is he?" Bill Thayer paused in the doorway of Lieutenant Moore's hotel room. His stout figure filled the opening as he frowned at the young soldier standing there. "I wondered where the lieutenant was all day. Hell, he near to drove me crazy standin' over me yesterday. He didn't look too good when he came in this mornin', so I figured somethin' had to be wrong when he didn't show up no more."

"He's all right, I guess. He's sleepin'." The youthful soldier shrugged. "Doc Stanley's been back a few times. He says the lieutenant will be fine in a couple of days."

"A couple of days . . ." Thayer gave a low snort. "That ain't goin' to sit well with him, I reckon. He's got things he wants to do. If he told me once, he told me a hundred times that he couldn't wait a couple of days."

"Yeah . . . well, it looks like he don't have much choice."

Thayer motioned with his chin toward the heavily painted young woman who busied herself beside the officer's bed. The yellow satin of her dress glowed in the semi-darkness of the room as Thayer asked more softly, "What's Jewel doin' here?"

"Jewel's been a real help. She helped bring the lieutenant here when he collapsed on the street, and then she got Doc Stanley."

"She don't look like she's dressed to do no nursemaidin' for a sick man."

"Did I hear somebody say my name?" Looking up, Jewel raised a hand to her upswept hair, her glance challenging as she started toward them. She halted a little too close for comfort, continuing huskily, "I thought I heard you sayin' somethin' about the way I look, Billie-boy. It can't be the dress you don't approve of. Only last week, when your wife was busy at that quiltin' bee with the other ladies, you made a point of tellin' me how damned good I looked to you wearin' this dress. I remember you told me you liked the feel of it . . . said it was real smooth . . . like my skin."

Thayer took an unconscious step backward. He clenched the sheet he held at his side, his face flushing. "I wouldn't go repeatin' that to nobody else, Jewel."

"I wouldn't think of it, Billie." Jewel smiled. "Especially since I had to do some heavy talkin' to you that night so's you'd remember that nice wife of yours wasn't no more than a few doors down the street." Jewel paused, appearing satisfied that she had made her point. Her smile dropped away. "Just to make things clear, I *have* been nursemaidin' here most of the day—because the lieutenant's a nice fella, and I like him. But I have to leave because the Maverick just can't get on without me. So I'm askin' you to make it quick. What're you doin' here?"

"I don't see how that's any of your concern, Jewel."

Jewel looked pointedly at Corporal Bell. Corporal Bell responded dutifully, "Is there somethin' I can help you with, Mr. Thayer? Lieutenant Moore ain't in no condition to talk right now."

Thayer glanced at Jewel. She didn't budge an inch, and he replied uncomfortably, "I'd say this is Army business."

"Army business . . ." Jewel was not to be ignored. "You're talkin' about that telegram the lieutenant sent to Major Bullen about what happened back at Fort Larned."

"Hell, ain't there nothin' this woman don't know?"

"Lieutenant Moore don't have no secrets from me." Jewel looked at the young corporal when his head snapped toward her. "Can't stop a sick man from mumblin' when he's in a fever. And just so's you'll both be clear, I know he was waitin' for Major Bullen's answer so's he could go back to the fort and push Major Bullen's orders back in that bastard captain's face."

"Yeah." Thayer held up the telegram he had come to deliver. "Well, he don't have to wait no more."

Jewel snatched the telegram from his hand.

"Wait a minute, Jewel!"

"Ma'am . . ." The young corporal's expression was sober. "I think that belongs to the lieutenant."

Pausing long enough to scan the contents, Jewel put the telegram into Bell's hand. "That must be some lady to make all these military fellas stand up and take notice like they are."

"I'll say she is," Bell agreed.

"Her name's Mallory?" she asked.

"That's right."

Jewel looked at the young soldier a moment longer. Her smile was forced. "Well, I'm leavin'. The lieutenant should be all right for the evenin'. I'll come back and check on him when I'm done workin'."

"That ain't necessary, ma'am. Corporal

Hodge will be relievin' me here, soon. We won't be leavin' the lieutenant alone through the night."

"You just tell that sweet Corporal Jamie Hodge that I'll be back, so's he'll be expectin' me."

Corporal Bell's hesitation was brief. "I'll do that, ma'am."

"Come on, Billie-boy . . ." Turning toward the older man, who had remained silently observing all, Jewel hooked her arm through his. "You can walk me down to the street. That'll give you a chance to tell me again how good I look to you when nobody's around to hear you." She winked. "You never know, it just might do you some good, this time."

Before she pulled the door closed behind them, Jewel looked at the young corporal and rolled her eyes.

The click of the door caused Lieutenant Moore to stir as the conversation had not. By his side in a minute, Corporal Bell leaned over him. The lieutenant's face was flushed and his eyes appeared unfocused. Bell saw what an effort it was for him to talk.

"Who was that?" he grated out.

"It was that fella from the telegraph office talkin' to Jewel." Bell raised the telegram into the lieutenant's line of vision. "Major Bullen answered your wire."

"He did?" Lieutenant Moore blinked. "What does it say?"

Looking down at the printed sheet, Bell responded, "Major Bullen reinstated your original orders, just like you thought he would. He says to proceed back to Fort Larned immediately, and he says that if Captain Tierney attempts to countermand his orders again, you may inform him that he'll suffer the consequences."

Bell glanced back up at Lieutenant Moore with a broad smile. "How about that, Lieutenant? He—"

Bell frowned. The lieutenant's eyes were closed. He was sleeping.

Bell shrugged. The day was almost over at Fort Larned. Tomorrow was another day, and there wasn't much more that could happen there that night.

Night was falling.

Captain Tierney paced his quarters with long, angry strides. Damn that woman! He was almost at the end of his patience!

Tierney's temper was rapidly rising out of control. He had extended an invitation for dinner to the arrogant Mallory Tompkins, and the witch had actually had the audacity to refuse him again! He had gone into the dining hall, half expecting to see her seated with the mute, but she wasn't there. She hadn't been there earlier, and she didn't arrive afterward. He discovered that she hadn't requested a tray for her quarters, either.

Tierney grunted. The mute had shown up, though. He sat down alone, he ate alone, and he left alone. Corporal Walker was the only one

who approached him, but their conversation—
conducted in awkward hand signals—had been
short.

Tierney felt his agitation rise as he considered
Bower. It irritated him that the bastard didn't
have the decency to look discomfited by his iso-
lation. Strangely, he almost believed Bower preferred it that way. It infuriated him that Bower
had actually made a point to pass his table on
leaving the dining hall, but it had been Bower's
gall, when he paused to look at him with those
eyes that cut like steel, that had almost brought
him to his feet for an all-out confrontation right
then and there.

Tierney's palm itched. He hadn't felt so strong
an urge to respond to that itch since Sand
Creek, when he had scratched it with the dying
cries of the savages he had personally hunted
down. He recalled with true relish dragging the
filthy beasts out of the burrows where they had
hidden to escape the attack on their village. Surrender meant nothing. He had not spared any
man, woman, or child to bring forth another
generation. He still gloried in the bloodshed
that day. He awaited Major General Cotter's arrival with great expectation, with the hope that
the army would then finish the job it had
started. Yet, deep inside was the realization that
the greatest satisfaction he could receive would
be in closing the pale, icy eyes of Matthew
Bower forever.

His breathing heavy, Tierney paused in bitter
reflection. No, that wasn't true. His satisfaction

would be just as keen when he finally had the arrogant Miss Tompkins cowed beneath him.

Tierney's breathing grew more ragged at the budding thought that perhaps that moment was near.

Taking time only to check his appearance in the mirror, Tierney grunted. He looked well, and he was a good actor. He had already ordered a tray sent to Mallory's room. It would seem perfectly natural for him to follow up by going to Mallory's quarters with feigned concern for her welfare. Darkness had already shrouded the fort. It would not be difficult to enter her room, even against her protests, and he was confident he would be able to control the situation from there. He was practiced in the deed, after all.

He would make her beg.

He would make her *enjoy* begging.

And when he was done, he would make certain she would never forget him.

Tierney's smile hardened as he turned toward the door.

Night had fallen.

Mallory glanced at the darkening fort yard beyond her window, then at the tray that lay untouched on the table nearby. The heavy aroma of beef filled the room, nauseating her. Her appetite had gone, and her spirits were low. She had avoided Captain Tierney the entire day, knowing she would be unable to face the man with any temperance.

Matthew still avoided her.

How many times had she wished she could snatch back the words that had turned Matthew against her? In the time since, she had gone through the whole catalogue of emotions—regret, disbelief, hurt, anger, *fury*, and the determination to make Matthew pay for the distress he had caused her—all useless emotions that had done nothing more than add to her anguish.

Mallory winced, again recalling the moment when Matthew's hands dropped from her arms, when his gaze turned to ice, when he turned away from her as if putting her forever behind him. Matthew would be forced to leave the fort in three days. Somehow she knew that if she did not straighten things out before then, nothing would ever be the same between them.

Having spent the major portion of the afternoon steeping in senseless regrets, she had then made a halfhearted attempt to put her mind to the business that had brought her to Fort Larned. Again using the fictional Joshua Barnes to her advantage, she had attempted to discover which men at the fort might be convinced to guide her to surrounding ranches so that she could get the firsthand accounts for which she came. The response was so poor that she had resorted to subtle bribes, and then to bribes that weren't subtle at all.

The result?

A few fellows had appeared interested . . . but not in guiding her to the surrounding ranches.

The others had flatly refused.

It galled her to admit that the only man who could change the situation was Captain Tierney.

Would she make an appeal to him?

Never!

Nothing had gone right after Matthew turned his back on her and walked away. Nothing would go right until she was in his arms again. She no longer sought to avoid that truth. She knew that if Matthew would only come to her door right now, she would—

Startled when a hard knock on the door shattered the silence, Mallory felt a sudden flush of heat warm her skin. She had known Matthew couldn't stay away! She'd explain to him that she hadn't meant what she had said—not the way it had sounded—and everything would be all right again.

Mallory jerked the door open. Her expression froze.

"Hello, Mallory. I was concerned that you weren't well when you didn't come to dinner."

Captain Tierney was smiling, and contempt as bitter as bile rose in Mallory's throat. She managed a curt, "I'm fine."

"Perhaps a walk in the fresh air would help you to feel better."

"I said, I'm fine."

"Mallory . . ." The captain's even features creased into convincing lines of concern, "I know we started off badly. I'd like a chance to start over with you, if I may. I know you came here with grave personal concerns . . ."

Grave personal concerns? Oh, the fictional Joshua Barnes. She had almost forgotten.

"I can help you. I *will* help you."

"I don't need your help."

"Mallory . . ." The facade of concern was cracking. "I'm afraid you do."

Mallory's composure snapped. "Why did you tell Matthew he'd have to leave the fort in three days? Why do you despise him? Are you jealous of him because he's a better man than you?"

The captain's jaw tightened. "A *better* man than I am?"

"In every way!"

Tierney's face turned a dark red that was visible even in the meager light. He repeated, "A better man than I am . . ."

Taking an unexpected step, Tierney shoved Mallory backward. Catching her arms while she was off balance, he slammed the door behind him and held her fast. Certain she had never seen such outright fury, Mallory felt fear prickle her spine as he rasped, "You are a supremely deprived woman, aren't you?"

"Deprived?"

"You obviously don't know what a *real* man is, or you wouldn't even mention the name of that voiceless coward in the same breath as mine!"

"Let me go."

"No."

"I said—"

"I don't care what you said! It's time for me

178

to teach you a lesson, Mallory, obviously one that's been a long time in coming."

"Let me go!"

"You're going to like this, Mallory."

Mallory gasped as Tierney jerked her tightly against him. She felt the rock-hard bulge of his passion as he pinned her against the wall behind her.

"You're going to like this very much."

His mouth was suddenly on hers, forcing her lips apart. His chest was crushing her breasts. One hand wrapped in her hair, he slid his other down to cup her buttocks and force her more tightly against him. She was squirming and fighting to be free, her screams muted by the pressure of his mouth, by the hand he then clamped over her lips when he withdrew to drag her toward the corner bunk.

Subduing her protests as easily as if she were a child, Tierney thrust her down on the firm surface and pinned her with the weight of his body. Looming over her, breathing hard, his face twitching with lust, he ripped open the front of her gown and slid his hand inside to cup her breast.

Mallory felt panic soar. Pressing forward against the hand covering her mouth, she bit hard. She heard his curse the moment before he struck her a stunning blow to the cheek.

Momentarily disoriented, Mallory felt a new fury rise as her mind cleared. Tierney's hand was underneath her skirt. He was tugging at her undergarment!

Bastard . . . bastard . . . *bastard*!

Rage endowing her with unexpected strength, Mallory swung her fist with all her might. Knocking Tierney off balance, she then sprang from the bed, her heart pounding in her ears as she dashed to the stool in the corner where her reticule lay. Searching frantically inside it for a few desperate moments, she withdrew her derringer with a shaking hand.

Surprise momentarily replaced the fury on Tierney's face. Contempt then sweeping his features, he started toward her.

"Stay where you are!"

He took another step.

Trembling so much that she could hardly speak, Mallory hissed, "If you think a gun this small can't kill you, you're wrong. If you think I don't know how to use it, you're wrong. And if you think I *won't* use it . . . you'll be *dead wrong*."

"Put that gun down, Mallory."

"Not another step, Arthur."

"Mallory . . ."

Mallory cocked the gun. She aimed it straight at his heart. Her finger twitched on the trigger.

"All right!"

Arthur took a step back, then another. Perspiration beaded on his forehead.

"Mallory . . ."

"Get out of here."

Tierney's chest was heaving. His color was high. She knew at that moment that he would kill her if he could.

"Do it!"

The moment that followed stretched to an eternity before Tierney turned abruptly and walked to the door. Her derringer steady now, Mallory watched as he turned again toward her, his face a wrathful mask as he rasped, "If you speak of this to anyone, you won't get out of this country alive."

"Get out!"

"To *anyone*, Mallory."

Mallory extended her arm to fire . . .

. . . as Tierney closed the door behind him.

Night had fallen.

No, he did not want her.

No, he did not need her.

The litany rang over and again in Gold Eagle's mind as he lay on his cot in the darkness. The fort had gone silent. Night had halted all activity, but for him there was no rest.

Gold Eagle strengthened himself against his own yearning, which had grown stronger as the night grew darker.

A hunger unlike any he had ever known rose again inside Gold Eagle as Mallory's image appeared in his mind. Her taste was in his mouth. Her scent was in his nostrils. Her remembered heat set his flesh aflame.

The woman had gained a hold on him that he had not foreseen.

Were he in his village, this need would be easily assuaged. Gray Dawn would gladly give him release. Summer Moon would vie for a place in his arms.

He knew that he had a choice of many. He also knew that there was only one woman he now desired.

Gold Eagle sought to understand the source of his hunger for this woman. Hair the color of sunset dazzled his eye, but it did not steal his heart. Eyes the color of the new spring drew him to her, but they did not hold him fast. Skin that was smooth and white tempted him, but it did not keep him captive. Lips, warm and yielding, raised a sublime heat within him, but they did not drive all else from his mind.

Yet her image remained.

Gold Eagle took a fortifying breath. He had made his plans. His time at the fort was limited. Owl Woman would do her best to ascertain the expected time of Cotter's arrival. She feared him too greatly to do otherwise. He would wait, knowing he had no other recourse. If Owl Woman failed, he would visit the captain before he left. He would gain his satisfaction—one way or another.

He would then return to his people with the knowledge he had gained.

As for the woman . . .

Gold Eagle expelled Mallory's image from his mind.

No, he did not want her.

No, he did not need her.

*   *   *

"How're you feelin', soldier boy?"

Jewel leaned over Charles's bed. Dawn was only hours away. She had come straight from the Maverick to the room where her thoughts had been centered during the long evening. She knew her makeup was faded and her hair was askew, that she smelled of tobacco smoke and cheap liquor, but she didn't care. She had never pretended to be other than what she was . . . and she knew the officer lying on the bed in front of her accepted her that way.

Jewel's heart warmed. She liked this fella. She leaned closer as his eyelids flickered fully open.

"I was on my way home and I thought I'd stop by." She frowned, noting the confusion in Charles's eyes. She touched his forehead. It was hot. She turned toward the soldier at the door. "Did you give the lieutenant the powder the doctor left for him?"

"No, ma'am. The doctor gave him somethin', though, before he left."

"When was that?"

"Before twelve, ma'am."

Jewel reached for the paper packet on the table. She felt the lieutenant's gaze following her as she mixed it with water and then pressed it to his lips.

"Come on—drink up, darlin'."

The lieutenant's dark eyes searched her face before he drank obediently. She listened intently as he attempted to speak.

"An imposter . . . Mallory, he's an imposter."

A painful knot tightened inside Jewel. "I ain't Mallory, Lieutenant. I'm Jewel."

"Mallory . . ."

The lieutenant grasped her hand and drew her toward him. He cupped the back of her head with surprising strength and pulled her mouth down to his. His kiss was brief, but it was sweet . . . so very sweet.

"Mallory . . ."

"My name's Jewel, Lieutenant."

His eyes closed, and the knot inside Jewel became painful.

She repeated, "It's Jewel, Lieutenant."

But she wished with all her heart it was not.

Dawn was a few hours away.

Mallory stirred when a sound broke the silence of her room. She came to full consciousness, stiffening in her bed when she heard the sound again. She reached a shaky hand under her pillow to withdraw the derringer hidden there. She was holding it cocked and ready when the window slid slowly open.

Mallory held her breath at the sight of the man silhouetted against the night sky. Her throat tightened. A slow sobbing began inside her when the figure slipped inside and walked toward her, the dim light behind him glinting on the fair hair that streamed over his shoulders.

Releasing the gun, Mallory raised her arms to welcome him.

"Matthew . . . I'm so glad you came."

He took her into his arms, and she felt him stiffen. His pale eyes narrowed, searching hers with concern. He sensed something was wrong. No, she couldn't tell him about Captain Tierney's assault. She knew, somehow, that the danger would be too great if she did.

"It's nothing . . . nothing's wrong." She repeated, "I'm just so glad you came."

Matthew's lips were on hers. His kiss warmed her. His body assuaged hers. She was caught up in the beauty he created within her, and all was well.

She loved him.

Oh, God, she did.

Matthew . . .

Chapter Seven

He felt like hell.

Staring for long moments at the gray morning light seeping though a rip in the stained window shade, Charles sought to clear his mind. He had opened his eyes moments earlier to the realization that the pounding in his head had ceased, but that little else about him seemed right. His throat was parched, his body ached as if he had been pummeled, and his stomach was still queasy. He turned at a sound in the corner of the room, frowning at the rotund fellow busying himself there.

As if sensing his scrutiny, the man turned abruptly toward him.

"Awake at last?" The fellow smiled. "You look confused, but I guess that's to be expected." He approached and placed a callused palm against Charles's forehead. "Your fever's down. That's a good sign."

The man's voice was familiar.

"My name's Doc Stanley, in case you don't remember. You collapsed on the street. Jewel and that little fella, Sam Clover, brought you here and called me. You were pretty sick."

Charles swallowed past the dryness in his throat. He frowned at the croaking quality of his voice when he responded, "I remember now."

He looked around the room.

"If you're wonderin' where your men are, they've been keepin' guard durin' the night. You must be doin' somethin' right, because they've been watchin' over you like mother hens. I just sent Corporal Hodge off to get some rest. He said Corporal Whittier will be right back to replace him." Doc Stanley paused. "Then again, if you're lookin' for Jewel, I'd say she's due to arrive here any minute. Talk about mother hens . . ."

Charles struggled to assimilate the information Doc Stanley was imparting. He remembered Jewel. He remembered Sam Clover.

Charles's heart jumped a beat. And he remembered what Clover had told him minutes before everything went dark.

Charles struggled to sit up. "I have to get out of here."

"You aren't goin' anywhere."

Sitting at last, his head swimming, Charles

fought to clarify his thoughts. "You don't understand. I have to get back to Fort Larned. It's urgent."

"I know. There's an imposter there—some fella named Bower—and you have to tell the fort commander."

Startled at his response, Charles remained silent as Doc Stanley continued, "You were delirious. You did a lot of talkin'. I chalked most of it up to the fever, but it looks like I was wrong."

Charles fought the weakness assailing him. "That damned red-eye . . ."

"It wasn't the liquor, Lieutenant. You picked up somethin' I can't rightly put a name to, but lots of folks hereabouts have been comin' down with it lately. Whatever it is, it doesn't seem to be serious—just a little debilitatin'. It'll be stretchin' it a bit, but you'll probably be able to travel tomorrow."

"Tomorrow!" Charles shook his head, regretting the spontaneous motion when the dizziness returned. "I can't wait. I've waited too long already."

"I don't see how's you have any choice, Lieutenant."

Turning at a knock on the door, Charles frowned at the sight of Jewel standing in the opening with Corporal Whittier behind her. Nodding a brief acknowledgment to Jewel, he snapped in the strongest voice he could muster, "Get the men together, Corporal. We're leaving for Fort Larned today."

"Fort Larned! You aren't strong enough to

travel yet." Jewel looked at the portly doctor. "Tell him, Doc!"

"I'm going," Charles insisted.

Whittier approached the bed. He handed Charles a note, his expression sober. "Your wire got through yesterday, Lieutenant. Major Bullen responded right away."

Charles read the wire. "Get me something to eat, Corporal. Then you can tell the men to be ready by noon. We're going back to Fort Larned."

"But—"

Charles turned toward Jewel, who stood beside the bed. Images returned—Jewel standing over him, talking to him, her cool hand against his forehead reassuring him, granting him relief while the fever sent his world spinning. It struck him that Jewel looked younger without her saloon makeup, and somehow more vulnerable.

For her sake, he softened his voice when he repeated, "I'm going back today."

Gold Eagle dressed slowly, his gaze intent on the bunk a few feet away. A gray, overcast dawn was lightening the sky. Snow would soon be falling.

His mind far from the weather, Gold Eagle looked down at the woman who still lay sleeping. The rough army blanket contrasted vividly with the delicate shoulders exposed to his sight. He knew that if he were to slip beneath that blanket right now, she would turn her womanly softness to him in her sleep as she had through the night. He knew his body would curve to accommodate hers, but he also knew that despite the hours of impassioned lovemaking recently past, it was not sleep that would soon occupy him.

Mallory mumbled in her sleep. He watched the movement of her lips. *Matthew* . . .

His body hardened and Gold Eagle smiled sardonically. So strongly did he respond to this woman that he reacted to the name she spoke in her dreams, although that name was not truly his own. But he remembered Mallory's enraptured whispering of that name as his own body had swelled inside her. He recalled that her lips had returned his kiss with true abandon, and that she had given herself to him wholly, without holding back.

But he remembered something else as well. He recalled that she had trembled in her sleep, that she had clung to him, and that she had awakened several times with a fear assuaged only when she saw his face. His gaze had asked the questions he could not voice, but she had given him no response.

The fear he had witnessed in her eyes tormented him. If someone had hurt her—

Suddenly recognizing the direction of his thoughts, Gold Eagle pulled himself erect and continued dressing. The woman was not his concern. There was no real bond between them. The man to whom she had given herself with so much passion did not truly exist.

Gold Eagle set his thoughts on the tasks before him. He would soon return to his village and he needed to prepare for the journey ahead. He had already delayed too long that morning in Mallory's bed. The fort would be stirring to life, and the possibility of being seen coming from Mallory's quarters grew greater with each passing minute. The whispers that would follow Mallory if he were seen did not concern him. She had made her choice. Of true concern was his realization that to increase Captain Tierney's jealousy would be to bring about unavoidable conflict.

He didn't want that—not yet.

Mallory stirred. She turned in her sleep, frowning, the twisting of the blanket exposing a firm, rounded breast. Gold Eagle recalled the taste of that sweet flesh, the feel of the rosy crest between his lips. . . . He remembered Mallory's gasps as he fondled it with his tongue. She had clutched him against her as he suckled it deeply, raising his passions almost beyond control.

A familiar danger loomed, and Gold Eagle steeled himself against his thoughts.

He did not want her.

He did not need her.

Gold Eagle opened the window and glanced outside. In a moment he was gone.

Captain Tierney walked briskly across the fort yard. The morning air was chill. The sky was gray and ominous.

Snow.

Damn!

The weather was against him. He couldn't expel Bower from the fort if it stormed. Bower was an Easterner, a novice in traveling in the wilderness. The damned mute had already made it known that his horse was weakened by previous travel. If he did expel him despite severe weather conditions and the bastard didn't survive . . .

Tierney paused to consider. Was the fool worth the trouble that might result?

Abandoning that thought abruptly when the dining hall came into view, Tierney adjusted his coat and stiffened his jaw. He had slept poorly, awakening countless times during the night to a fury that would not abate. Mallory's image had haunted him—that ridiculous gun in hand, her eyes spitting hatred, the mark of his blow still on her cheek.

Cursing when his body hardened in unexpected response to that image, Tierney slowed his pace, almost tempted to laugh at the sheer perversity of his damned male organ. The woman had been one step away from shooting him through the heart!

His amusement faded as a familiar wrath returned. If he hadn't backed off, the witch would have done it, too! Despite her shaking, her gun was level and her mind was set. Her finger had actually twitched on the trigger!

But she *didn't* fire.

Tierney's expression tightened.

She'd never get another chance.

And in the end, he would have her . . . any way he pleased.

Allowing himself the succor of that thought, Tierney pushed open the dining hall door and stepped inside.

Mallory awakened to the morning chill of her quarters. She glanced at the empty pillow beside hers. Matthew was gone. She had known he would be. But he had come to her despite the anger that had driven a wedge between them.

They had had little time for talk during the night.

Matthew's inability to speak didn't hinder communication between them. She understood whatever he wanted to say, and she knew he had sensed something was wrong when he first came to her room. She was uncertain why she denied his unspoken concern. Matthew was not a violent man, yet she sensed that his control was being sorely tested. She did not want to be responsible for another confrontation between him and the fort commander.

The memory of Captain Tierney's attack returned with unexpected clarity, bringing Mallory to her feet. A glance in the washstand mirror revealed a purple bruise on her cheek where Tierney had struck her, and Mallory felt a moment's panic. The shadows of the night had hidden the mark from Matthew, but she knew she would not be able to conceal it in the full light of day.

Mallory's heart pounded with anxiety. She didn't want Matthew to see the bruise for the first time when they were in public. She needed to talk to him privately first. She needed to explain that she had settled the matter to her satisfaction, and to make him understand that she didn't want him to retaliate in any way.

Suddenly eager to see Matthew so she might dispel her growing anxiety, Mallory reached for her clothes with trembling hands. She would go to Matthew's room now, before he left for his morning meal. She would talk to him—plead with him if need be. She would tell him that retribution was not worth the danger it posed to him.

And she would tell Matthew that she loved him.

Because she did.

She would tell him that she would not be able to bear losing him.

Because she would not.

And she would tell him *now*.

Dressed in minutes, Mallory stepped out into the fort yard.

"Gold Eagle . . ."

Gold Eagle stiffened, halting as he prepared to pull the door of his quarters closed behind him. He turned toward the whisper to see Owl Woman concealed in the shadows nearby. He glanced around. His lips tight, he responded,

"You speak unwisely when you call me by that name here."

Owl Woman did not respond to his rebuke. Instead, she said, "I bring you the information you seek."

Gold Eagle searched her expression before he pushed open the door of his quarters and motioned her inside.

"No, I cannot." Owl Woman shook her head. "If I am seen coming from your quarters, my husband would suffer ridicule. He is a strong man accustomed to taunts, but I will not give opportunity to those who would jeer at him."

Scrutinizing her expression, Gold Eagle pulled the door shut, then drew Owl Woman into a point of concealment nearby. He scanned the fort yard briefly before he asked, "What do you have to tell me?"

Owl Woman's small face twitched revealingly as she whispered, "I spoke to my husband of the great general's approach. I talked of my concern for the safety of my child, and he replied to me in confidence, as is his custom. He trusts, believing I will never betray him."

Gold Eagle's light eyes singed hers. "Tell me what you came to say."

Owl Woman began. "My husband say the Great White Father believes that the tribes will meet to attack the forts when the sun melts the snow. He say the great general comes here with many men, some mounted, some not. He say the general brings great guns and a bridge to float on the rivers so the men may walk across."

Gold Eagle nodded. The general would be bringing cavalry, infantry, artillery, and pontoons.

"The great general goes to Fort Harker, then Fort Zarah, and he then comes here. He will arrive before the grass is again green and Indian ponies are again strong."

Owl Woman shuddered. "My husband say the great general is angry. The great general hears many bad things. The great general believes the chiefs show no respect for peace. My husband say the great general will send for the chiefs to come to this place, and they must come, because if they do not, he will punish. The great general say there are many things he will demand if he is not to make war. The chiefs must speak softly to him. The chiefs must tell our people they cannot travel the roads the white man travels because there is often fighting. The chiefs must return prisoners some say they have taken. They must return horses some say they have taken. The great general say that he is ready for peace or war, and that it is for the chiefs to decide which it will be because his demands must be met."

Gold Eagle waited for Owl Woman to continue. When she did not, he spoke, controlling his anger. "Do you have more to say?"

Owl Woman nodded. "My husband say that the great general does not wish to allow Indian agents to speak for him. He say *he* will speak, and the chiefs will listen. He say his soldiers are strong and well fed, and that their horses did not suffer for the long winter, unlike the Cheyenne and Arapaho warriors, who are hungry and whose horses are weak from winter cold. He say that he will not leave unless all these things are settled with the chiefs—one way or another."

Gold Eagle's eyes narrowed as Owl Woman spoke again.

"I have done what you asked. I have brought you the information you seek. Now I return to my husband."

Owl Woman attempted to leave, only to be stayed by Gold Eagle's tight grip on her arm. The sound of his deep voice reverberated softly on the silence between them as he instructed, "Speak of this to no one—no one, or you will speak no more."

In a moment, Owl Woman was gone.

Speak of this to no one—no one, or you will speak no more.

Incredulous, Mallory took a short backward step into the shadows. She held her breath as Penelope stepped out of concealment near Matthew's door and scurried past without glancing her way. Frozen into motionlessness, she waited for the second person to emerge—the person who had been conversing with Penelope in a voice that had halted her in her tracks as she approached Matthew's quarters—a voice hauntingly familiar to her ears.

She heard a footstep and her heart stopped. The person emerged into view and her heart shattered into countless pieces, never to be whole again.

It was Matthew.

No . . . Gold Eagle.

Mallory watched as Matthew strode in the opposite direction, toward the dining hall. Her breath coming in short, pained gasps, she surveyed the familiar width of his shoulders, the light hair visible under his hat, the stride that was both bold and silent—Matthew's own—until he disappeared from sight.

She had heard Matthew speak to Penelope, addressing her as Owl Woman. She had heard Penelope speak to Matthew, addressing him as Gold Eagle.

She had heard Matthew *speak*. . . .

Who was he?

Why had he pretended he couldn't speak?

Why had he come to Fort Larned?

Why had he been conversing with Penelope—Owl Woman—in secret about Cotter's advance?

Oh, God . . . who was he?

Trembling so badly that she could hardly walk, Mallory turned back in the direction she had come. She neared her door, then stopped short as Corporal Walker approached her.

"Are you all right, Miss Tompkins?" His youthful face was concerned. "You look kind of pale."

Mallory blinked, uncertain. "Y-yes, I'm all right." She swallowed. "What do you want?"

"Ma'am . . ." The young soldier shifted uncomfortably. "You were talkin' to the men yesterday, askin' if any of them could help you."

"Yes. No one would."

"I'm sorry about that, ma'am." Walker shifted again. "I'm ashamed for them . . . and I'm ashamed for me, for refusin' to help you just because of Captain Tierney. I've been thinkin' about it all night, and I'm here to tell you now that I'm willin' to help you any way I can."

"You are?" Hysterical laughter bubbled up inside Mallory. Could she trust him? Perhaps he wasn't who he seemed to be, either. Perhaps he wasn't really an army corporal after all. Perhaps . . . perhaps . . .

Mallory took a stabilizing breath. "Would you be willing to talk to me now, Corporal?"

"Now, ma'am?"

"Just for a little background information I need." The laughter bubbled again, stealing her breath.

"Are you sure you're all right, ma'am?"

"Yes." She pushed open the door to her room. "Please come in."

Waiting until Walker was inside, Mallory pushed the door closed behind them.

Mallory hadn't been at breakfast. Neither had the mute. If he didn't know better . . .

Captain Tierney walked across the fort yard, his stride purposeful. Time was slipping away from him, damn it! Major Abbott would be back soon, and he would lose absolute authority at the fort. He needed to rid himself of Bower and put Miss Mallory Tompkins in her place before that happened. But he had to be careful in doing so. Cotter was on his way. He would arrive in a few weeks at the latest. His record must be spotless so that nothing would stand in the way of the post he expected Cotter to grant him.

Tierney grunted. His threat to Mallory had not gone unheeded the previous night. He had seen no change in the expressions of the men when they looked his way in the dining hall; apparently she had spoken to no one about their violent exchange. With that victory under his belt, he was eager for another. He had already planned his strategy. After the mute left, Mallory would mellow toward him. He would be contrite, and she needed his help, after all. And if he didn't get her one way, he'd get her another.

Captain Tierney caught a glimpse of light hair and broad shoulders disappearing through the stable doorway. So, the bastard was working in the stable without bothering to come in for the morning meal. What could possibly be so important?

Tierney looked up at the overcast sky. It would start snowing before noon. Bower couldn't possibly be preparing to leave the fort.

Changing direction abruptly, Tierney headed toward the stable. Bower's head turned toward him as he walked through the doors. The silent bastard looked at him, his hands halting in mid-task as he assembled supplies.

"Getting ready to leave, Bower? I'd say that's wise of you."

The bastard's eyes narrowed into slits and Tierney silently cursed. Something wasn't right. The man was mute, but he wasn't blind. He could see that it was going to snow. He had already been caught in a snowstorm. He wasn't fool enough to go out there and get caught in another—was he?

Tierney glanced around the stable. Catching movement near the doorway, he called out to the half-breed, who was attempting to escape his detection, "Penelope, come over here. I need someone to translate so I can speak to Mr. Bower."

The woman approached haltingly. She glanced at Bower out of the corner of her eye and Tierney snorted. Shifty-eyed, the whole damned breed of them. . . .

Tierney faced Bower. "I want to know what you're doing."

Bower's expression did not change as he signed sharply in reply.

"Mr. Bower say he is getting ready to leave the fort as you ordered."

"Is that right?" Tierney almost laughed aloud. If the damned fool was too stupid to see that it was going to snow, it was on his head. Barely restraining a smile, he inquired, "When do you plan to leave?"

Bower signed again.

"Mr. Bower say he will leave as soon as he is ready."

"Today?"

Bower signed.

"Yes, today."

"Good. I'll make sure to inform the watch—just to make it official. And don't bother to stop by to take your leave. I'll enter your departure in my records as soon as I get back to my office. Good-bye."

Tierney turned on his heel, nodding briefly to the half-breed in passing. He had to leave before he told the mute bastard what a damned fool he was, and before he boasted that the haughty Miss Tompkins would soon be his alone to deal with.

That thought appealed to him. He'd approach Mallory right now. And he'd apologize. That was always a good tack.

It occurred to Tierney as he walked across the yard with a new spring in his step that the half-breed had looked nervous, almost frightened when she glanced between Bower and him. Stranger still, she had seemed somehow more frightened of Bower than she was of him.

Tierney considered that thought. Frightened of Bower—a voiceless coward whose most potent weapon was an icy glance? Tierney laughed . . . then laughed again.

"It's going to snow, sir."

Charles turned toward Corporal James Hodge. His temper was short, time was even shorter, and he still felt damned sick. But he was going to leave for Fort Larned that afternoon, or die trying.

"Sir?"

"I know it's going to snow, Corporal. Are the other men ready?"

Hodge glanced at Doc Stanley. Pretending he didn't see the disapproving wag of the doctor's balding head, Charles continued, "Tell them we'll be leaving within the hour."

"Yes, sir."

Hodge had barely cleared the doorway when Doc Stanley quipped, "Bound and determined to kill yourself, are you?"

Taking a new lease on his patience, Charles turned toward the man and attempted a smile. The smile failed. He just wasn't up to it. Instead, he stated, "You're right, Doc. I'm not well yet and I'm probably making a mistake starting out so soon, but I'm going anyway." Regretting the curtness of his statement a moment later, Charles said, "I'm sorry. I don't want you to think I don't appreciate what you did for me, but you said yourself that this fever I picked up isn't serious."

"Not serious if you rest and allow yourself to recover."

"I don't have the time to rest, Doc." Somehow needing to make this concerned physician understand that he wasn't the fool he seemed to be, Charles made another effort to explain, "I don't know how to make you understand, except to say that I was given an order—the responsibility for a woman's welfare. When I reached Fort Larned, my instincts told me that there was something wrong there, but I allowed myself to become distracted by my personal feelings. I was wrong, Doc. I should've paid attention to my instincts and looked into things more deeply, but I didn't. As a result, an imposter has the run of the fort. His disguise is elaborate and I don't think his intentions are honorable. I think he's a danger to the fort . . . and specifically a danger to the woman I was ordered to protect. I don't intend to let this fellow take advantage of either situation."

Doc Stanley's wiry brows arched with thoughtful speculation. "The woman *and* the fort are in danger . . ." He posed an unexpected question. "Is she pretty?"

"She's beautiful."

"Care about her a lot, do you?"

"Yeah." Charles gave a weary sigh. "I have to be going." He extended his hand. "Thanks."

Doc Stanley accepted his hand and shook it solemnly. "Give your second in command authority to take over for you so you can rest whenever possible. Take the powders I gave you if you feel physical distress mounting. When you get to the fort and straighten things out, take some sick time and sleep until you're slept out . . . and tell that lady of yours that she's a lucky woman."

"Good-bye, Doc."

Charles turned toward the door and stopped abruptly. Jewel stood in the opening, saloon makeup bright against her pallor as she forced a smile. She offered, "Mallory's her name, right?"

Charles managed a smile in return. "Yes."

"She's beautiful."

"Yes."

Jewel paused, as if contemplating that thought. "Well, if that beautiful, lucky lady shouldn't happen to realize how lucky she is for any reason, you turn yourself right back in this direction and come see me, you hear?" Jewel walked boldly toward him and slipped her arms around his neck. Her voice cracked, but her smile did not falter as she whispered, "You're my kind of fella, Lieutenant . . . the kind that could make an honest woman out of me if he had half a mind to."

Jewel planted a firm kiss on his lips, a kiss that lingered appealingly before she drew back and rasped, "You heard what the doc said. Rest . . . take your medicine. I'd take it real unkindly if you let somethin' foolish happen to you, you know."

Charles brushed a dark strand back from Jewel's cheek. "Thanks, Jewel."

Jewel breathed deeply, her smile dimming. "The good ones always get away."

He liked her.

"I'll come back to see you, Jewel."

"Yeah."

Somehow knowing it was kinder not to say more, Charles picked up his hat and walked out the door.

Gold Eagle walked briskly toward his quarters. He glanced up at the snow just beginning to drift downward in whirling spirals. He recalled the look on Captain Tierney's face when he'd said he was leaving. The man thought he was a fool for leaving with a storm approaching. Perhaps he was—but only for having allowed the man to get out through the doorway alive.

He had achieved his purpose in coming. He would warn Two Bears of Cotter's approach and intentions. He would see that the Cheyenne were prepared for what was to come.

Gold Eagle pushed the door of his quarters open and walked inside. He halted sharply, startled into motionlessness by the familiar female voice which broke the silence with a harsh command.

"Stop there! If you make any sudden moves, believe me, I'll shoot you dead."

Gold Eagle turned slowly to see Mallory standing in the shadows a few feet away. Her face colorless, her eyes devoid of warmth, she instructed softly, "Say my name."

Gold Eagle remained silent.

"Say my name. I heard you speaking to Penelope. I know you can talk."

Gold Eagle saw the wrath that held Mallory rigid as she confronted him. He saw the small gun in her hand.

"It's a derringer. It fires like any other gun, and it kills just as effectively. If you don't believe me, just take a step and you'll learn the hard way."

Gold Eagle did not doubt her.

"Say my name."

Gold Eagle scrutinized Mallory more closely.

She was shuddering, but there was no fear in her. Her breast was heaving with a passion as cold as death. Her face was pale, but her courage was undaunted. The heart of a warrior shone in her eyes. And her finger was curled around the trigger.

No, he did not doubt her.

Gold Eagle held her warrior's gaze with his.

"Mallory . . ."

A chill ran down Mallory's spine and her throat closed tight. His voice was deep and rich in timbre as it caressed her name. It was the same voice she had heard speak her name during the first night they were together—a night of lies from beginning to end.

"Say it again."

"Mallory."

"Again!"

"Mallory."

A frigid rage spread through Mallory's veins and she whispered in return, "You made me believe I was dreaming when I heard you say my name that first night. You made me believe a lot of things that weren't true, but before we leave this room, you're going to tell me the reason why." Mallory raised her chin. "You're going to tell me why, *Gold Eagle* . . . "

Gold Eagle stiffened and Mallory smiled. "That's right, I know who you are. Your name isn't Matthew Bower. It's Gold Eagle. You're well known in this section of the country. You're a white man who lives with the Indians, a white man who fights with the Indians."

"I am Cheyenne."

"Yes, you're Cheyenne. Corporal Walker told me—"

Gold Eagle's expression flickered, and Mallory paused before continuing, "No, I didn't tell him who you really are. I had only to mention the name Gold Eagle, and the rest was easy. He told me that Gold Eagle is a Cheyenne warrior, that the soldiers say he kills without mercy, and that they hate him more than any other Cheyenne because he's white. Walker said there's a standing reward for the man who brings him down."

Mallory waited as Gold Eagle returned her stare. She realized abruptly that she no longer thought of him as Matthew, and the reason was suddenly clear. No trace of Matthew, the gentle, considerate lover with whom she had communicated without words, remained in this man who stood before her. He looked the same. He dressed the same. Yet the sound of his voice had dispelled the other man forever. This new man with Matthew's face and body was a stranger.

The stranger responded emotionlessly, "All of these things you say are true."

"Everything Walker said?"

"Yes."

Gold Eagle's clear gray eyes scrutinized her in the momentary silence before Mallory demanded, "Where's Matthew Bower?"

"He's dead."

"You killed him."

"No, I did not."

When no further explanation was forthcoming, Mallory demanded, "Why did you come here pretending to be Matthew Bower?"

Again the almost imperceptible flicker of Gold Eagle's expression. She waited.

"I came for information."

"About what?"

"About Cotter's arrival. I will warn my people what Cotter plans and when he comes, so they may defend themselves."

"What makes you think your people need to defend themselves against him?"

Gold Eagle's deep voice rang with rebuke. "You are not a fool. Do not ask a fool's question."

Mallory raised her chin. "It's strange that you should say that, *Gold Eagle*, when you made so complete a fool out of me."

"I did not fool you." Gold Eagle's eyes held hers. "I allowed you to believe what you chose to believe."

Memories of the nights past returned to flush Mallory's face with heat, and she took a spontaneous backward step. She heard herself rasp, "And what did you believe, Gold Eagle?"

Silence stretched long and taut between them before Gold Eagle replied, "I believed in the moment . . . and nothing more."

Pain as quick and sharp as a penetrating blade pierced Mallory's heart. The last treasured vestiges of Matthew Bower seeped from the wound, leaving her empty and dry.

"Penelope—Owl Woman—knew who you were all along, didn't she?"

"Yes."

"She was your confederate."

"An unwilling confederate."

So Penelope had not deliberately deceived her.

Mallory forced herself to continue. "She gave you the information you needed."

"Yes."

"What were you planning to do now?"

"I was going to leave."

Steeling herself against his reply, Mallory forced herself to ask, "Did you intend to see me before you left?"

"No."

Needing long seconds to digest Gold Eagle's words, Mallory began slowly, "You know your fate is in my hands."

Gold Eagle did not respond.

"I have only to fire a shot, or call out into the yard and you'll be taken into custody. You'll watch Cotter's arrival from behind bars and nothing you learned will be worth anything at all."

Silence.

"Your secret has been discovered." Mallory paused. "What you don't realize is that my secret hasn't."

Gold Eagle looked startled, and Mallory felt a momentary gratification. She proceeded with bittersweet enjoyment, "Strange, isn't it, that I should be here under false pretenses, too. You see, Joshua Barnes, the man I supposedly came here to find, doesn't exist. I came here for information, just as you did, to write the true story about what's going on between the Indians and the army for *The Examiner*, the largest newspaper in Chicago. I invented Joshua Barnes to suit my convenience, just as you used me to suit yours."

Mallory searched Gold Eagle's face. Seeing not a trace of Matthew Bower to refute the harshness of her last statement, she continued, "The main difference between you and me right now is that you have the information you need. I don't.

"I want the information I came here for. I won't return without it, and I think Captain Tierney will drive a hard bargain before he'll let me go where I can get it. So, I have a proposition for you . . ."

Gold Eagle waited for Mallory to continue. It occurred to him as the words of her "proposition" were about to unravel, that this woman was a warrior who would not allow herself to be defeated. Her gun hand was steady and her eyes were cold. One move from him and she would shoot.

Gold Eagle studied Mallory. He dwarfed her in size and strength, but the formidable power surging from within her held him motionless as she stated flatly, "I'll let you go back to warn your people . . ."

A brief silence stretched long.

". . . on three conditions. The first is that you

take me back with you so I can bring the truth about what's happening here to the American people."

Gold Eagle almost laughed. He knew what this woman's truth would be.

"The second is that all intimacy between us will cease."

Gold Eagle did not respond.

"The third is that we will speak only the truth to each other from this point on."

Gold Eagle's reply was instinctive.

"No."

Mallory raised her derringer toward the ceiling, her lips tight. "One shot, and this room will be swarming with soldiers."

"No."

Mallory's delicate jaw hardened. She extended her arm toward the ceiling and pulled the trig—

"Yes!"

The clear green of Mallory's eyes flashed with triumph. "What did you say?"

"I said, yes. I will take you back with me. I will keep the conditions of our bargain."

"I have your word on that?"

When Gold Eagle did not answer, she demanded, "I want to hear you say it!"

"You have my word."

Mallory lowered her gun and Gold Eagle marveled at her gullibility. She had just uncovered the many lies he had allowed her to believe, yet she would now trust him with her life. He was possessed of a sudden desire to laugh.

But he did not. Instead, he said, "I will take you with me, but you must follow my directions without question." Pausing, he instructed curtly, "Go back to your room and gather your things. We leave within the hour."

Mallory stepped out fully into the light, and Gold Eagle stopped still at the sight of the dark bruise on her cheek. Hardly realizing his intent, he grasped her arm to hold her fast as she attempted to brush past him. He demanded, "Why is your face bruised?"

"It's nothing." Mallory raised her chin. "Let me go."

Filled with incomprehensible anger, he hissed, "Only the truth between us . . ."

Remembered ire flashed in Mallory's eyes. "All right. Captain Tierney came to my room last night. He didn't like it when I made him leave."

Gold Eagle released her arm. "We leave within the hour."

Mallory drew the door open, then turned back to face him with a frown. "It's snowing!"

"Within the hour."

Mallory pulled the door closed behind her.

"How do you feel, Lieutenant?"

The frigid wind flayed his face with razor-sharp flakes of snow as Charles turned toward Corporal Bell. They had been on the trail for more than two hours. The snow was constant, he was cold to the bone, and it took all his strength to hold himself upright.

213

He responded, "I'm fine."

"Yeah, I can see that."

Hodge interjected, "Whittier's cold, sir. He wants to stop for a while and rest."

Whittier turned toward Hodge with a look of surprise that ended in a belated nod of confirmation. If he wasn't feeling so damned poorly, Charles knew he would've laughed at the obvious ruse. Instead, he addressed the silent corporal.

"Do you want to stop, Whittier?"

"Yes, sir."

"I don't, so we're not going to."

"Lieutenant . . ."

"Look, I know what you're all trying to do, but I'm all right. I'll rest when we get to Fort Larned."

"Sir . . ."

Pointedly ignoring Bell, Charles stared straight ahead. He didn't want to tell them why he was driving so hard. He knew they'd think he was getting delirious again, but the truth was that he had a bad feeling—a feeling that if they didn't hurry, they'd be too late.

Mallory . . .

Charles kicked his mount into a lope.

Waiting only until Mallory disappeared in the direction of her room, Gold Eagle stepped out into the yard and closed his door behind him. Without conscious decision, he started toward Captain Tierney's quarters.

. . . Captain Tierney didn't like it when I made him leave . . .

Rage stirred.

Tierney had gone to Mallory's room the previous night. Gold Eagle had not needed to ask Mallory the reason for Tierney's visit. He remembered her trembling when he came to her shortly afterward, and he knew what that man had attempted to do.

Tierney had struck her. The image of Tierney's hand crashing against Mallory's cheek increased ·Gold Eagle's pace until he stopped before Tierney's door.

There was no answer to his knock.

"You lookin' for Captain Tierney, Mr. Bower?"

Gold Eagle turned at the sound of Corporal Walker's voice. He signed an affirmative response.

"I'd stay away from him for a while if I was you. He ain't in too good a mood." Walker glanced around them, then added, "I saw him knockin' on Miss Tompkins's door a while ago. He didn't like it much that she wasn't there. I've a feelin' that he's got an eye for Miss Tompkins and she ain't cooperatin' like he wants her to. To tell you the truth, he ain't the kind of fella to take no for an answer."

Gold Eagle signed a rapid response.

"Hell, even a blind man could see that he was mad as a hornet when Miss Tompkins wasn't in her room. I think he's lookin' for her now. It ain't like him to go strollin' around the fort the way he's been doin' for the past hour, and I got the feelin' that the harder it is for him to find her, the madder he's goin' to get."

Gold Eagle signed again.

"The last time I saw him he was walkin' out back, by the stable."

Gold Eagle turned on his heel.

"Hey, where're you goin' in such a hurry?"

"Where in hell is she?"

Growing more irritable by the minute, Captain Tierney walked past the stable for the third time. He scrutinized the interior. Bower's horse was still there, saddled and ready, but Bower wasn't.

Tierney's jaw twitched. He didn't like that—Bower and Mallory *both* nowhere to be found.

Tierney stopped abruptly. No, she wouldn't. Mallory wouldn't try to get back at him by leaving the fort with that voiceless bastard!

Tierney considered that possibility. She had probably told that mute coward what had happened in her room the previous night. That was why the bastard was so anxious to leave—so he could take her away with him!

His chest heaving with agitation, Tierney considered the situation again. There was one way to be sure what was going on. If Mallory was leaving, her horse would be saddled and waiting for her. If it was . . .

"Dolan!" Striding into the stable, Tierney called out again, "Dolan, where are you?"

Frustrated when there was no response, Tierney approached Bower's horse in the rear of the stable. The animal was fully packed and prepared for a journey. A quick glance around the surrounding area revealed no other horses similarly accoutered. All right, so she wasn't leaving. Where was she? When he did find her, he would make her—

An unexpected flash of movement behind Tierney left him no time for defense. An arm snaked around his neck holding him captive.

A knife pressed to his throat, drawing blood!

The low hiss that sounded in his ear as he struggled to breathe was unfamiliar as it spat, "Do you know who I am, Captain Tierney?"

A chill as cold as death crawled up Tierney's spine. No, it couldn't be.

The voice deepened with fury. "Tell me who you think I am."

"Bower . . ." Tierney croaked.

The blade pressed deeper as his captor continued, "You are wrong. Matthew Bower is dead. He died beside the fire of a Cheyenne shaman, but not before he passed to me the legacy of his name. I put aside my Cheyenne name and accepted his, knowing it would suit my purpose here better than my own."

Tierney's mouth went dry in sudden realization. "You're Gold Eagle."

"Too late, Captain."

"Let me go!" Tierney grated. "You can't get away with killing me. If you do, Major General Cotter will make you pay! He'll hunt you down and destroy your whole tribe!"

"And who will make you pay for what you tried to do last night?"

"Pay . . . last night?" Tierney panicked. The witch *had* told him! He gasped, "She knew who you were all along, didn't she?"

"Who will make you pay, Captain?"

Gold Eagle felt Tierney trembling, and he was filled with contempt. This man who had derided him for cowardice even now stained his uniform in fear.

"Sh-she asked for it! She led me on! She invited me into her room. She was enjoying every minute until—"

"Lies!"

Tierney stiffened as Gold Eagle pressed his blade painfully closer. He felt the captain's blood against his fingers as he rasped, "You struck her, but she repelled you with her warrior's heart!"

"She had a gun!"

Amusement touched Gold Eagle's mind. "A very small gun."

"It was a gun, damn it! And she would've used it!"

Yes, she would have.

"Let me go. I'll make it worth your while." Gold Eagle felt Tierney shudder as he continued, "Cotter will listen to me. I'll tell him to leave your tribe alone. I'll tell him the Cheyenne want peace."

"Peace—but not at the price you ask."

Gold Eagle jerked Tierney backward, his knife against the man's bloodied throat as he dragged him toward a dark corner of the stable.

His voice a choked squeak, Tierney rasped, "What're you going to do?"

Satisfied only when the shadows shielded them both, Gold Eagle whispered into the shuddering man's ear, "I would have you remember this moment. I would make it clear that as you marked the woman, I mark your body and your mind, so you will never touch her again. Will you remember, Captain?"

"Yes . . . no! Let go of me, damn you!"

Raising his knife, Gold Eagle sliced sharply.

"My ear! You cut off my ear!"

Gold Eagle felt the blood gushing. ". . . So you will remember."

Turning the man toward him in a quick shift of movement, Gold Eagle saw Tierney's eyes flare wide the second before his fist crashed against his jaw.

Breathing heavily, his pale eyes narrowed with contempt, Gold Eagle held his temper under firm control as Tierney slumped to the ground.

Mallory glanced around the room. Satisfied that she had left nothing behind, she fought to steady her inner trembling as she pulled her hat down on her head and picked up her bag. The heavy traveling clothes that she had worn on her journey to the fort felt comfortably familiar. It brought Charles to mind, and she regretted that when he returned, she would be gone. She looked at the letter she had left on the chest nearby. Reconsidering, she snatched it up and stuffed it into her pocket.

Striding into the stable moments later, Mallory halted when Gold Eagle appeared abruptly at her side. She saw Matthew's face, but Gold Eagle's eyes—those damned light eyes as cold as ice.

Allowing no time for second thoughts, Gold Eagle snatched her bag from her hand and tied it on her saddle with the other bundles there. He grasped her tapestry reticule and the derringer inside it slapped against his hand. His gaze met hers in silent acknowledgment before he slipped the straps over the saddlehorn, then swung her easily up onto the saddle.

Momentarily flustered at his effortless power, Mallory snapped, "I could've mounted by myself!"

Not choosing to reply, Gold Eagle mounted his horse in a fluid movement, then instructed softly, "The guards at the gate have been notified that I am to leave."

"But they aren't expecting me to be with you. What should I do if—"

Gold Eagle spurred his mount forward without waiting for her to finish, and Mallory's anger flared. A savage . . . yes, he was a savage, after all!

Her heart pounding as they rode across the fort yard, Mallory searched the surrounding area with a furtive gaze. Somehow this was too easy. Where was Captain Tierney? She had expected some sort of reprisal from him for the blow she had dealt his pride the previous night. The man's conceit was so enormous that she had half expected him to approach her with a coy apology, with the expectation that she wouldn't be able to resist it or him. Was he waiting somewhere for the right moment to make his appearance?

"Mr. Bower . . ." They were at the gates. The pounding of Mallory's heart increased to thunder as the guard glanced between Gold Eagle and her. "I was told you'd be leavin', but I wasn't expectin' Miss Tompkins to be with you."

Gold Eagle turned to scrutinize the area. His gaze stopped on Corporal Walker, who approached through the rapidly thickening snowfall.

"I heard you were leavin', Mr. Bower. I'm real sorry to see you go." Gold Eagle signed to him, and Walker turned to the guard. "Mr. Bower said he's already told Captain Tierney that Miss Tompkins would be leavin' with him."

The guard appeared wary. "I don't know about that."

Gold Eagle signed again.

"Mr. Bower says that's its startin' to snow harder and he wants to get started."

The guard continued shaking his head. "Captain Tierney didn't tell us nothin' about this."

Mallory's composure snapped. "Open the gates, Private! Open them immediately!"

"Ma'am . . ."

"You are aware that I came here with special instructions from Major Bullen that I am to be

221

accommodated in every way, aren't you, Private?"

"Yes, ma'am."

"If you don't open those gates immediately, you may be sure I'll see to it that Major Bullen hears about your unwillingness to follow his orders!"

"But ma'am . . ."

"Excuses will mean nothing when you're brought up on a reprimand!"

"But . . ."

"Are you going to open those gates or not?"

Wilting under Mallory's unwavering stare, the soldier gave a reluctant nod.

"Yes, ma'am." He turned to address the men behind him with a touch of sarcasm that did not escape Mallory's ear. "Open the gates. Miss Tompkins is in a rush to leave."

Pausing only long enough to direct a deadly glance the young fellow's way, Mallory was startled when Gold Eagle leaned down and extended his hand toward Corporal Walker. She noted the respect that flashed between the two men as they shook hands.

"Real pleased to have met you, Mr. Bower."

Mallory inwardly scoffed. If he knew . . .

Mallory stared at Corporal Walker a moment longer. A sudden decision made, she dug into her pocket and withdrew the envelope she had put there minutes earlier. She held it out to him.

"Lieutenant Moore should be returning to Fort Larned within the week." Ignoring Walker's obvious surprise, she continued, "When he gets here, would you see to it that he gets this letter?" She forced a smile. "I'd appreciate it if you'd put it right into his hands. It's important to me, Corporal."

"Yes, ma'am. I sure will."

Mallory turned back to Gold Eagle in time to see that his gaze had turned frigid. The gates swung open and Gold Eagle urged his horse forward.

The open portal suddenly drove home the immensity of the step she was taking, and Mallory hesitated. This was crazy! She was riding into the wilderness with a man who was a stranger to her . . . a man who had already deceived her . . . a man who was known to the civilized world as a savage who killed without regret.

She was putting her life in his hands!

As if sensing her thoughts, Gold Eagle turned back toward her. His light eyes met hers. She read the challenge there. She saw contempt dawning as her hesitation continued. Suddenly angry, she jammed her heels into her mount's sides, spurring him into a jump forward.

Her heart pounding as the fort gates swung closed behind them, Mallory guided her horse in line behind Gold Eagle. She stared at his back as they moved steadily along the trail, seeing in his proud posture the male arrogance she had faced so many times in her life.

Gritting her teeth, Mallory again dug her heels into her mount's sides. When her horse came abreast of Gold Eagle, she reined back to ride beside him in a position of equal power.

Satisfied, vowing she would never follow silently in his wake again, Mallory held her gaze straightforward as the snow continued falling.

Chapter Eight

"I think it's time to stop for the night, sir."

Corporal Bell's voice slowly penetrated the frozen haze that had overwhelmed Charles's mind. He looked around, straining to see through the heavy curtain of snow that had whitened the desolate terrain. For the first time he realized that daylight was fading.

He turned to address Bell, abruptly discovering that it was an effort for him to speak as he rasped, "I suppose you're right, Corporal." It occurred to him belatedly that he was swaying in the saddle, that if Bell hadn't spoken up when he did, he probably would have fallen.

Charles strained to concentrate. The snowfall was unrelenting. He was able to calculate at last that they had traveled a shorter distance than he had hoped, but a longer distance than he had expected.

He was tired.

Assessing his physical condition with as much clarity as he could muster, he concluded that his fever had not returned, but that he had reached his limit for that day's travel—and that he was temporarily in no condition to continue commanding his detachment.

Charles silently assessed the qualifications of his men. Hodge, Whittier, Knoll—all were older than Bell, but none was as sharp and quick. His decision was made.

"Corporal Bell." Charles turned with the last of his remaining strength toward the soldier riding beside him. "It's going to be up to you to find us a place to camp for the night. I'm putting you in charge until morning." He paused. "*Only* until morning, at which time we'll continue on to Fort Larned. Is that understood?"

"Sir . . ."

"Is that understood?"

"Yes, sir."

It occurred to Charles that Bell was looking at him strangely. He wasn't sure why. He was about to ask, when the snow-covered ground rose up to meet him with a deafening crash that turned the world to darkness.

Captain Tierney cursed. His stomach was sick. The taste of blood was in his mouth—*his own* blood—and his body was painfully stiff.

Mumbling repeated curses through the

blood-soaked gag tied across his mouth, Tierney listened to the voices of the soldiers who again passed him by in their search. It was obvious that the entire fort had been alerted that he was missing. They had been looking for him the entire day, coming close to the pile of hay under which he lay tied hand and foot, but not close enough to hear his muffled calls for help.

Matthew Bower was Gold Eagle. He still could not comprehend how he had been so completely taken in by the disguise. He had looked Gold Eagle directly in the eye without recognizing him. He had dismissed the man as a coward. He had not suspected for a moment that Gold Eagle was anyone but the man he pretended to be. He had been fooled by an ignorant primitive who wore the face of a white man, but who, in the end, had shown himself as the savage he truly was.

The bastard had cut off his ear!

Filled with rage, Tierney struggled against his bonds. He had awakened from Gold Eagle's blow to find himself bound and gagged and lying beneath a pile of hay in what he remembered was a filthy, isolated corner of the stable. His ear had stopped bleeding but the pain would not relent.

Tierney's heart began a ragged pounding. The bastard would pay! When he was back on his feet, he would make it his mission in life to bring the arrogant savage to a day of reckoning.

The sound of heavy footsteps nearby alerted Tierney to someone's approach, and he struggled more fiercely against his bonds. Shouting through the gag he wore, he kicked and squirmed, unmindful of the indignity as he sought to catch the attention of the men.

The footsteps drew closer. He heard the rumbling of voices. He saw the hay atop him moving.

"He's here! The captain's here!"

It was Sergeant Riker. The idiots had finally found him!

The bloody gag was ripped from his mouth and Tierney gasped, drawing fresh air into lungs deprived for tormented hours.

"Are you all right, sir?"

"Untie me!"

"Yes, sir." The fellow gasped. "Sir . . . your ear is gone!"

"Untie me, damn it!"

Riker labored to untie his bonds as others gathered around him where he lay so thoroughly disgraced.

Freed at last, Tierney suffered the further humiliation of being unable to stand. He grated, "Help me up, you fool!"

On his feet at last, Tierney struggled to square his shoulders with a semblance of military correctness. Breathing heavily from the effort, he scrutinized the men around him, his gaze falling on the fellow who had been on guard earlier in the day.

"When did Bower leave the fort, Private Drummond?"

The fellow swallowed, his overly large Adam's

apple bobbing almost comically as he replied, "This mornin', sir. We was expectin' him, so we let him leave."

"How long ago was that?"

"It's almost nightfall, sir."

His ear throbbing so painfully that the guard's statement almost escaped him, Tierney grated, "What did you say?"

"I said . . . I said we was expectin' Mr. Bower to leave, but we wasn't expectin' Miss Tompkins to leave with him."

"What?"

"I said Miss Tompkins left with him."

Tierney went still. It had all been planned, and she was in on it! The savage and the witch were probably now laughing at the retribution they had served him!

Tierney took a shaky step forward, then another. He saw the speculation in the eyes of the men around him, and humiliation burned. He need make no explanations to them! Everything would be clear when Gold Eagle stood under his gun at last, and when the red-haired witch *begged* for his mercy. Then it would be his turn to make the blood flow.

And that day would come.

He would make sure of that if it was the last thing he ever did.

The snowfall, which had continued through the day, showed no sign of abating as daylight waned. The merciless wind would not relent. Charles came again to Mallory's mind as she pulled her shapeless woolen hat farther down on her forehead and adjusted the collar of her heavy coat against her neck in defense against the chill that was sinking into her bones.

Mallory silently acknowledged that were it not for Charles, she would be even colder than she presently was—which would have been cold indeed, considering that she was already shivering like a leaf in the wind. She had done a lot of thinking during the long day, and her regrets were many when she reviewed her treatment of Charles. The letter she had left for him was inadequate in so many ways, but she had wanted to alleviate some of the concerns he would suffer when he returned and found her gone.

She had realized abruptly on leaving her room, however, that Charles would never get the letter if the captain saw it first. She had known she needed to put it into safe hands, but she had not known whose hands they would be until she saw Corporal Walker. She had trusted Walker to see that Charles received her letter. She hoped she had not again misplaced her trust.

Mallory glanced at the big man riding beside her. Charles would be shocked when he discovered who Matthew Bower really was. Or . . . perhaps he wouldn't. Charles had told her he didn't trust Matthew—Gold Eagle—but she had been so certain he was wrong. In the letter she had done her best to explain the reason she'd made her bargain with Gold Eagle, but it had been difficult to explain something she didn't truly understand herself.

Mallory was suddenly disgusted with her own attempt to avoid the difficult truth. She understood the reason for the dangerous bargain she had demanded of Gold Eagle. It could be explained in two words. *Humiliation* and *pride*. She had been humiliated to have been so thoroughly deceived, and she had been too proud to allow Gold Eagle total victory.

Mallory's frozen face twitched. She had learned belatedly, however, that the price of her victory was to traverse a snow-swept wilderness with a man who was immune to the cold that numbed her, and to the hunger that gnawed her stomach—a man who did not even suffer the demands of nature's call, if she were to judge by the desperate discomfort she had endured before finally forcing him to call a halt so she might relieve herself.

Mallory sneaked another glance at Gold Eagle out of the corner of her eye. The man was made of stone! He had not glanced behind him a single time during the day to see if anyone from the fort was following them, while she had spent the first few hours expecting Captain Tierney to come riding up behind them at any minute. His expression revealed nothing, and he had spoken so few words to her since leaving the fort that he might just as well be the mute he had pretended to be.

Another shudder wracked Mallory's frame. It was getting dark and the temperature was dropping. Her body was so stiff, she doubted she would be able to dismount from her horse. She was cold, miserable, and more exhausted than she had ever been in her life.

The wind gusted, abrading her face with icy particles of snow, and Mallory held herself rigid against it.

But she'd be damned before she'd give up one minute before he did!

Wh-what was that sound?

Mallory silently groaned. Her teeth were chattering so hard that she feared they might shatter.

Oh, damn . . . damn, damn, damn!

Gold Eagle scrutinized the surrounding terrain—it was pure and white, unmarked by animal or man. The snow that had fallen throughout the day had been to his advantage, erasing all trace of the trail they had taken, but he had no fear that they would be followed soon, in any case. No one at the fort other than Captain Tierney knew his true identity, and it would be hours before Tierney would be found.

Gold Eagle's jaw hardened. When he'd seen the mark on Mallory's cheek, the need for vengeance had been so strong that he had given no heed to the possible consequences. In truth, it had taken all his control to leave the man still breathing.

That realization made him uncomfortable.

Mallory rode abreast of him along the trail. The reason she maintained that position did not escape him. Her pride would not allow her to ride behind him in a position of secondary importance. It mattered little to her that in riding ahead, he would break the trail for her mount, that his larger body would act as a buffer against the weather's assault, and that she accomplished little by causing both herself and her horse needless exhaustion. Keenly aware that her discomforts had worsened through the day, he secretly marveled at her endurance. He had betrayed no emotion when she finally submitted to her body's demand by calling a halt for relief. He refused to acknowledge that the loud complaints of her stomach and the growing stiffness of her slender form wore more heavily on his mind than he liked.

Gold Eagle reminded himself that there was no reason for him to explain to her that their relentless pace throughout the day had been calculated so they might reach a specific place to camp that night—a spot he knew would afford them adequate shelter from the storm. He told himself that she had challenged him, declaring herself his equal under circumstances in which she was lacking. He knew she would recognize her shortcomings only by paying the price of that error.

Gold Eagle forcibly dismissed Mallory from his mind to review again the facts of Cotter's approach. Cotter's reputation preceded him. He was a dedicated officer said to be relentless in battle, one who was rumored to believe that all Indians were enemies of the government he represented. Gold Eagle did not doubt Owl

Woman's claim that Cotter's men were well fed, well armed, and well mounted. He knew his own people could not match the power of the army's great guns with their outdated weapons, and that they would not be at full strength until the sun again brought the earth to bloom. His people's ultimate victory, entrusted to him in the sunlight of a sacred hilltop, had never appeared more difficult to achieve.

A wind gusted, lifting frozen strands of his hair to whip his face as Gold Eagle surveyed the darkening landscape more closely. His gaze halted on a wooded copse in the distance, and he smiled in satisfaction. He glanced at Mallory again, and was startled to see that she was shuddering visibly. He noted her mortification at not being able to control the chattering of her teeth. He knew her strength was rapidly fading.

Gold Eagle spurred his horse to a faster pace.

It was still snowing.

An hour had passed since Captain Tierney had been discovered. He had walked off his stiffness, bathed away the blood of his ordeal, and changed into a clean uniform that almost restored his self-esteem.

Almost . . .

Tierney reached up to touch the bandage on the side of his head, his lips twisting in a silent snarl. In the absence of the fort doctor, Sergeant Ulrich had been the man most familiar with wounds such as his, but Tierney had only reluctantly allowed Ulrich to treat him. The reason was simple. Ulrich hated him. Until now he had never been bothered by Ulrich's hatred. Nor had he ever tried to ascertain the true reason for it. He suspected it was because he had shot Ulrich's pregnant mongrel dog when the animal barked at him in the fort yard. The bitch was ugly. He had hated it from the moment he saw it. It had seemed to him somehow representative of the half-breeds that were gradually infesting the country—neither Indian nor white, racial lines blurred into oblivion, an inferior class that threatened the entire race of man.

He had killed the animal without a second thought, considering that he had done the canine species a favor. He cared little what Ulrich or anyone else had to say about it. He recalled that a few men had forcibly held Ulrich back from coming after him when the dog lay dead on the ground, but he had never truly understood the man's reaction. Mongrels were worthless, whether they were canine or human. If he had his way, he'd do away with them all.

Tierney recalled Ulrich's expression when the fellow entered his quarters to treat him. The bastard had almost smiled. His touch had been less than gentle, and had he not realized Ulrich's intention to make him look ridiculous, he would now be wearing a bandage the size of a sultan's turban over the stub of his ear.

Tierney's agitation swelled. He was scarred for life. He would never again look into the mirror without remembering what Gold Eagle had done to him. What Gold Eagle did not know, however, was that the day would come when he would look into the mirror and remember what he had done to Gold Eagle in return.

It was still snowing. He had no doubt that Gold Eagle and Mallory were presently exposed to the fury of the biting wind that was even now driving icy pellets of snow against the window. The closest Indian village could not possibly be reached in less than two days' travel. They were doubtless attempting to find shelter from the elements right now, unable to make a fire to warm their frozen bones. . . .

A soft knock turned Tierney sharply toward the sound. The door opened at his response and Tierney's jaw hardened at the sight of the half-breed, Penelope Dolan, standing tentatively there.

"Come in." Tierney's voice was less than inviting. "Close the door behind you."

The woman was silent. A familiar disgust rose inside him when he studied the umber tone of her skin and the ink-black color of her hair.

He addressed her sharply. "You knew about him all along, didn't you!"

The woman took a backward step.

"Answer me, woman!"

Penelope's small face twitched. "I do not know what you mean."

"I'm talking about Gold Eagle! *Gold Eagle*! You knew all along that Matthew Bower and Gold Eagle were the same man!"

"No."

"Don't lie to me! One Indian always recognizes another!"

"Gold Eagle is not an Indian."

"He is, damn it! He claims to be Cheyenne, and he is! You know what he did to me. No white man could be so savage!"

Penelope's lack of response silently refuted his statement, and Tierney's rage deepened. Closing the distance between them in a few short steps, he grasped her arm. "I'm not going to argue with you. I know you were a part of Gold Eagle's scheme, and I know you know the reason why he came to this fort. I want you to tell me why he came, and I want you to tell me now!"

"I know nothing."

Tierney squeezed her arm tighter, almost lifting the small woman from her feet as he spat, "Tell me, or I'll throw you, your husband, and your child out into the snow tonight! I have a right to do that, you know. As commandant of this fort, I have the right to expel anyone I feel is a threat to the safety of this post."

"As you attempted to do with Mr. Bower."

Tierney's fury heightened. "Yes . . . as I attempted to do with *Gold Eagle*, and I was right! What he did bears me out. It will give me more credibility when I explain to Major General Cotter how I saved the fort from another half-breed spy as well!"

"I am not a spy. I know nothing."

"Tell me, damn you!"

The woman's gaze did not falter.

Releasing her with a snarl of revulsion, Tierney watched as Penelope staggered backward. He waited until she stood steady once more, until he was also stable enough to maintain a semblance of dignity before grating, "You, your husband, and your child—I want all three of you out of this fort at sunrise."

The woman blinked as Tierney continued, "If you don't leave voluntarily, you will be forcibly ousted and all your possessions will be burned."

"You cannot do that."

"I can and I will."

"My husband—"

"Nothing your husband says or does can change my orders. Only *you* can change them— by telling me why Gold Eagle came to this fort disguised as someone else."

"I know nothing."

"Start packing!"

Unable to bear the woman's expressionless mein a moment longer, Tierney called out, "Private Sanders!" Addressing the guard who entered the room, he ordered, "Get this woman out of my sight!"

Turning away from her with a repugnance so deep that he was almost nauseated, Tierney strode to the window to stare at the snowflakes still falling thickly.

Yes, it was still snowing. Gold Eagle and Mallory would be shivering in the midst of the storm right now, hungrier and colder than they had ever been. That thought giving him bitter solace. Tierney muttered, "Right now they're probably saying . . .

"Don't fall behind! Keep up with me!"

Gold Eagle's sharp admonition snapped Mallory from her stupor. She reacted automatically, digging her heels into her mount's sides, but there was little response from the weary animal. She squinted, forcing her cloudy mind to concentrate. Gold Eagle was a few feet ahead of her. He was looking back at her. The snow that had accumulated on his clothing, hair, and brows gave him the appearance of a huge, glowering snowman.

A snowman . . . Mallory's mind wandered. She had built many snowmen with her father as a child. He had made it a point to come home from the office at the first true snowfall of the season so they could perform their yearly ritual. No snowman had ever looked more out of place than theirs did each winter, standing proudly on what normally was the great lawn of the white-columned family mansion. She had loved her father for that. She had waited with bated breath when the first snowflakes fell for him to come home.

She would like to build another snowman . . . but her arms and legs were so stiff. And she was so cold. She felt as if she would never be—

"Mallory!"

Mallory snapped out of her foggy reverie to see Gold Eagle staring back at her.

"Do you hear me, Mallory?"

Mallory spat, "Of course I hear you!"

But the words were a hoarse squeak.

Gold Eagle reached back toward her. He snatched the reins from her numb fingers.

"Hold onto the saddle horn."

Mallory protested, but the words were swallowed by her gasp as her mount was pulled suddenly forward.

She didn't like this! She didn't like being towed around like so much baggage. She didn't like having command of her own person snatched from her hands as if she were an incompetent child! She didn't like . . . She didn't like . . .

She couldn't remember what else she didn't like.

It slipped from her mind as her horse continued its steady forward pace.

Her horse stopped. She saw the outline of a shed amidst the thickly falling snow. No, it was a cabin.

"Mallory . . ."

Mallory looked down to see the huge snowman standing beside her horse. Pale eyes ridged with ice-crusted lashes stared at her.

The snowman swung her from her horse.

"Let me go!" The words were uttered through frozen lips. "I can get down by myself!"

Her statement went unheeded as she was carried across the snow-covered ground in the snowman's arms.

The snowman kicked the door open. The cabin was dark and cold.

She commanded, "Light the lamp."

Her words were garbled. The snowman looked down at her.

"It's dark."

She hadn't spoken those words any more clearly. What was wrong with her?

The snowman placed her on a musty bunk in a shadowed corner. She didn't like it when he walked away from her. She tried to get up, but she couldn't. She was so confused.

She saw a flicker of light. A fire in the fireplace. She forced herself to her feet and started toward it. The snowman steadied her. The snowman—no, Gold Eagle.

He sat her on the floor.

"Stay here."

He was stripping away her coat, and she fought him.

"I must take off your coat."

"I'm cold."

He took off her coat, anyway. Then her hat. She groaned with relief when a blanket fell around her shoulders, when strong hands wrapped her tightly in its folds, then positioned her closer to the fire.

But she was still shivering.

She turned as a horse neighed close by. Quaking, she watched as Gold Eagle brought both horses into the small cabin and secured them by the door. She looked up at him as he crouched beside her. The snow had melted from his brows, but his face was reddened from the bite of the storm. His long, light hair had become unbound. It lay against the shoulders of his coat in damp strands.

She was cold. She couldn't stop shivering. Gold Eagle studied her a moment longer. He disappeared from her side, reappearing with a bottle in his hand.

"Drink."

She was thirsty. She took a long gulp, swallowing automatically, then coughed as the fiery liquid burned all the way down to her stomach. Mallory turned toward Gold Eagle, accusing hoarsely, "That's . . . that's . . ."

"Whiskey. It will warm you."

Mallory watched as Gold Eagle took long swallows. She grated, "Liquor . . . it's illegal for Indians."

Gold Eagle returned her gaze with a raised brow and Mallory frowned. "Oh . . . I forgot."

She shuddered, then shuddered again. Her stomach was on fire, but the rest of her was unaffected by the inner blaze.

"I'm cold."

Gold Eagle's light eyes held hers.

She shivered again.

Gold Eagle stood up abruptly. She watched as he stripped off his hat and coat; the wet clothes fell on the floor beside the fire. When he crouched beside her again, the bare skin of his chest glowed in the flickering light. She remained silent as he unwrapped her blanket and drew her into his arms, then lay down and pulled the blanket around them both. He took another blanket from the shadows and stretched it out atop them. He adjusted her against the curve of his body, and a slow heat began permeating her veins. He drew her closer, so close that she felt the steady beating of his heart beneath her ear and the warmth of his bared flesh against her cheek.

She wasn't sure when she stopped shivering. His palms stroked her back, warming her, and she pressed herself tightly against him. Her stomach was unstable and her concentration was uncertain, but other, unfluctuating constants consoled her.

She was safe.

She was warm.

She was where she wanted to be.

Mallory closed her eyes.

Owl Woman stood over the cradle of her sleeping son. He was a beautiful male child. His cheeks were round and his skin was flushed with returning health. She loved him more than the life that flowed through her own veins.

Owl Woman jumped as her husband slipped up unexpectedly beside her.

"He's all right, Penelope." Dolan studied her concerned expression, uncertain, and Owl Woman felt guilt nudge her mind as he continued, "His fever's gone. That medicine Matthew Bower gave him practically worked a miracle."

Owl Woman nodded. Her husband had spoken the truth. Gold Eagle had given her son back to her when his life was almost gone.

Dolan was suddenly frowning, just as she

was. "I talked to Sergeant Ulrich after he left Captain Tierney's quarters. He said there ain't nothin' more than a nub of his ear left. The rumor is that Bower did it before he left the fort." Dolan paused. "The rumor is that Bower wasn't really Bower . . . that he was the Cheyenne warrior called Gold Eagle." He paused again. "You didn't know nothin' about that, did you?"

Owl Woman raised her gaze to meet her husband's. He was a good man, who loved her. They had suffered much at the loss of their first child and the bond between them was strong—but she had told him nothing. She regretted the secret she kept from him while knowing she spared him by doing so.

Dolan did not know she had been called to Captain Tierney's office. Nor did he know the threats that man had made. She did not doubt the captain would follow through with his threats, nor did she doubt he would enjoy the moment should she allow it to come.

Dolan's question hung on the silence between them. Dolan broke the silence first. "You knew. I figured you did. There ain't much that gets past you." He took a short breath. "Don't tell anybody you knew. If Tierney found out, there'd be hell to pay. I wouldn't put it past him to throw us out of the fort—all three of us—on some kind of pretext or another, just to get even." Dolan reached down to touch stubby fingers to his son's forehead. "He wouldn't give a damn about Joseph. He ain't got a heart."

Owl Woman watched her husband's fingers

as they stroked their son's cheek. Dolan drew his hand back abruptly and walked to the window. "It's still snowin'. I'm sure glad we ain't in Gold Eagle's spot right now—or Miss Tompkins's. Joseph would never survive."

Owl Woman looked up to see her husband shake his head sadly . . . and her decision was made.

"Hey, where're you goin', Penelope?"

Owl Woman turned back to her husband as she pulled her wrap around her. "The cook is ill. I must see to the bread that is rising in the kitchen."

Dolan did not question Owl Woman as she slipped out the door and disappeared amongst the whirling snowflakes.

The whiskey had been a mistake.

Gold Eagle drew Mallory closer.

The day had been long and the snow incessant. He had been more cold than he had allowed his mind to accept. He had intended that the burning heat of the white man's liquor would renew the heat within Mallory, and it did. He had intended that it would renew him as well, but it had renewed a heat of another kind.

Gold Eagle stroked Mallory's back.

She was sleeping now. She nestled closer, her shivering almost gone, and he settled her flush against him. He brushed the hair from her cheek. The dark bruise that marred the perfection of her skin was evident, and rage again stirred within him.

Gold Eagle struggled to reconcile his warring feelings. He reminded himself that this woman who now lay silent and warm against him was the same woman who had aimed a gun at his heart. He forced himself to recall that she had suffered the freezing cold without complaint rather than allow him an advantage over her, and that if she were in full control of her faculties now, she would despise herself for snuggling against him.

Mallory sighed, a sound of contentment that stirred his blood. She was beautiful—as white women were sometimes beautiful. She was brave—as white women seldom were. But she was a white woman, a stranger to the world of the Cheyenne, where she would always remain an outsider.

Mallory stirred. Her lips brushed his skin and Gold Eagle caught his breath. The conditions of their bargain chafed as the whiskey heated his blood. It would be so easy . . .

The flickering light of the flames danced against Mallory's fiery hair as Gold Eagle struggled against himself. He tightened his fingers in the bright strands. He indulged himself in her beauty. He remembered nights past when Mallory's parted lips had sought his, when her body had come alive at his touch, and she had gasped his name in ecstasy.

Gold Eagle frowned. She had not gasped *his* name. She had gasped the name of a man who did not exist. She was with him now only because her pride had caused her to act unwisely.

But a bargain had been struck, and he had given his word.

Staring down at Mallory for moments longer, Gold Eagle lowered his mouth to hers. The taste of her was familiar, and he drank of it deeply. His body swelled despite himself, and he pulled back abruptly. Mallory protested his withdrawal in her sleep, and Gold Eagle's stomach clenched as he repeated a familiar litany in his mind.

No, he did not want her.

No, he did not need her.

The litany rang over and over as he drew her back into his arms.

"Do you think he's all right?"

"Yeah, he's all right. The snow softened his fall."

Lieutenant Moore was sleeping. Corporal Bell looked at him more closely as the cold wind whistled. They had lit a fire and rigged up a shelter with some branches and one of the blankets. They had drawn the horses in close to block the wind and had eaten a meager meal. They would soon be joining the lieutenant under their shelter for the night.

The lieutenant had slept through it all.

Bell was worried.

"I ain't never seen a man sleep so sound."

"He don't have a fever, does he?"

"Hell, he's killin' himself gettin' back to that fort!"

Bell scrutinized the men's frosty faces. "If you was responsible for a lady like Miss Tompkins, if you knew she was waitin' for you to come back to the fort, trustin' somebody who ain't to be trusted, and if you had some special feelin' for her, wouldn't you drive yourself as hard as the lieutenant is?"

"Maybe." Whittier looked unsure.

Knoll shrugged.

"I ain't got no doubts that I would"—it was Hodge's turn to shrug—"but I don't expect I'll ever have nobody like Miss Tompkins waitin' for me."

Bell knew what his answer would be.

"He ain't ate nothin'."

Whittier's concern was real. Bell responded, "The lieutenant will eat tomorrow mornin'. The snow'll probably stop by then, and we'll be able to cook up somethin' warm."

"Like what?"

"Hell, what do you want me to do?" Bell's frozen blond brows rose in pale half moons. "Recite a menu?"

The snickers that followed were halfhearted, but they were the first signs of levity since afternoon.

The men wrapped themselves in their blankets and slipped under the shelter.

"You really think it'll stop snowin' tomorrow?"

Bell looked at Hodge, suddenly realizing that

the question was directed at him. He pulled his blanket closer and closed his eyes.

"Yeah, sure it will. Didn't you see the sky before it got dark? Them clouds is almost snowed out."

"It'd better stop snowin'."

"If it don't, this much damned snow won't melt until July."

"Yeah . . . July."

Bell opened his eyes for a last look at the lieutenant. He didn't even have a bump on his head from the fall. He was sleepin' like a baby. He'd be fine tomorrow.

He hoped.

Bell closed his eyes. Yeah, he sure did.

The door closed behind Penelope Dolan. Alone again in his office, Captain Tierney controlled the urge to laugh out loud. The half-breed bitch had returned to turn on Gold Eagle and save herself! She had told him that Gold Eagle had come to the fort seeking information about Cotter's arrival. She told him that he had gotten all the information he needed by listening at doors and keyholes, and that he had left satisfied that he would be able to prepare his people to defend themselves against Cotter's advance.

The half-breed had told him all she knew, he was sure. He had seen the fear in her eyes. He had allowed it to linger with true enjoyment before he dismissed her.

As for Gold Eagle, the man was a fool! There was no defense against a force the size of Cotter's, or against the artillery they carried with them. He hoped Gold Eagle *did* stir up those Cheyenne savages, so much that they would refuse to negotiate with Cotter when he came. That would clear the way for another Sand Creek . . . and he'd be the first man in line to see that the Army finished the job it had started then!

His ear began to throb anew, and Tierney winced against the pain. Good! Pain was a strong reminder that his debt would not be settled with Gold Eagle until that white savage knew he was responsible for the annihilation of his tribe. That would be a rare vengeance, indeed.

As for Mallory Tompkins, he had the feeling vengeance of another kind would be his once Gold Eagle was out of the way.

Scar him for life, would he?

Oh, yes, Gold Eagle would pay.

The quaking inside her had ceased. Mallory turned toward the source of heat that warmed her back, feeling strangely bereft. The circle of security that had alleviated the cold, that had pillowed her cheek, that had held her safe, was gone.

A delicious fragrance reached her nostrils, stirring her from her semi-sleep. She opened her eyes, momentarily disoriented. The room was dark and dank. The only source of light came from a fire burning in a fireplace nearby. She was alone in a strange cabin.

Alone.

A soft whinny turned her toward the door. Horses . . . inside the cabin.

Reality returned with a sudden jolt. Yes, she remembered. The snowman . . . Gold Eagle had carried her into the cabin.

Mallory's face flamed. He had *carried* her because she had been unable to walk.

Mallory scrutinized the cabin more closely. Where was he? The cabin was empty. Had he decided that she was too much trouble? Had he left her?

No. He couldn't go anywhere without the horses. She was confused.

A sound at the door turned her in that direction the moment before it was kicked open and Gold Eagle walked inside, his arms heavily loaded with logs. Pushing the door closed behind himself, he spared her no more than a glance before proceeding to the fire. He turned toward her when the logs were in place.

"Are you hungry?"

Mallory nodded, unwilling to trust her voice. Gold Eagle dipped a cup into the pot bubbling over the fire. He put it on the floor beside her. Every bone in her body ached when Mallory attempted to sit up, and she fell back again. She heard Gold Eagle mumble under his breath the moment before he drew her up to a seated position.

"I was off balance." Recognizing that her voice was as feeble as her excuse, Mallory persisted, "I could have sat up by myself."

Gold Eagle did not reply.

Somehow embarrassed by her own defensiveness, Mallory picked up the cup. She gulped down the gruel, then gasped as it scalded her throat.

Gold Eagle sipped from his own cup slowly, without comment.

She should have realized it would be hot. What was wrong with her?

Suddenly too tired for further effort, Mallory attempted to lie back, only to feel Gold Eagle's arm slip around her to hold her upright. He held the cup to her lips.

Mallory turned her head. "I . . . I'm not hungry."

Her stomach growled just at that moment, and Mallory frowned. "I'm *not* hungry," she insisted.

Gold Eagle's face was so close, she could see the rough spots on his cheeks where the icy snow had abraded his skin. His eyes were tired, his face drawn. His hands were red and raw from the elements as he raised the cup to her lips again.

"Drink slowly."

"I don't want—"

Gold Eagle tilted the cup and Mallory drank. She had never tasted anything so delicious. She drank until the cup was empty, but the effort wearied her. She did not realize her eyes had drooped closed until she felt herself lowered back to the blanket underneath her.

Mallory heard movement around her as she

drifted into an uneasy sleep. She opened her eyes to see Gold Eagle lying a short distance away. Her eyes drifting closed again, she twisted, then turned, mumbling her discomfort. She was about to despair when the blanket atop her was raised and a familiar, muscular length slipped underneath. Strong arms closed around her, drawing her close. A hard body molded to hers, cushioning her against her discomfort. A warm breath fanned her cheek and Mallory moved closer.

Warm, safe . . . where she wanted to be.

Chapter Nine

Mallory glanced at the bright yellow rays shining through the mottled window of the cabin. The previous day's frigid nightmare had been banished with the rising of the sun, but her exhaustion lingered. She had awakened a short time earlier to see a familiar pot bubbling over the fire, but to find that the cabin was again empty. She had experienced a momentary fear when she noted that the horses were no longer secured near the doorway. When the door opened and Gold Eagle stamped in from the cold, she was profoundly relieved.

Mallory stifled a groan as she drew herself to her feet. Ignoring her, Gold Eagle busied himself at the fire. It galled her that her muscles protested every movement she made, while

Gold Eagle moved easily around the fire with no apparent ill effects from their horrendous journey the previous day.

Mallory approached the fire with as much dignity as she could muster. She did not dare to consider her appearance. Her clothes were oversized and wrinkled, and she was personally disheveled. She knew the Mallory Tompkins who had originally come to the wild frontier would have died before allowing herself to be viewed in such a state, but just now she cared not a damn.

Mallory glanced at Gold Eagle. His demeanor was unchanged. He was silent, uncommunicative, and cold—the same man who had made a reluctant bargain with her the previous morning and the same man who had driven them both relentlessly through a blinding snowstorm without a word of encouragement or consolation.

Mallory filled her cup and raised it cautiously to her lips. She had been ill-prepared for the rigors of the journey she had undertaken. It had taken a greater toll on her than she had considered possible. She supposed that was the reason for the hallucinations she had experienced during the night—the sensation of Gold Eagle's lips against hers, of his callused palm stroking her back and his hard body warming hers as she slept in his arms.

Mallory stiffened as Gold Eagle looked briefly in her direction. One frigid glance, and she realized how foolish she had been to believe those hallucinations for a moment.

Mallory averted her face. She was relieved. She did not want to believe that she had really slipped eagerly into Gold Eagle's embrace, had luxuriated in his proximity and heat.

Gold Eagle stood up abruptly. He turned toward her and Mallory's thoughts halted abruptly. His hair was unbound. It hung in brilliant, uneven strands of gold against the massive stretch of his shoulders. His eyes were gray ice against his weather-roughened skin, and his strong features were composed. All trace of Matthew Bower had been erased so thoroughly that she could not presently understand how she had ever believed this man to be other than the Cheyenne warrior she knew him to be.

In a brief flash of insight, Mallory realized that the journey that had so debilitated her, had actually strengthened Gold Eagle. The wilderness that had so weakened her had actually augmented him, until he now stood powerful and overwhelming in the silence.

Mallory was suddenly angry. She resented his silent intimidation. Gold Eagle had permitted her to ride beside him, but figuratively, she had still been riding behind him because he had kept her ignorant of their course, their status, and his expectations of the journey—as if she were unable to comprehend whatever complexities were involved! In diminishing her position, he had elevated his own.

No, she would not allow that to happen

again—no matter how great the physical demands of the journey or how loudly her body complained!

Mallory emptied her cup and lowered it to the dusty table beside her. She saw the narrowing of Gold Eagle's eyes. She had no choice in what she must do.

"Captain Tierney, riders approaching!"

Tierney turned toward the sentry atop the wall. He had been up since dawn, walking the fort grounds. He knew the barracks were rife with gossip about what had transpired between Gold Eagle and him the previous day. He also knew that to remain out of sight would be to allow the gossip to slant against him. He intended to demonstrate that although he had been wounded, his ordeal at the hands of Gold Eagle had not daunted him.

Squinting as the glare of sunlight on the newly fallen snow briefly blinded him, Tierney shouted back, "How many?"

"Three, sir." The sentry looked back. "They're in uniform." He paused again. "It's Major Abbott!"

Abbott.

Fury flashed hot and deep within him. The bastard had returned early! He hadn't planned on relinquishing command of the fort for another week!

Tierney's mind raced. He couldn't abide Major Bernard Abbott. The man had disgraced his military training by proving to be an Indian-lover. Abbott made no secret of the fact that he despised the army's actions at Sand Creek and that he'd do his best to see that they were never repeated. Aware of Abbott's leanings, Tierney had hidden his own opinions when he was transferred into Abbott's command, knowing he stood little chance of advancement if he didn't. He had hoped Abbott would be delayed in his return to the fort, so that when Major General Cotter arrived, he might have an opportunity to speak to him confidentially about Abbott and arrange a transfer. Now it appeared he would not have that chance.

"He's here!"

Barely controlling his annoyance, Tierney shouted, "Open the gates!"

A welcoming smile fixed firmly on his face, Tierney watched as three uniformed men rode into the fort. His smile did not last long.

Dismounting, Abbott turned toward Tierney, his unshaven face dour. "I need to talk to you in my office, Captain."

Cautiously respectful, Tierney replied, "Is something wrong, sir?"

"Yes, something's wrong." Sweeping his saddlebags from the saddle as a soldier appeared to take his mount, Abbott motioned toward his traveling companions. "We've been on the trail since daybreak. Corporals Hale and Windsor will only stay the night. Tell Sergeant Riker to arrange for sleeping quarters for them, then come to my office." Abbott's expression darkened. "Be there in fifteen minutes, but get your

things together first. Tell Corporals Greer and
Bailey to do the same. I want the three of you
to start out as soon as possible for Fort Zarah."

"Fort Zarah?"

"Major General Cotter is presently marching
in that direction. I want you to be there to meet
him. I want you to take him my report and a
personal message from me. I'll define your orders more clearly in my office." Abbott paused,
appearing to notice the bandage on Tierney's
head for the first time. "What happened to your
ear?"

"It's a complicated story, sir."

"In my office—fifteen minutes."

"Yes, sir."

Hardly believing his luck, Tierney followed
Abbott's wiry form with his gaze as the man
strode briskly away. He was being *ordered* to
meet Cotter at Fort Zarah!

Silently jubilant, Tierney turned toward his
quarters.

She was angry.

Gold Eagle scrutinized the ire that had leaped
to life in Mallory's gaze. He had no need for anyone to tell him that her physical discomfort was
intense. The life to which she was accustomed
had not prepared her for the hardships she had
suffered during the previous day's journey. It
had taken all her strength to draw herself upright a few minutes earlier. Her body had protested every step she took. Her stomach had
proclaimed its emptiness loudly, yet with only

one cup of strengthening gruel, her fiery spirit had returned.

Gold Eagle prepared himself for Mallory's assault.

She spoke abruptly. "I see you've made preparations to leave." Mallory raised her chin as she proceeded. "I know what you're trying to do, you know."

Gold Eagle raised his brows.

"It's not going to work."

Gold Eagle did not respond.

"You're trying to wear me down. You're trying to show me that I'm out of my depth with this agreement that we've struck, but you're wrong." Mallory took a short breath that Gold Eagle recognized as an attempt to bring her escalating wrath under control. She continued, "With everything happening so quickly yesterday, I had no time to set the rules for our arrangement. I allowed you to lead while I followed docilely, without knowing in what direction we traveled or how long it would take to reach our destination. I don't intend to take another step today until that situation is changed."

Gold Eagle almost smiled at the sheer audacity of Mallory's statement. They were alone in a frigid wilderness with which Mallory was unfamiliar. Had he so chosen, he could have brought their agreement to a swift and final end the previous night when she was cold and helpless. Instead, although she obviously chose to forget it, she had slept in his arms, her body clinging to his warmth. In the light of the new day, she was still dependent on him for her life and sustenance—yet her tone was almost threatening.

Gold Eagle took an almost imperceptible step closer to Mallory, allowing her to feel a full appreciation of the physical inequity between them. She was tall for a woman, but her size was meager compared to his. She was strong for a female, but he could crush the slender white column of her neck with the grip of one hand. He moved nearer and Mallory retreated a step that brought her up against the table. Her hand slipped out of sight behind her.

When he looked down, Gold Eagle saw a familiar derringer pointed at his stomach. He looked up to see that Mallory's jaw was set.

"I want you to know that I'm not the fool you think me to be."

She was wrong. He did not consider her a fool.

"Nor am I merely a woman who can easily be manipulated by a man."

He had never thought she was.

"I want to know where we're going. I want to know how long it's going to take us to get there. And I want to know now, before we leave this cabin."

"That was not part of our bargain."

"Yes, it was."

"No."

"Tell me . . . *now*."

A warrior's heart.

Gold Eagle replied, "We go directly to my village to tell Two Bears of Cotter's approach. If we leave as soon as the horses are loaded, we will arrive at the village after midday." He paused, adding, "But today you ride behind me."

"No, I won't." Mallory's face flushed. "I'm not an Indian squaw and I won't act like one."

Gold Eagle snapped, "No, you are not an Indian squaw, nor do you have the sense of one. If you did, you would realize that your horse is small and tired, and that breaking a path through fresh snow wearies her unnecessarily and slows our progress—while my mount is larger and stronger and can clear the trail more easily."

"If your horse is stronger, I can ride him!"

"Would you also lead the way?"

Mallory stiffly conceded. "All right, but I intend to hold you to the full extent of our agreement from here on."

Mallory lowered her gun, her expression unyielding. "I hope there won't be any need to use threat again in order to make my point."

"A gun is little threat . . ."

"Isn't it?"

". . . when it is not loaded."

Turning abruptly toward the door, Gold Eagle ignored Mallory's startled expression. He heard her gasp when she discovered his claim to be true, and he pulled the door closed behind him.

"How are you feelin', Lieutenant?"

"I'm fine. Let's get going."

Charles's response to Bell's concerned inquiry was perfunctory. Of course, he wasn't fine, and his men knew it.

Charles walked unsteadily toward his mount. It was morning. The day had dawned bright and clear, but he knew the brilliant morning sunshine that glinted off the surrounding snowdrifts was not the cause of the unnatural heat that flushed his skin.

The few steps he took to his horse's side exhausted him, and Charles silently cursed. The damned fever would not quit!

Charles closed his eyes briefly as he was swept by another wave of weakness. His condition had been so poor the previous day that he remembered little of what had transpired on the trail, and an endless parade of frantic dreams had disturbed his rest during the night. His condition was worsening, but he knew he couldn't allow his men to see how quickly he was weakening. They would slow their pace to accommodate him, and he couldn't afford additional delay. His mind was foggy, but his conviction that Mallory was in true danger at Fort Larned was never clearer.

Inhaling deeply, Charles slid his foot into the stirrup and heaved himself up onto the saddle. The effort was almost his undoing.

Bell rode up beside him.

"You're sure you're all right, sir?"

Ignoring Bell's question, Charles fought to clear his gaze as he inquired instead, "What's your estimate of our traveling time to Fort Larned?"

"Three hours . . . maybe four."

"We'll do it in three hours."

"Only under the best of conditions, sir."

"Three hours, Corporal."

Charles spurred his horse into motion.

"It's a complicated affair, sir." Tierney's expression was a portrait in sincerity under Major Abbott's scrutiny. Seated across the desk from his superior officer in the solitude of the older man's office, Tierney continued earnestly, "Miss Tompkins was obviously taken in by the renegade, Gold Eagle, as we all were. His disguise was excellent. I can only assume the true Matthew Bower is dead at his hand, since he had all the man's belongings."

"You're telling me that Gold Eagle came here disguised as a man named Matthew Bower?" Major Abbott shook his head. "That's strange. I've never met Gold Eagle, but I know his reputation. He's well respected among the Cheyenne."

"He's not so well thought of in other circles."

Abbott's expression tightened. "There are some circles where *no* Indian is well thought of, but I don't happen to agree with those who think that way. Why did he attack you?"

"I'm not certain. I think it's because I was suspicious of him from the first. There was something about him that didn't seem right. I taunted him at times, sir, trying to rattle him so he might lose his composure. I suppose I made him angrier than I realized."

Abbott shook his head. "I'm baffled. Why would he come here in disguise, and why would he attempt to kidnap Miss Tompkins?"

"Maybe he was looking for a way to gain some leverage. Miss Tompkins comes from an influential family. She'd make an important hostage."

"Taking a hostage at this particular time isn't to the Cheyenne's advantage. From what I understand, Gold Eagle is intelligent enough to understand that."

"Maybe he is . . . and maybe he isn't."

"What about this Lieutenant Moore? Why did he disobey Major Bullen's orders by leaving Miss Tompkins when he had been assigned to her protection?"

"I ordered him back to his command."

"You what?"

Feigning discomfort, Tierney began with an uncertain smile, "Well . . . to be honest, I noticed an uneasiness between Lieutenant Moore and Miss Tompkins. I think he was getting romantically involved, and Miss Tompkins was finding it difficult to discourage him."

"Are you telling me that Lieutenant Moore took advantage of his position with Miss Tompkins?"

"No, sir."

"Then what *are* you saying?"

"I'm saying that I was afraid he might." Tierney paused again. "I made a judgment call, sir. I hope I didn't overstep my bounds, but I felt it was necessary to cool Lieutenant Moore off before he did something that might damage the potential for a very bright career."

"All right. I'll accept that." Abbott looked him directly in the eye. "My next question is, do you think Miss Tompkins was coerced to leave with Gold Eagle?"

"No, there's no evidence of that. I think she went voluntarily, believing he would help her discover the whereabouts of the man she was looking for—a Joshua Barnes."

Abbott contemplated his response. "I suppose we have no recourse, then, but to inform Major Bullen of what happened here and to wait for his response. We'll do that . . . but first we must deal with a more pressing problem."

Pleased with the success of his deception, Tierney replied, "Yes, sir."

Abbott's demeanor grew more intense. "I want you to know that I consider this mission I'm sending you on to be of the utmost importance, Captain. Major General Cotter's advance may be the turning point in our relations with the Indians in this area of the country. Peace or war. That's what this is all going to come down to in the end."

Abbott paused briefly, continuing, "For the sake of clarification, I want you to know that I believe it's our duty to follow whatever course Cotter decides to take, but I also intend to make sure Cotter gets only *factual* information to guide his decisions . . . not wild rumors with no basis at all."

"Sir?"

"Damn it, rumors are running rampant in the surrounding area! I never heard such nonsense—five hundred Cheyenne lodges gathered with hostile intentions, ready to make war in the spring! Only a fool would believe that! Everyone with any sense at all knows that the Cheyenne have been through a long, hard winter encampment and that neither their people nor their horses are in any physical shape for an attack. Then there's the talk about white prisoners who were taken by the Cheyenne. Anyone who took the time to investigate would discover that it was the Kiowa who took those prisoners and that neither the Cheyenne nor the Arapaho had any part in it. Lastly, everyone knows that Two Bears wants peace—only a true man of peace would stand by his convictions after being present at Sand Creek—and it's up to us to recognize him for what he stands for!"

"What do you want me to do, sir?"

Major Abbott drew himself back as he struggled against obvious emotion. Slapping the flat of his hand against the sheaf of papers on the desk in front of him, he stated, "I want you to get to Cotter before he reaches here. I want you to personally put this report into Cotter's hands, and I want you to answer any questions he puts to you, earnestly and with great conviction." Abbott's expression became almost grim. "I've chosen you for this assignment for a special reason, Captain."

"Sir?"

"I'm aware of your family connections with Cotter. I know he'll receive you well, and I know he'll listen to what you have to say. I want you to do your best to convince Cotter. He's an excellent soldier, but he's woefully ignorant of the customs of the Indians. He could easily misunderstand their actions if he's led to believe they're hostile."

"Yes, sir."

Major Abbott leaned forward, tensely serious. "I want you to travel with Cotter, to oversee things during the march to Larned. I want you to make sure that Cotter clearly understands existing conditions, and I want you to make certain that he doesn't go off half-cocked and start a war before he gets here. I'll be ready for him when he arrives. Have I made your assignment clear, Captain?"

"Yes, sir."

"All right, then there's nothing left to say. Get going, and remember, I'm depending on you."

"I won't let you down, sir."

Mounting his horse minutes later, Tierney signaled his men into motion behind him as he rode out of the fort.

Looking back as the gates closed behind them, Tierney could no longer stifle his elation.

Yes, sir.

You can depend on me, sir.
Tierney laughed out loud.

She was riding *behind* him.

Staring at Gold Eagle's broad back, Mallory could not believe her own pure stupidity. Gold Eagle didn't have any choice but to allow her to take her guns with her when they left Fort Larned, but he wasn't a fool. He had taken his first opportunity to clip her claws—when she was asleep and helpless.

Embarrassment again burned. She had boldly threatened Gold Eagle with an empty gun. The revolver she had kept secreted in her case was now also empty. She supposed she should be thankful that Gold Eagle hadn't laughed aloud at her meaningless attempt at intimidation.

Staring at Gold Eagle's back with growing resentment, Mallory stubbornly refused to accept his explanation for her need to ride in such a humiliating position. Agreed—her horse was smaller and weaker than his. So why hadn't he arranged for her to be riding a *bigger* horse?

She knew why.

And she didn't like it.

She liked even less seeing herself as she would look through the eyes of the Indians in Two Bears' camp when she arrived. The prejudice against her as a white woman would be difficult enough to overcome, but she—

Gasping with fright as her mare whinnied sharply and lurched forward, Mallory fought to retain her seat. The animal struggled to right herself in the knee-deep snow, but the effort was to no avail. Tossed violently from the saddle, Mallory saw the surface of the hard-crusted snow rising to meet her the moment before a strong arm snatched her to safety.

Breathless, Mallory turned to see Gold Eagle's face only inches from hers. He was panting, his chest heaving underneath the heavy coat he wore. He searched her face with an expression that looked like fear, and Mallory was struck with an absurd need to comfort him, to tell him she was all right.

Mallory realized she'd misjudged his reaction when Gold Eagle lifted her onto the saddle in front of him with little delicacy and then snapped, "Remain here!"

Mallory did not respond as Gold Eagle dismounted and approached her limping mount. She winced at the animal's whinny of pain when Gold Eagle examined its leg.

"What happened to my horse?"

"Her leg is injured. She cannot be ridden."

She cannot be ridden. . . .

Gold Eagle attached her mount's reins to the rear of his saddle and Mallory frowned. Keeping her seat, she inquired, "Are you going to walk?"

Gold Eagle's icy gaze froze her.

Mounting behind her, Gold Eagle adjusted her position in front of him on the saddle, shifting her as easily as if she were a child until he had arranged her back against him to his comfort. As discomfited by his presumption as she was by his touch, Mallory snapped, "I was fine the way I was!"

Ignoring her as if she hadn't spoken, Gold Eagle slid his arm around her waist and held her in place with the flat of his hand. Annoyed when he drew her back even tighter against him, until her buttocks rested firmly against his groin, Mallory withheld comment with pure strength of will.

Gold Eagle's male heat pressed warmly against her as he heeled his mount into motion, and Mallory struggled to deny the awareness that crawled up her spine. His strong frame supported her easily, shielding her against the bite of a breeze that chilled despite the sun. Mallory struggled against the memory of intimate nights when Gold Eagle's body had supported her just as effortlessly, when his strength became loving gentleness, and his hunger became her need.

Suddenly furious at the direction of her thoughts, Mallory forced her mind back to the present. She stiffened her posture, reminding herself that she had been fooled badly by this man once before, that she had promised she would not allow herself to be manipulated again, and that she was as strong as he was.

The horse missed a step, jolting her body unexpectedly, and Mallory barely restrained a groan as her sore muscles protested. Gold Eagle's arm tightened around her waist in a motion that was too fluid to be touched with stiffness or discomfort.

Damn the man!

Mallory glanced back at the mare limping pitifully behind the strong stallion, which supported both Gold Eagle and her.

Pitiful . . . yes, *they were.*

"Do you think he'll make it?"

Charles heard the question echo through the shadows that clouded his mind. He turned toward the voice. His vision was blurred; he struggled to identify the soldier who spoke encouragingly to him.

"It's only a little farther, Lieutenant."

Fort Larned . . . yes.

He heard a horse ride up beside him. He did not protest when his mount's reins were taken from his hand, choosing instead to grip the saddle horn to maintain his balance. He was uncertain how long he rode that way before he heard excited mumblings behind him.

His mount moved faster, and Charles gripped the saddle horn tighter.

"Open the gates!"

The shout startled Charles from his lethargy.

"Hurry up! The lieutenant's sick!"

He was moving forward again, and he was glad. He couldn't hold on much longer.

"Watch out! He's going to fall!"

Who was going to fall?

Oh . . . he was.

*   *   *

Gold Eagle sat his horse with ease as the animal moved steadily along the snow-covered trail. Morning had long since faded, and afternoon was on the wane. They had stopped once after Mallory's mount became injured, but they had spoken little.

Gold Eagle surveyed the familiar landscape. They would reach his village soon. He would speak with Two Bears, and then his work would begin.

Mallory shifted on the saddle in front of him, interrupting his thoughts, and Gold Eagle's lips tightened as her firm buttocks moved against his already tormented flesh. She struggled to maintain her rigid posture.

Gold Eagle was bitterly amused at the effort. Mallory did not choose to remember the long afternoon hours when she had dozed with her head lolling against his shoulder and her body curved comfortably back against him. She had instinctively turned her face into his neck to shield herself from the crisp breeze, and he recalled with a pleasure just short of pain the moment when her lips brushed his skin. The touch had scorched him. He recalled with annoying clarity the heat that instantly transfused him. It irritated him even more to admit that he had taken comfort in the realization that the unspoken battle between them was temporarily dismissed.

But she had awakened. He knew the exact moment when she became aware of her relaxed

273

posture. Her back stiffened, and the silent battle was resumed.

Gold Eagle frowned, suddenly grateful that their journey would soon be at an end. He had made too many mistakes with this woman. In taking her body, he had somehow allowed her to gain a foothold in his mind—a foothold that even now threatened him. His village would soon appear in the distance and his thoughts should be devoted to his confrontation with Two Bears. Instead, they were centered on the woman who rode reluctantly in his arms.

Gold Eagle squinted into the distance. He stiffened as familiar lodges appeared on the horizon.

Mallory reacted to the subtle change in his posture by turning toward him. "What is it? What do you see?"

Her lips were only inches from his. They twitched with mounting agitation as she rasped, "Tell me!"

He did not feel compelled to respond.

"If I had my gun—"

"—you would threaten me. And if your gun was loaded"—Gold Eagle took perverse pleasure in her obvious discomfort at his reminder—"you might even shoot me, which would then bring my whole village down upon you."

Mallory's temper flushed hot. "Do you think I care!"

"No, I do not think you do." Gold Eagle held her gaze. "For that reason, I give you fair warning. When you walk on Cheyenne land, you would be wise to walk in our footsteps, and not expect that we will walk in yours."

"I know what I'm doing!"

"Do you?"

Mallory's face flamed. "While we're clarifying things, let me remind you that you agreed to help me get the information I need for my articles."

"No, I did not."

"You agreed to help me send my reports back to my newspaper in Chicago when they were ready!"

Unyielding, Gold Eagle corrected, "I agreed to help you bring the truth back to your people."

"You're splitting hairs!"

"I think not."

"I'm a newspaperwoman! I only write the truth—supported by facts. That's why I'm here."

"You write *your* truth."

"What are you saying? Are you trying to back out of our bargain?"

His attention diverted by the appearance of a rider on the horizon, Gold Eagle was suddenly alert. He did not deceive himself that Mallory would be well received by all in the village. That thought was reinforced when he recognized the rider's mount—a brightly marked animal whose rider bore his name.

Spotted Horse was the most aggressive of his opponents, a man whose hatred of the white blood that ran in his veins would forever hold them apart as brothers. Gold Eagle recognized the danger Spotted Horse posed to him and to the peace Two Bears sought. He knew Spotted Horse could be even more dangerous to a white woman whose heart was that of a warrior, and whose tongue was not easily tamed.

His gaze intent on the approaching rider, Gold Eagle did not observe the uncertainty that marked Mallory's expression the moment before she turned to follow his gaze. He felt the jolt that shook her when she saw the rider approaching, and he sensed the moment she pushed her fear aside.

Recognizing the peril there, Gold Eagle whispered into Mallory's ear.

"Take care."

Gold Eagle's whisper echoed in Mallory's mind. She glanced up at him, noting that his gaze was intent on the Indian riding toward them. She saw an armed caution in his demeanor, the same quality she had sensed in him when they left the fort.

A fellow Cheyenne—his enemy?

Gold Eagle continued his steady forward pace despite the rapid approach of the other rider. She felt his body tense as the Indian neared. His supportive arm tightened around her . . . as his other hand moved cautiously toward the knife at his waist.

Take care.

Mallory remained silent as the Cheyenne's laboring horse was reined to a halt a few feet from them. The man appeared to be of medium height and stature, and of Gold Eagle's age. He addressed Gold Eagle in the Cheyenne language, and Mallory was disconcerted at the realization that she would not be able to understand a word of their conversation. What could not be misconstrued, however, was the distaste with which the other Cheyenne appraised Gold Eagle's appearance. When he spoke, his words were uttered with a hatred that overcame the language barrier. She wished she knew what he was saying . . .

"So, you return!" Spotted Horse addressed Gold Eagle, openly taunting. "You have changed your Cheyenne dress for white man's clothes. Does your blood still flow through your body as a Cheyenne, or has that changed as well?"

Gold Eagle responded in the Cheyenne tongue, "My heart is Cheyenne, and in all I do, that remains true."

"Yet you return wearing white man's clothing!"

"These are the clothes of the white man who died in Walking Buffalo's lodge. His name and his clothing have served my purpose well."

"The dead man's clothing." Spotted Horse scoffed. "I know of that man. He drew pictures in place of the words he could not speak."

"He was a healer who sought to learn from our people."

"He was a white man, and he was not welcome on Cheyenne land!"

"He was a good man who sought only the

good in others. Walking Buffalo read the goodness within him."

"Walking Buffalo pays homage to those with white blood. He is a fool to think they will ever be friends of our people."

Unwilling to continue the conversation, Gold Eagle attempted to ride around him, only to have Spotted Horse spur his mount into his path, demanding "Why do you bring this white woman here?"

"Get out of my way," Gold Eagle grated.

"White women bring trouble to the Cheyenne. She is not wanted here."

"Move out of my way."

"A hostage will bring the soldiers down upon us before we are ready to defend ourselves."

"This woman is not a hostage. She comes here willingly."

His hand tight on the knife at his waist, Gold Eagle watched as Spotted Horse urged his mount closer. His gaze surveyed Mallory with bold intimacy as he laughed. "White women serve only one purpose here, and this one will serve me well."

Spotted Horse reached out to grasp a lock of Mallory's hair, and Gold Eagle's response was spontaneous. Slicing at the offending hand, he drew blood, rasping, "My knife tastes your hand this time in fair warning. The next time, it will taste your heart!"

Allowing a moment for his words to register clearly, Gold Eagle spurred his mount into motion, leaving Spotted Horse behind him. He remained rigidly alert, his posture relaxing only when Spotted Horse turned his horse into a circular course back to camp, avoiding his trail. Relieved that more drastic measures had not been necessary, he looked down at Mallory.

"Was that necessary?" she demanded. Not waiting for his reply, she hissed, "That man was merely curious about the color of my hair!"

"No, it was not necessary"—Gold Eagle's tone was cold—"if you wanted to lie beneath him this night."

Gold Eagle felt the jolt that shook her. "He wouldn't!"

"You are safe now."

Mallory spat, "You object when your people are called savages, yet you tell me that man has so little regard for civilized behavior that he would—he would *force* himself on a white woman just on a whim?"

"As our women have often suffered at the hands of your men."

"No, I don't believe that! Such behavior would be contemptible!"

Gold Eagle snapped, "Believe what you like!"

Her breast heaving, Mallory pressed, "I want you to tell me the truth! You agreed there would be no more deception between us. We made a bargain."

"I have already told you the truth."

Mallory searched his gaze. The pain that grew in her eyes was reflected in her voice when she said, "It can't be true."

Momentarily silent, Gold Eagle replied, "Savagery shows its face in all people. You asked me to speak the truth. Now I ask you to do the same. Do you doubt that Captain Tierney would act any differently than Spotted Horse if the situation were reversed?"

Mallory blinked. Her face paled.

Sensing more in her lack of reply than she chose to reveal, he pressed "Do you?"

"I don't want to talk about it."

The extended silence spoke a truth Gold Eagle had not expected. He fought to curb a sudden rage. He had severed Captain Tierney's ear, but a greater justice would have been served if he had taken a more intimate part for that man's offense.

Staring rigidly forward, Mallory shuddered unexpectedly. Gold Eagle followed the direction of her gaze to see a crowd gathering as they neared the village. He was about to speak a word of comfort when he noted the almost imperceptible rise of her chin, and he knew words were not necessary.

Scrutinizing the faces of those assembled, Gold Eagle went still as a familiar gaze met his.

The gates of Fort Zarah loomed in the distance, and Captain Tierney kicked his mount to a faster pace. He turned back to the men riding at his rear as he found himself outdistancing them.

"Keep up with me, you fools!"

The gates swung closed behind him as twilight darkened to night, and Tierney turned triumphantly to the guard. "I have an important dispatch for Major General Cotter. I was advised that he's on his way here. Do you have any information about his expected time of arrival?"

"A courier arrived an hour ago saying he'd be here by midday tomorrow, Captain."

"That's good . . . that's good." That would give him enough time to clean up and make a good impression. Then he'd handle that old fool, just the way he always did.

A sudden twinge raised his hand to the bandage on his ear, and Tierney's satisfaction faded. He snapped at the waiting guard, "I need to see the commandant now. Notify the fort doctor that I'll see him immediately afterward." He frowned. "You do have a doctor here, don't you?"

"Yes, sir."

Tierney sneered. Half an ear or not, he was ten times the man Gold Eagle was. He'd prove it to the bastard. He'd make him admit it—say the words aloud—and then he'd kill him.

"This way, sir."

"Where is she? I don't see her."

Twilight elongated the shadows of the room as Charles spoke in a voice slurred by his rising fever. "I need to tell her . . . warn her . . ."

"What's he trying to say, Corporal?"

Addressing the young soldier who stood near the doorway, Major Abbott frowned. "Your name's Bell, isn't it?"

"Yes, sir."

"Lieutenant Moore put you in charge of his detachment during his illness?"

"Yes, sir."

"Answer my question, then. I'm waiting for your report."

Uncomfortable under the major's scrutiny, Bell was momentarily flustered. The lieutenant was sick . . . real sick. They had traveled to Fort Larned as quickly as was humanly possible under difficult circumstances, and the truth was that he had half expected the lieutenant wouldn't make it alive. Another day was coming to an end, and another truth was that he still wasn't sure the lieutenant would make it. And it looked like the major didn't give a damn.

Major Abbott's scrutiny did not abate.

"Lieutenant Moore's worried about Miss Tompkins, sir. He was charged with escorting her here to find somebody she was lookin' for. He didn't want to leave, but Captain Tierney ordered us back to Major Bullen's command."

"I know all about that." Major Abbott's expression darkened. "Before he left, Captain Tierney explained that he was forced to order Lieutenant Moore back to his command because of extenuating circumstances."

Bell was confused. "He did? He's gone?"

"Continue, Corporal."

Bell frowned. "Like I said, the lieutenant was

worried about Miss Tompkins. He didn't trust that Matthew Bower fella. He said somethin' was wrong there. We stopped to wire Major Bullen about his orders bein' changed at the first town we came to, and that's when he found out that Matthew Bower was an imposter. The lieutenant figured the fella was up to somethin'. Major Bullen wired back, reinstatin' the lieutenant's orders just when we was ready to come back to warn the fort. The lieutenant was sick, and now he's sicker, but all he was worried about was gettin' here in time to prevent any trouble."

"Unfortunately, you're too late."

"Sir?"

"We know about Matthew Bower. Actually, he was a Cheyenne named Gold Eagle. He attacked Captain Tierney, then left the fort with Miss Tompkins."

"Mallory . . . Mallory's gone?"

Major Abbott's head snapped toward Lieutenant Moore's weak interjection. Approaching the bed, he inquired, "How do you feel, Lieutenant?"

"Mallory's gone?"

Major Abbott frowned at the young officer's obvious confusion. "Yes, she's gone. Apparently she left of her own accord, believing Matthew Bower would help her find the man she was looking for."

"He's not Matt Bower."

"Yes, we know."

The lieutenant struggled to rise. "I have to go after her."

"No, Lieutenant." Major Abbott's frown darkened. "Relax. You're sick. We'll take care of things."

"Major Bullen said—"

"I said we'll take care of things on this end."

"He said . . . he said . . ."

The lieutenant faded into unconsciousness, and Major Abbott turned to the woman who stood silently beside his bed.

"Can you do anything for him, Penelope?"

"I have some medicine that made my son well when he was sick."

"Give it to him, then. If you have something that'll keep him quiet, give him that, too."

"Miss Tompkins was his good friend."

"Captain Tierney told me all about it."

"Miss Tompkins did not like Captain Tierney."

Major Abbott stiffened. "We all appreciate that you volunteered to care for the lieutenant, Penelope, but I wouldn't offer my opinion so lightly if I were you."

"I do not speak lightly. Miss Tompkins did not like Captain Tierney. Lieutenant Moore was her good friend."

"She's right, Major."

Corporal Bell's interjection turned Major Abbott toward him. "When I want your opinion, I'll ask for it, Corporal."

"Yes, sir."

Major Abbott turned back to Penelope. "Do

the best you can for the lieutenant. Let me know if there's any change."

"Yes, Major."

Approaching Penelope as the major strode out of the room, Bell whispered, "Seems to me that Captain Tierney did a lot of talkin' before he left. The lieutenant's goin' to have his job cut out for him when he tries to straighten Major Abbott out." Bell paused. "He's goin' to make it, don't you think, Miz Dolan?"

"The medicine is good."

"When that Captain Tierney gets back, the lieutenant's sure goin' to give him an earful, that's for sure."

"Yes . . . an earful."

Surprisingly, Penelope smiled.

Waiting outside the door, Corporal Walker snapped to attention as Major Abbott emerged from Lieutenant Moore's room. The major eyed him dubiously, then questioned, "What're you doing here, Corporal?"

Corporal Walker was at a momentary loss. He was confused. Matthew Bower, who was really Gold Eagle, had left the fort with Miss Tompkins, but nobody was sure whether she'd left willingly, knowing who he really was, or if she'd left willingly, thinking he was Matthew Bower. In fact, nobody was really sure she'd left willingly. He was as uncertain as everyone else about what had really happened, but he knew one thing for sure. Whether he was Matthew Bower or Gold Eagle, the man who had looked him in the eye and extended his hand in friendship before leaving the fort was a man he could count on. He also knew for certain that Captain Tierney was a bastard who couldn't be trusted—yet, somehow, everything had gotten all turned around.

He didn't understand it.

And he wasn't sure what he should do.

Aware that Major Abbott was still waiting, Walker replied, "I was . . . I was just waitin' to see how the lieutenant was."

Major Abbott's scrutiny deepened. "Know him well, do you?"

"No, sir. I only met him when he came to the fort with Miss Tompkins."

"But you're concerned about him."

"Yes, sir."

"I understand you were friendly with the man who represented himself as Matthew Bower."

"Yes, sir."

"And Miss Tompkins."

"It was Mr. Bower who was friendly with Miss Tompkins, not me, sir."

"Oh . . . friendly enough to leave the fort voluntarily with Mr. Bower?"

"I was there when they left, and in my opinion, she left voluntarily."

"Do you think she was aware of Gold Eagle's true identity?"

"I don't know, sir."

Major Abbott paused. "Do you have anything else to add that might be of help in clarifying the situation?"

The letter in his pocket weighed heavily, but Walker made a quick decision. "No, sir. I don't know nothin' at all."

Major Abbott stared at him a silent moment longer. "There isn't much point in your going in to see the lieutenant. He's delirious. He doesn't really know what's going on. Penelope is doing the best she can for him."

"Oh."

"You can try again tomorrow. There should be some kind of change in his condition by then."

"Thank you, sir."

Releasing a relieved breath as the major turned out of sight, Walker reached into his pocket to touch the letter.

No, he didn't understand any of it. But the letter was addressed to Lieutenant Moore. Miss Tompkins had asked him to put it right into the lieutenant's hand.

Right.

Walker settled back to wait.

Mallory held herself erect in the curve of Gold Eagle's arm. She squinted to discern the expressions of those who had gathered to watch their approach to the Cheyenne camp. The fading light of day shadowed their faces, but one thing was abundantly clear. They did not look at her with welcome.

Mallory forced her fear aside. Gold Eagle had said she was safe. He had agreed there would be no deceit between them, and she trusted him

287

to keep his bargain. She would be a fool to think anything else. He had had plenty of opportunity to harm her if that was his intention.

Yet, uncertainty nagged. She was a stranger in this Cheyenne camp. She had seen hatred in the eyes of the man who had ridden out to meet them. Were there others like him? Would Gold Eagle be able to protect her from them all if there were?

They neared the village and the faces became clearer. An old man stood apart from the others. His hair was gray, his face creased with age. A feather hung limply in his tangled locks and his body appeared lean under the blanket wrapped securely around him. Several women stood nearby, but there was only one who caught Mallory's attention. She was young, her own age. The blanket she wore wrapped around her did not fully conceal the womanly curves underneath, or the pride in her carriage. The woman's features were well drawn, and her hair and eyes were as black as the night. The woman swept her with a gaze that needed no interpretation, and her expression spoke for itself when she then looked at Gold Eagle.

She was Gold Eagle's woman.

Mallory fought to subdue the sudden tightening in her throat. She should have expected something like this, but somehow she had not. She marveled that she could have been such a fool.

The old man stepped forward, and Mallory felt Gold Eagle turn subtly toward him. She looked up at him to see respect in his gaze as the man addressed him in halting English that she suddenly realized was calculated to keep the others ignorant of their exchange.

The old man's voice was level, devoid of expression, as he said, "I saw your return, Gold Eagle. Your image danced in the flames, as did the image of this woman with hair the color of fire. I saw anger, and I saw the drawing of blood."

Mallory turned toward Gold Eagle when he did not respond. She realized belatedly that his silence signaled confirmation. The old man continued, "There is danger to come. I saw it clearly before the smoke clouded my mind and my vision."

The old man turned to study Mallory for a long moment.

Take care.

Gold Eagle's words rang in Mallory's mind as the old man's perusal intensified. Its heat singed her.

"This woman's spirit blazes hotly. Her mind is keen and her tongue is sharp. She has much to learn. She does not see the world through the eyes of most people. Want has made no demands on her. No man has truly challenged her will. With her comes a test of the destiny that awaits you. Caution."

Startled by the old man's words, Mallory looked up at Gold Eagle. His frown spoke his thoughts clearly, and an unspoken protest rose to Mallory's tongue.

Turning back to the old man, Mallory was surprised to see that he had already started back toward a nearby lodge.

Mallory looked again at Gold Eagle, chafing at the silence imposed upon her. Surely Gold Eagle saw the injustice of the old man's pronouncements!

Gold Eagle nudged his mount into motion.

The flickering flames of evening danced against the walls of Two Bears' lodge, emphasizing the lines of disapproval that drew the man's strong features into downward lines as he returned Gold Eagle's direct gaze. The uneasy silence continued for long moments before Two Bears spoke again.

"I have talked to the great generals of the white man. I have told them that our people do not want war. They will not march against us."

Frustration knotted Gold Eagle's brow as he studied Two Bears' determined expression. The fire had burned low during the time he had spent talking to the aging warrior chief who was determined to fight no more. Aware that the bond of his given word held the great chief immobile despite the advancing threat, Gold Eagle proceeded cautiously.

"The general who now advances rides this land for the first time. The ways of our people are unknown to him, and our faces blend into one. He seeks to punish all for the crimes of a few who turn their back on peace. He is a warrior who speaks but who will not listen, and who sees justice only in shedding blood for blood that has been shed."

Two Bears' gaze searched Gold Eagle's face with an almost palpable touch. Gold Eagle saw the chief's hesitation. He saw the moment Two Bears made an abrupt decision.

"Tomorrow you will speak to the warriors who follow Many Horses and Wolf in Waiting. With them you will watch for the advance of this great force so we may be warned if it approaches. I pray the great general's eyes will be opened to the truth so we need not seek a hiding place until the sun warms the land and we are at full strength again." Two Bears paused, continuing, "Your Cheyenne heart beats brave and true. The fate of your people is in your hands."

With that thought resounding in his mind, Gold Eagle breathed deeply of the cold evening air as he turned in the direction of his lodge. Hardly aware of the full moon that glinted on the surface of the snow, he reviewed Two Bears' charges in his mind. Many Horses and Wolf in Waiting were friends who would not doubt his word. They would watch and wait, as would the warriors who followed them. Cotter would not be able to advance upon them without warning.

Satisfied with the task he had accomplished that night, Gold Eagle slowed his steps as he neared his lodge. The fire he had lit before leaving burned low. There was no sign of movement within. Remembering Walking Buffalo's warning, he had left Mallory there without any explanation. He had told himself that he had provided her shelter from the cold and food to satisfy her hunger—that her needs had been met.

Her needs . . .

But it had not been Mallory's needs that had been foremost in his mind when he had taken Mallory into his arms the previous night. Her sigh when his arms closed around her had echoed his own, and the warmth of their intimate posture on horseback had kindled a heat within him that the advancing night cold could not cool.

Hair as bright as firelight . . . smooth skin . . . parted lips . . . a female warmth that took him in and held him tightly as he worshipped her sweet flesh . . . He had denied its sweet lure and he—

His thoughts halting at the sound of a step, Gold Eagle turned in a flash of movement to grasp the shadowy figure behind him. His blade ready, he heard a familiar voice whisper, "If you would take my life, Gold Eagle, I give it willingly."

Gray Dawn.

Turning toward him, Gray Dawn pressed herself full against him. A shaft of silver moonlight lit the planes of her face as she slid her arms around his neck. Her musky scent filled his senses as she offered him her lips.

Gold Eagle felt the heavy pounding of her heart as Gray Dawn's mouth touched his. The taste of her was familiar. He remembered that her body had always welcomed his, and that her lips had given him comfort in many ways.

Gray Dawn moved intimately against him. She slid her hand down to stroke him warmly as she whispered, "I have missed you. I have awaited your return. My lodge is warm and my blankets are ready. You are weary, but I will give you ease."

Gray Dawn's touch grew bolder. Her voice dropped to a throbbing caress, and her tongue licked at her lips in a way that signaled her desire.

Studying her impassioned expression as if from a distance, Gold Eagle recalled the times when Gray Dawn had taken him to her sleeping bench, when she had labored long into the night to pleasure him, speaking her love for him freely while receiving no response in kind. He remembered that he had reacted with a bodily heat that had matched her own, but that his heart had remained untouched. With growing sadness, Gold Eagle realized that despite that physical bonding, only affection remained.

Gray Dawn's dark eyes glowed up into his. The beauty of their people was reflected there, and Gold Eagle's regrets were many as he closed his hand over hers to halt her intimate touch. Pain flashed in Gray Dawn's eyes as she whispered, "Do Cheyenne women no longer please you, Gold Eagle? Do you now desire only women with white skin that matches your own?"

Still holding her hand, Gold Eagle drew it to his lips before dropping it to her side. Gray

Dawn gasped at his unspoken response. Unwilling to accept it, she drew both his arms around her, beseeching, "Come with me now, Gold Eagle. My lodge is warm and waiting. The white woman will not please you as I would please you. Like all white women, she holds her own pleasures above all. She seeks to take rather than to give. Come with me now and I will love you as a Cheyenne woman loves."

Realizing he could no longer withhold the truth, he whispered sadly, "Our time together brought me great comfort, Gray Dawn. It will live in my mind. My heart is filled with gratitude for the succor you have given . . . but our time together is past."

"No, it is not!" Panic touched Gray Dawn's expression. "The white woman is not for you!"

"She is not my woman." Facing a truth he could not allow himself to ignore, he continued, "She comes to our land with a purpose, and once it is done, she will return to her people with no thought of those she has left behind."

"But you want her."

Gold Eagle made no reply.

Her voice growing hoarse, Gray Dawn whispered, "I will make you want me again." She reached up to draw his mouth down to hers, continuing, "I will make you long for my flesh, and I will please you in all ways. Come with me now, Gold Eagle." Pressing his hands to her breasts, she whispered . . .

* * *

"I don't like this, damn it!"

Mallory's ardent statement echoed in the solitude of the Indian lodge where she sat, a blanket clutched tightly around her, as the blaze in the fire pit flickered low.

Jerking her blanket closer, Mallory gritted her teeth with mounting frustration. Where was he? What was he doing? What had she gotten herself into? Somehow, back at Fort Larned with the heat of Gold Eagle's deception scorching her, she had not considered that the bargain she had forced upon him might backfire, that she might ultimately find herself abandoned in a cold Indian lodge in the middle of a frozen wilderness, surrounded by a hostile people who had alternately denounced her, spoken of using her for sexual pleasure, and then treated her as a pariah while she dutifully followed Gold Eagle to the lodge where she now sat—alone.

Frustration burned. He had left her without explanation. Did he intend to come back? What was taking him so long?

She was cold, damn it!

Mallory looked around the small lodge. The fire was dying and there was no fuel in sight. If she weren't afraid that she might be mistaken for an intruder—or that the abominable Spotted Horse might sneak up behind her, or that she might just fall into a hole somewhere and freeze to death before anyone found her—she might venture outside to find some firewood in the dark. It was humiliating to sit shivering helplessly until Gold Eagle returned.

If he returned.

Mallory considered that thought. A tremor shook her. For all she knew, he could be bartering with Spotted Horse for her services right now. He might even be—

Faced with a suddenly painful moment of truth, Mallory was suffused with shame. Courage was so simple when there was no threat. Noble claims were so easy when there was no challenge. Pursuing a dream was so elementary when the path had been carefully cleared. It was time to see what she was made of.

Mallory straightened her spine. She needed fuel for the fire, and she was going to get it.

Standing up abruptly, Mallory tugged her blanket more tightly around herself. She turned toward the doorway, pausing when she heard Gold Eagle's voice in low conversation. The sudden surge of warmth she felt was more revealing than she chose to acknowledge.

Not pausing in her stride, she pushed aside the flap and walked outside—her step freezing and her heart going still at the sight of Gold Eagle and a woman in tight embrace.

No!

Her heart and mind wildly protesting, Mallory closed her eyes.

She opened her eyes as they drew apart.

Struggling to conceal her pain, Mallory watched as the woman leaned against Gold Eagle with casual intimacy, her hand on his chest. Mallory wanted to scream her anger! She wanted to strike the woman, to push her out of

Gold Eagle's arms. She wanted to claim that place as her own.

But she would not.

Instead, her jaw stiff as she held her fury under tenuous control, Mallory turned to walk past them.

"Where are you going?" Gold Eagle's question reverberated on the chilled night air.

Mallory responded flatly, "I'm going to find some firewood."

His strong features sharpened by the gilding light of the moon, Gold Eagle ordered, "Go back inside."

Her emotions barely controlled, Mallory snapped, "No."

"Go . . . inside."

The woman's eyes narrowed at the exchange. She pressed closer to Gold Eagle, and Mallory's composure snapped. "I'm going to get some firewood, whether you like it or not!"

Beside her in a moment, Gold Eagle snatched her up into his arms. Pushing the flap aside with his shoulder, he deposited her inside the lodge, his stance rigid with anger as he ordered, "Stay here!"

He was giving her orders as if she were . . . as if she were . . .

Mallory faced him squarely. Her reply was succinct.

"No."

Stunned by Gold Eagle's unexpected reaction, Mallory gasped as he thrust her hands behind her and secured her wrists with a leather thong that had hung from a nearby pole. Moving too quickly to allow her time for effective resistance, he again swept her from her feet and placed her on the sleeping bench nearby. Mallory struggled wildly to no avail as he secured her ankles as well.

She glared up at Gold Eagle as he towered over her, his jaw as hard as stone. She watched, trembling with rage, as he left the lodge as quickly as he had entered.

The indignity of her position was almost more than Mallory could bear. Struggling against her bonds, she twisted and turned in contortions that landed her on the floor of the lodge with a thud. Unwilling to allow Gold Eagle total victory, she strained against the bonds on her wrists, but without success. Furious, she scanned the lodge, her gaze halting on a smoldering stick that lay at the edge of the fire. She edged her way toward it, grasping it at last. She awkwardly attempted to apply it to the thong binding her wrists.

Cursing as the smoldering stick burned her skin, Mallory ignored the sting and tried again. She gasped aloud when she was burned more painfully a second time.

Determined, Mallory gritted her teeth and tried again.

His lips tight, Gold Eagle drew Gray Dawn along beside him as he strode across the snow-covered ground. He halted in front of her lodge, his anger dimming at her obvious distress.

"I am sorry, Gray Dawn." Suddenly realizing he had never meant those words more, he raised a callused hand briefly to her shoulder. "I must go."

"That woman is not for you." Gray Dawn's eyes grew moist. "She causes you anger. She will not be a good wife."

"I know."

"She will make you unhappy."

Gold Eagle could not refute her statement.

"You will see the truth in my words." Gray Dawn raised her chin. "And you will remember the nights when our bodies were joined and our hearts sang with joy. I would give that joy to you each night, Gold Eagle, until our bodies wither with age and only memories remain. You will come back to me."

Gray Dawn fled into her lodge. Lingering only a moment longer, Gold Eagle turned back in the direction from which he had come.

Mallory heard the lodge flap open a moment too late. The smoking stick was pulled from her hand, and she rolled to her back to see Gold Eagle looking down at her with a silent fury matching her own.

Refusing to be intimidated, she demanded, "Untie me!"

Gold Eagle made no move to comply.

"Untie me, you bastard!" Mallory fought an escalating rage. "Is this what you brought me here for? To humiliate me?"

"You cause your own humiliation."

"Untie me!"

"And if I do not, would you burn the skin from your wrists?"

"If I have to!"

Gold Eagle's chest was heaving with obvious wrath as Mallory spat, "To think that I stood up for you when you first came to Fort Larned! I thought I saw something in you—something special! I must have been crazy!"

"You chose to be deceived."

"I chose—"

"Just as you now choose anger over common sense."

"Common sense—"

"It was unsafe for you in the darkness."

"It was safe for you and that woman!"

"Gray Dawn is familiar with the dangers of this camp."

"You're the only danger here!"

"You speak foolishly!"

"Do I? Is that why I lie here, tied up like—like an animal?"

Gold Eagle crouched over her. The flickering shadows of the fire lent a menacing quality to his shadowed features as he gripped her chin with his palm, holding her gaze fast. "You lie here tied because your strong will would not allow you to submit to my authority—even though you knew I spoke for your benefit."

"You ordered me back into the lodge. I don't care what you meant or what you said. I don't take orders from anyone!"

"You were angry." He leaned closer. Seeming

to peer into her soul, he whispered abruptly, "But that was not the true reason for your anger."

"Yes, it was!"

"The truth—that was our bargain."

Those damned light eyes! She couldn't avoid them. They were devouring her.

She was beautiful in her anger. Her pale skin was flushed, and her eyes spat fire. She was helpless against him, but her warrior heart would allow no retreat.

Sensing a greater truth that Mallory withheld, Gold Eagle felt sudden promise expanding within him. It escalated the pounding of his heart, increasing his hunger for this woman, despite his struggle to deny it.

He pressed, "The truth."

"You left me here without any explanation. I was cold and I was angry. Then I went outside and saw you with that woman, and I knew why you had been gone so long."

Gold Eagle searched Mallory's gaze for a sign of deceit, but he saw none. A slow elation grew within him.

"You were angry because you saw Gray Dawn in my arms."

Mallory's face twitched. "Yes."

Gold Eagle leaned closer. His throat was tight. "You wished it was you I held in my arms instead."

Mallory closed her eyes.

"Truth."

"Yes."

Mallory was shuddering, but Gold Eagle knew there was no fear within her. Suddenly struggling again to free herself, she rasped, "Untie me!"

Turning her to her side, Gold Eagle flicked open the knots securing the thongs on her wrists and ankles. He sat back on his heels, abruptly shuddering as well, as Mallory sat up to rub her ankles and wrists, avoiding his gaze.

"You are free." His emotions under tenuous control, Gold Eagle whispered, "Now it is my turn to speak some truths—as I did with Gray Dawn when I told her that the moments we once shared are past, as I did when I declared to her that my Cheyenne heart yearns for one woman alone, as I do when I say to you that my heart speaks only the name of the woman who now sits before me, and that the angry words between us mean nothing when I hold her in my arms."

Gold Eagle paused, concluding in a ragged whisper, "My heart and mind long for that woman, but my promise remains an obstacle that cannot be overcome, even while I hunger to take her."

His impassioned declaration hung on the air between them as Gold Eagle waited. He had opened his heart to another as never before; now he twisted in the throes of painful expectancy as Mallory continued to avoid his gaze, as she shifted, the flickering embers casting a soft glow on her sober profile.

His torment grew. "Truth, Mallory."

Still refusing to meet his gaze, Mallory raised herself to her knees. When she was so close to him that their heartbeats mingled, Mallory looked up at Gold Eagle at last. Her eyes were gloriously full as she whispered, "The words have all been said. There's only one truth left between us."

Sliding her arms around Gold Eagle's neck, Mallory pressed her mouth to his.

The lodge was warm, the fire fed and banked. The soft sounds of rapture had faded, but the echoes lingered in his mind as Gold Eagle raised himself above Mallory, indulging himself in the beauty of the woman for whom his heart sang.

Lowering his head, Gold Eagle brushed the rosy crest of her breast with his lips. The sweet taste of her skin raised a yearning for more, and he covered it more fully, suckling gently.

The sound of Mallory's gasp brought his gaze up to meet hers. He lowered his head to drink from her parted lips, gradually aware that he was growing hard again.

Mallory shuddered.

Gold Eagle questioned, "Are you cold?"

"No."

Her gaze dropped to his lips, and Gold Eagle understood the reason for her quaking. Gold Eagle threw back the blanket partially covering them to indulge himself in her naked splendor. Mallory made no protest as he caressed the contours of her cheek with his hand. Her skin was soft and smooth. He worshipped it with his lips. Her breasts were small and rounded, and he cupped them gently as he favored each in turn. A waist so narrow . . . hips gently curved . . .

Sliding his callused palms against the flat of her stomach, Gold Eagle passed the warm delta to gently separate her thighs. Mallory trembled at his touch, and he whispered, "Your flesh is mine to taste and consume. I do it lovingly."

Sliding down upon her, Gold Eagle pressed his mouth to her warm delta. The taste of her sent his senses reeling, and he drew deeply. He heard the gasp of Mallory's rapture. He felt her hands reaching to restrain him as she labored to catch her breath. He heard the echoes of her passion pounding within her when she separated her thighs more fully at last, allowing him the access he sought.

His heart pounding, his body quaking with a hunger that would not be appeased, Gold Eagle coaxed the bud of Mallory's passion to bloom. He reveled in her response, drinking deeply. The tone of each unintelligible word she uttered reverberated within him to raise his passion to new heights. Her body was quivering; the moment was near. He raised his head to whisper with ardent urgency, "This moment is mine. Give to me now, Mallory, so I may hold it forever in my heart."

Lowering his mouth to the womanly font once more, Gold Eagle heard her rapturous gasp. He felt her body shudder; his elation soared as she gave to him fully with unbridled abandon.

Gold Eagle raised himself above Mallory when her body stilled. Pausing to savor the moment, he then thrust himself home inside her, closing his eyes as Mallory's moist heat closed around him.

Wonder grew. Passion soared. Culmination was mutual, hot and searing as he quaked to ultimate fulfillment within her.

In the silent bliss that followed, one thought reigned.

She was his.

Breathless in the aftermath of Gold Eagle's passionate assault, Mallory slowly opened her eyes. The ice had melted from the gaze that met hers. In its place she saw the lingering remains of a scorching heat that had illuminated her heart.

But in the pale depths, a shadow remained.

Struck with a sudden, perverse uncertainty, Mallory forced herself to demand, "Truth, Gold Eagle."

Gold Eagle responded simply, "My heart is yours."

"For this night alone?"

"For this night."

Mallory's heart stilled.

"And for all the nights that follow."

Her throat so tight that she could not speak, Mallory responded in the one way that could not be misconstrued. She raised her lips to his.

Chapter Ten

It was morning. The dim light of dawn slanting into the room was indisputable, but Charles was certain of little else.

Looking around him, Charles fought to clear the shadows that clouded his mind. His surroundings were unfamiliar and he was strangely weak, capable of little more than raising his head from the pillow.

Looking up as the door opened, Charles strained to identify the small woman who entered and approached his bed.

Penelope Dolan.

Charles took a relieved breath. He was in Fort Larned.

Penelope leaned over him with a cup in her hand, and he rasped, "I have to talk to Mallory."

"You must take this medicine, Lieutenant." The half-breed spoke with soft determination. "You have been very ill."

"I want to see Mallory."

"Medicine first."

The door opened again. Charles addressed Corporal Bell in hoarse command as the young man approached. "Find Mallory, Corporal. Tell her I need to see her. Tell her it's urgent."

"She ain't here, sir."

The agitation was making his head swim and Charles paused, uncertain. "What?"

"Miss Tompkins is gone, sir."

Penelope mumbled a short word of caution, turning Bell's head toward her, and Charles reacted sharply.

"What happened? What's wrong?"

Penelope urged, "Your medicine, Lieutenant."

"I don't want medicine! Where's Mallory?"

"Medicine first."

"You'd better take it, sir. Miz Dolan's been takin' care of you since you got here, and she ain't about to let her care go to waste."

Emptying the cup that was pressed to his lips, Charles grimaced at the sharp taste, then turned back to Bell as he repeated, "She's gone, sir. She left the fort with Mr. Bower."

"Bower . . ."

"But Bower ain't Bower after all. It turns out, his name is Gold Eagle."

No, he must be delirious.

"Yes, sir. Seems like he fooled us all."

Bell's face was beginning to waver as Charles pressed, "Where . . . where did they go?"

"Nobody knows."

Charles's breathing was becoming labored. Maintaining his concentration was difficult. He turned toward the woman standing beside him.

"What did you give me?"

"Medicine—the same that Mr. Bower gave to my son when he was similarly ill."

"Mr. Bower . . . you mean Gold Eagle?"

"Yes."

"You gave me that savage's medicine?"

Penelope's expression twitched, but Charles had no time for niceties. Addressing Corporal Bell through the haze that was overwhelming his mind, he rasped, "How many patrols have they sent after her?"

"None, sir."

"None?"

"She left willingly. Everybody's agreed on that, and Major Abbott didn't see the need."

Charles fought the heavy weight of his eyelids, instructing, "Round up the men. Tell them we're going to be riding out soon." The haze was crowding his mind. Turning again toward the silent woman beside them, he grated, "What was in that medicine?"

"You will sleep for a little while."

"I don't want to sleep." His words strangely slurred, Charles looked back at Bell. The damned fellow was fading.

* * *

Silver shafts of light slithered beneath the doorway flap, announcing the approach of morning as Mallory slowly awakened. A warm sense of well-being permeated her senses despite the unaccustomed stiffness of her muscles.

Suddenly aware that she was alone underneath the blanket she had shared with Gold Eagle the previous night, Mallory looked around her. The lodge was empty but the fire was flickering warmly and a steaming bowl sat on a cloth nearby.

Annoyed with herself, Mallory sat up. The blanket fell away from her naked breasts as she reached for her clothes. Where was Gold Eagle? The memory of Gray Dawn standing familiarly in the circle of his arms drew her brows into a frown. She needed to see him.

The sound of approaching footsteps outside the lodge raised Mallory's head the moment before the flap was lifted. Her breath catching in her throat, Mallory clutched her blanket to her chest at the sight of the Indian who stood in the opening, his features obscured by the light beyond.

The man entered, dropping the flap closed behind him, and Mallory was stunned into speechlessness. An eagle feather hung in his unbound hair. Weathered buckskins molded his muscular proportions and moccasins muffled his steps as he approached her. The aura of the man was feral, as untamed as the intractable terrain around them. He was Gold Eagle as she had never seen him before—the hunter, the warrior, the Cheyenne whose exploits were legend among his people and whose reputation made settlers cringe.

Expressionless, he looked down at her. Mallory remained still as he crouched beside her.

"I must go," he said abruptly.

She looked at the lips that uttered those gruff words. They were the same lips that had bathed her with gentle kisses, raising her to the heights of an emotion so strong that she—

"Are you listening?"

But the gentleness was now missing from his tone as he continued, "Stay here. It is not safe for you to wander the village while I am gone."

Stay behind?

"No, I won't stay here."

"I have no time to talk. Others await me."

"I'm going with you."

"No."

"I am." Mallory stood up abruptly and reached for her clothes.

Gold Eagle stood beside her. "Two Bears has placed the welfare of the tribe in my hands. I will not fail him or my people."

"I'll help you."

"No."

"Gold Eagle—"

"You will stay here."

In a moment he was gone.

"Who did this to you?"

Dr. Rudolph Day stared down at him with bloodshot eyes, his warm breath fetid with the stale smell of liquor. Contempt twisted Captain Tierney's lips. The doctor had been bleary-eyed, his hands shaking, when he entered the fellow's office after his discussion with the fort commander the previous night. It had taken only one look at Dr. Day to send him back to his temporary quarters with his mutilated ear throbbing and unattended.

Tierney winced as the fellow cleaned the bloody stump and examined it more closely. "It don't look to me like this was an accident. Your ear was severed quite neatly. There aren't any ragged edges for me to trim except for this little nub. It looks strange, I admit, but I think it would be best to leave it just the way it is." He gave an unexpected laugh. "You must've gotten somebody pretty mad for this to happen!"

Tierney seethed. The old sot thought it was funny, did he! The fort commander had questioned him about his wound during his interview shortly after arriving. He had avoided giving the man a direct answer, and he had no intention of satisfying this drunken dunce's curiosity, either.

Tierney snapped, "It's none of your business who did it or how it happened!"

"You sure have a way about you." The amusement in the older man's voice remained. "Talk is that you tried pushing the wrong fella this time. There are some men here who say that's your style. If it is, it don't look like you learned much. Seems to me you'd better watch out you don't lose the other ear."

"I'm not interested in your advice. Just do your job so I can get out of here!"

The doctor reached for a roll of bandages and Tierney growled, "Make sure you make the bandage *small*."

"I can understand that. The smaller the bandage, the less comment you're likely to hear."

Tierney glowered.

On his feet the moment the bandage was secured, Tierney heard a shout from the fort yard. A soldier appeared in the doorway, announcing, "Major General Cotter and his contingent are approaching, sir."

Dismissing Dr. Day with a deprecating glance, Tierney started toward the door. The fellow commented behind him, "Guess it's true what they say about them Cheyenne being so good with a knife."

The gibe hit its mark with pinpoint accuracy and Tierney stiffened. He glanced at the soldier beside him. Was the fellow smirking? He ordered, "Get my horse, Private, and tell your commander that I'll be riding out to welcome Major General Cotter."

"Yes, sir."

He'd show them. He'd show them all!

The wind was sharp, but the mid-morning sun radiated a welcome warmth as Mallory urged her mount across the deserted, snow-laden landscape. She swept her surroundings with a cautious glance. She was intensely aware of the dangers of the desolate wilderness, but her mind was set. She had no intention of being left behind at the Cheyenne camp to await Gold Eagle's return—whenever that would be.

A blanket clutched around her, she had stood at the doorway of the lodge, watching Gold Eagle as he rode away at daybreak. Were it not for the bright color of his hair and his distinctive size, he would be indistinguishable from the braves with whom he traveled. He was one of them. He was well suited to the buckskins he wore and to the Indian pony he rode bareback with ease. He carried himself with the same instinctive pride as his companions. The few words they exchanged in conversation as they started off had been conducted in the Cheyenne language. Most significant of all was the common purpose she had glimpsed in their eyes. She abruptly understood in a way she never had before that the young men who rode with Gold Eagle were his brothers as those with white skin would never be.

Turning back to the fire as they slipped out of sight, she had glanced only briefly at the bowl still steaming beside it. Someone had prepared it for Gold Eagle to bring to her.

A woman.

She would not eat it.

Emerging from the lodge minutes later, she had discovered that the horse that had carried Gold Eagle and her to the camp was tied a short distance away. She had saddled him immediately, noting the curious glances she received as she mounted up and rode out without speaking a word. Now, hours later, she was still following the same trail broken through the fresh snow—and she was still hoping it was the right one.

Rounding a small rise, Mallory stopped at the sight of riders in the distance. They were Indians, but she could distinguish little else about them.

Mallory's throat tightened. She had ridden through this same wilderness with Gold Eagle only a day earlier. But without him, the situation had drastically changed. Mallory remained motionless, unwilling to alert the riders to her presence before she could identify them.

Her horse whinnied unexpectedly, and Mallory saw the riders turn her way. They hesitated only briefly before starting back toward her. Realizing the futility of attempting escape, Mallory held her breath as they drew closer.

Sunlight glinted on the pale hair of the lead rider, and Mallory breathed again. She remained sober, anticipating Gold Eagle's anger when he drew up alongside her.

The men beside him commented briefly in their native tongue as Gold Eagle fixed her with his stare. She was uncertain what to expect when Gold Eagle urged his horse closer.

"You would not remain behind as I asked."

"No."

Turning abruptly toward his men, Gold Eagle snapped a short, Cheyenne command that sent them back in the direction from which they had come. Silent, he took up a position beside her as they followed behind.

* * *

Charles looked up from Mallory's letter. It was past midday. He had awakened earlier, his mind clear and his body stronger. He had not started shaking until Corporal Walker put her letter into his hand.

Astounded, Charles read it again. How could she have done it? How could she have gone off with that man, knowing that he had been misrepresenting himself all the while he was at the fort—knowing that he was the white savage, Gold Eagle?

Charles read further, shaking his head with incredulity. She related briefly the abuse Captain Tierney had continued to heap on the man they believed to be Bower. His anger flared when she mentioned Tierney's "improper advances" and "threats."

Surely she had not believed herself safer with Gold Eagle than she would be at the fort with Captain Tierney?

Then had come her confession that she had come to the fort misrepresenting herself, just as Gold Eagle had done. The man named Joshua Barnes did not exist. She had come to make a name for herself as a reporter for her father's newspaper.

She asked him to forgive her deceit. She said he was her true friend. She asked him not to worry about her, that Gold Eagle was going to help her get the information she needed for her articles. *He had given his word.*

315

Charles lowered the letter to the bed beside him. He closed his eyes in despair.

"Lieutenant?"

Charles opened his eyes as an unsmiling officer entering the room.

"How are you feeling, Lieutenant? I'm Major Abbott, the commander of this fort." Abbott stopped beside his bed. "We spoke shortly after you arrived here, but I'm not sure you remember."

"No, sir, I don't." Charles's heart doubled its rhythm. "I'm glad you're here. I want to talk to you about Mallory Tompkins."

Major Abbott frowned. "Yes, I know. I understand you and she were friendly."

"Major Bullen assigned me to her safety. Captain Tierney countermanded Major Bullen's orders and sent me back to Major Bullen's command. If he hadn't, I wouldn't have allowed Miss Tompkins to be taken in by Gold Eagle."

"Captain Tierney and I spoke at length about the situation before I sent him to Fort Zarah to meet Major General Cotter."

. . . sent Tierney to meet Major General Cotter at Fort Zarah . . .

"Captain Tierney informed me that he was faced with some difficult decisions while I was gone—decisions he felt forced to make because of extenuating circumstances."

. . . extenuating circumstances . . .

"In any case, she's not your responsibility any longer. From what we've been able to ascertain,

316

she left this fort with the Cheyenne, Gold Eagle, of her own accord."

Charles's hand closed spasmodically on Mallory's letter as he replied, "Yes, she did."

Abbott's frown darkened when he noticed the carefully handwritten sheet in Charles's hand. "Is that a letter from Miss Tompkins?"

"Yes, sir. She left it for me to receive when I returned."

"Where did you get it?"

The major's suddenly grim expression evoked Charles's caution. "It was on my bed when I awakened."

Major Abbott looked up at the woman standing in the corner of the room. "Do you know anything about this, Mrs. Dolan?"

"No, I do not."

Major Abbott nodded, obviously unconvinced. He questioned, "Does Miss Tompkins clarify any of the circumstances precipitating her departure, Lieutenant?"

"I think you'd get a true picture of the situation if you read her letter, sir."

The major accepted the letter Charles held out to him. His face was flushed and his stance rigid when he finished reading and handed the letter back to him. "Thank you, Lieutenant."

"What about Miss Tompkins, Major? Someone has to go after her. It isn't safe for her in that Cheyenne village."

"I'm sorry. Miss Tompkins went there voluntarily. We now know that for sure."

"She wasn't cognizant of the danger!"

"It's out of the question, Lieutenant. General Cotter will arrive here soon. I'm sure he'll prefer to handle the matter with the Cheyenne himself."

"When is he due to arrive, sir?"

"Within the week."

"A week! By that time Mallory could be—"

"That's the end of it, Lieutenant! As for Captain Tierney, you may be assured that I'll deal with him appropriately when he returns."

"Yes, sir."

Major Abbott paused. "I'm sorry, Lieutenant."

"Yes, sir."

Waiting until the major's footsteps faded, Charles called out, "Corporal Bell!"

Entering the room from his position outside the door, Bell responded, "Yes, sir!"

"You heard what Major Abbott said."

"I sure did."

"He made a mistake when he said Miss Tompkins is no longer my responsibility. My orders from Major Bullen were reinstated and I intend to follow them. I want you to tell the men to get their gear ready—and to be quiet about it. We're going to ride out after Miss Tompkins."

"Glad to hear that, sir."

"We're leaving tomorrow."

"Tomorrow? You ain't goin' to be well enough to travel by then, Lieutenant!"

"Tomorrow, Corporal."

Bell shook his head. "All right. Tomorrow."

* * *

The sun was making its descent in a gloriously colored sky, and the temperature was falling. Mallory rode silently beside Gold Eagle as she had most of the day. Strangely, the silence had been no barrier to communication between Gold Eagle and the men who followed him. A single word, a glance, a quick sign was all that was needed to send a man off to scout briefly in a different direction.

Gold Eagle had explained Two Bears' charge to him when they halted briefly. She could understand that Gold Eagle believed his village needed to be warned of Cotter's approach, but she could not make herself think, even for a moment, that an officer with Cotter's reputation could be a threat to any man—Indian or white— who sought peace.

But it was obvious that the other men in their small party agreed with Gold Eagle. Two Horns, Many Horses, Yellow Fox, Burnt Antelope—all made that clear without a spoken word. It surprised her that they accepted her presence with so little comment, except when they halted briefly and she saw Many Horses look at her, then speak to Gold Eagle in their native tongue. Gold Eagle did not respond.

The sun slipped behind a cloud, and the chill was immediate. Mallory shivered. She cursed the involuntary reflex when Gold Eagle looked at her.

Denying the chill that was creeping into her bones, she replied to his unspoken question, "I'm not cold."

319

"We will be back at camp soon. You will be warm then."

"I'm not cold!"

This time it was Yellow Fox's turn to make a comment. The others responded with soft laughter.

Suspecting a joke at her expense, Mallory kicked her horse forward. She gritted her teeth as Gold Eagle came up alongside her and they continued at a steady pace.

The laughter still stinging her pride, Mallory was unable to restrain herself. Squinting at Gold Eagle, she repeated in a voice that dared contradiction, "I said . . . I'm not cold."

The moment had finally come!

Riding toward the vast military contingent that approached Fort Zarah, Captain Arthur Tierney rode his horse proudly. His uniform had been meticulously tailored to fit his muscular frame, and even under the present difficult circumstances, he knew his appearance was a cut above the others. He had made sure it would be, by commandeering the services of an unnamed private to see that his buttons were polished, his trousers freshly pressed, and his boots glistening. He was well aware of Major General Wallace Cotter's obsession with the code of military attire—he had even seen to it that his mount's coat was brushed to a polished sheen.

His handsome features composed into a welcoming smile, Tierney decided that the bandage on his ear added just the right touch to the picture of the consummate professional soldier which he presented—a man of honor, integrity, and discipline.

Major General Cotter smiled broadly as he neared. In that moment Tierney knew that the years he had spent listening to Cotter's endless war stories, and the sacrifice he had made in pretending to heed every pompous syllable of advice the man offered, were about to pay off.

Major Abbott's report lay snug in his saddle-bag. He intended to present it to Cotter at the first feasible moment. He would wait patiently while the report was read . . . until Cotter asked him the inevitable question.

What do you think of this report, Arthur?

He would avoid out and out disagreement with Abbott's opinion that the Indians were friendly—that they wanted peace. He knew Cotter, and he knew that Cotter's opinion of the Indians was not unlike his own. He would allow the man to draw him out, and he would finally confess at Cotter's urging that he felt Major Abbott had made a grave mistake in his assessment of the situation. He would imply that Abbott was simply the wrong man for the job, a man who refused to see the Cheyenne for the bloodthirsty savages they were. He would follow with a subtle barrage that was certain to appeal to the fighting man in Cotter, and he would conclude with an equally subtle reference to the accolades Cotter would receive when he settled the Indian problem on the frontier, once and for all.

General Cotter would accept the picture he presented, simply because he wanted to believe it.

Tierney almost laughed. When he arrived back at Fort Larned, he would be riding right beside the big man—he was sure of it. And when they attacked Two Bears' village, he would draw first blood! But first or last blood, he would draw Gold Eagle's blood, just as Gold Eagle had drawn his.

His chest heaving with the stimulation of his thoughts, Tierney kicked his horse to a canter. Halting dramatically a few feet from General Cotter, he snapped a sharp salute.

The great man returned his salute, then offered him his hand.

Smiling, Tierney shook it warmly.

She was freezing.

Abandoning her unaffected facade the moment the lodge flap dropped closed behind her, Mallory snatched up a nearby blanket and wrapped it around herself before sitting as close to the blazing fire as was possible. The last few hours' ride had been exhausting. She was hungry, tired, and irritable. Gold Eagle had yet to comment on her refusal to remain behind, but she knew the time was fast approaching when he would make his thoughts known.

Gold Eagle's footsteps crunched against the frozen snow outside the lodge, alerting her to his approach, and Mallory thrust the blanket aside. She stiffened when he entered, followed by a young woman who smiled shyly at her and then placed two steaming bowls beside the fire. The young woman looked up at Gold Eagle and spoke softly to him. It had not missed Mallory's notice that the young women of the village deferred to Gold Eagle, smiling at him when he passed, while they looked at her assessingly— as if she fell short in their opinion.

She didn't like it.

The young woman left and Gold Eagle sat beside her. His expression sober, he said, "I do not ride out tomorrow. Others go instead."

Mallory drew back. "Is it because I followed you?"

"No."

She asked abruptly, "Are you angry that I followed you?"

"I was, as I am each time you choose not to accept that I act for your welfare."

"I don't need anyone to look out for my welfare. I came here with a job to do, and I can't do it if I stay here, hiding in this lodge."

"You are irritable."

Mallory's frown darkened.

"Because you are cold and hungry." He motioned toward the food the woman had left. "You should eat while the food is hot. It will warm you."

Mallory looked at the steaming bowls. It was a stew of some kind, she supposed, warm and thick with gravy. It smelled delicious.

"I don't want any."

"You are not hungry?"

"No."

Mallory's stomach took that inopportune moment to growl, but Mallory ignored it. She asked abruptly, "Who was that woman? Is she a friend?"

"She is very close to me."

A sharp emotion slashed viciously at Mallory, prompting her reply. "Yes, I could see that."

She turned her back deliberately on the steaming bowls.

"The food loses its appeal because of the woman who brought it."

Mallory's response was to reach for a piece of the stringy jerky that was fast becoming a staple in her diet. Gold Eagle stayed her hand, curling it in his much larger palm as he turned her back toward him. His face was close to hers. She wondered how she had ever thought his gaze cold as he whispered, "Your belly burns in anger that another woman caters to my needs."

"No."

Silence.

"Yes."

"Singing Spirit is my sister."

"Your sister?"

"She is daughter of the woman who found me when I was a child of less than three summers. I was alone in the wilderness, standing beside the wagon where my family lay dead from the white man's fever. All in the village feared that I would bring the fever to them as well, but

Running Deer took pity on me. She kept me with her, risking her life as she tended to my needs far from the camp until the people no longer feared I would bring the sickness to them. Running Deer is the only mother I remember, and Lame Wolf was my only father. Singing Spirit brought new joy to our lodge with her birth, and although Running Dear and Lame Wolf no longer live, our spirits are still joined."

Mallory did not reply as Gold Eagle continued, "The fire that burns in your belly burned in mine as well when Spotted Horse talked as he did of taking you to him. When he touched you, my knife spoke my fury without words."

Mallory studied Gold Eagle's face. A smile tugged at her lips. "I suppose I should be glad I don't carry a knife."

"That is what Yellow Fox said when you became angry this afternoon."

Mallory's discomfort returned. "They were laughing. What did they say?"

"They said the white woman I took to my lodge has a strong mind and a spirit that will not relent. They said she has a warrior's heart that challenges mine and will give me little peace."

"Do you agree with them?"

"I cannot deny their words. Your warrior's heart shines for all to see in your eyes. I saw it that first day in Fort Larned when you stood against everyone to speak for me when you believed I could not speak for myself. My kindred spirit called out to yours, although I sought to deny it."

"Is that what it was, Gold Eagle?" His words a sudden revelation, Mallory turned fully toward him. "Is that what it was, the force that drew me to you, displacing all others in my mind with a feeling that a link between us had formed without the need for words?"

"Warriors' hearts beating as one . . ." Gold Eagle frowned. "But a warrior's heart bears a heavy burden. It cannot surrender. I say this now so you may know that I recognize the force that impelled you to follow me. But there are difficult days to come, and I ask you now to understand that I must follow the path that has been set for *me* as well."

A chill crawled up Mallory's spine. "What do you mean?"

"I follow the path that will bring my people to ultimate victory."

"To victory—over Cotter's forces?"

"To victory, wherever that path leads."

"But you couldn't possibly win if you opposed Cotter!" Panic invaded Mallory's senses. "Cotter's force is extensive—well fed and well armed. He has artillery. You will not win if you fight him—much less survive!"

"The blood of my people is valuable to me. I would not see it shed, but the choice may not be mine."

The inference of Gold Eagle's statement stunned her. "Major General Cotter doesn't want war with the Cheyenne!"

"Then I must believe that he approaches with his well-armed force, with the great guns you speak of, because he wishes to talk peace?"

Her trepidation expanding in the face of Gold Eagle's irrefutable logic, Mallory rasped, "I'll speak to him if he comes here. I'll tell him that your people don't want war. He'll listen to me. He has to."

Gold Eagle stroked her cheek. He smoothed away a tear that she did not realize she had shed as he whispered, "My path was set long before Running Deer found the child who now stands here as Gold Eagle. I can only follow where that path leads."

Silent, Mallory looked up at Gold Eagle. She saw an honesty that could not be doubted in the pale eyes that returned her gaze. She saw unyielding conviction and honor.

Her decision abruptly made, Mallory said simply, "Your path is mine."

Charles awakened as the first light of morning sliced through the window of his room. His first thought was that he must remove Mallory from the Cheyenne camp before Cotter advanced.

Slinging his legs over the side of the bed, his head swimming, Charles stood up. A wave of weakness shook him and he staggered. He forced himself to take a step, then another, but the room was whirling around him.

He couldn't do it. Damn it all, he couldn't do it!

Lowering himself back onto the bed, Charles

breathed deeply, struggling to order his muddled thoughts. What had Major Abbott said? He had sent Tierney to meet Cotter at Fort Zarah? He silently calculated—it would be two days before a force of that size could possibly reach Fort Larned, then another few days before they could reach the Cheyenne village.

Four days, at the bare minimum.

Despairing, Charles raised a shaky hand to his head. He would be a fool to start out in his present condition. He wouldn't last a mile, and it was crucial that he be fully recovered when he faced Gold Eagle.

Mallory's face flashed before him, and Charles steeled himself against the myriad regrets assaulting him. He shouldn't have left Mallory alone. He should have convinced her to accompany him to another fort until he could get his orders reinstated. He should have heeded his instincts and checked on Matthew Bower more carefully. He should have realized that the ice he saw in that man's eyes reflected a contempt so deep that no course of action was beyond him.

Charles struggled to control his anger. One day, maybe two, and he'd be ready to travel. He would bring Mallory back, and he would deal with the savage imposter then. If Gold Eagle had hurt Mallory in any way, if he had touched her—

A blood rage rose inside Charles.

He'd kill him.

* * *

Mallory came slowly awake as the new morning dawned. Gold Eagle lay facing her as he slept, his arm curled around her. She inched closer to his warmth, taking comfort in the sweet intimacy of flesh against flesh, and in the knowledge that this day would be theirs to spend together.

Mallory looked around at the interior of the lodge. It had proved a surprisingly adequate shelter against the winter chill, especially when its heat was shared. Her gaze strayed back to Gold Eagle, her stomach tightening at the pure male power he exuded, even in sleep—tight muscles, taut skin, strong features, long strands of unbound blond hair augmenting an innate virility. But she saw something else as well. She saw the man she had unknowingly sought and never thought to find in the "civilized" world that presently seemed so far away.

What would her father say to her if he could see her now?

She knew what she would say to him.

She would say that she loved this man.

Daybreak . . . the rumble of wagons . . . the shuffle of marching feet . . . the whinnying of horses echoing on the frigid air as the great contingent began its forward push across the frozen ground.

Captain Tierney surveyed the impressive sight of fourteen hundred men marching steadily forward. His heart pounded. It was the most powerful force to enter the frontier, just as the rumors had claimed. It was everything he had hoped it would be—and he rode with its leader!

His back rigidly erect, Tierney glanced at the slender, tightly muscled man who rode beside him. Major General Wallace Cotter, West Point graduate, veteran of the Mexican and Civil Wars, a man fresh from the battlefields of the South—the same man who had listened intently to his earnest discourse the previous night, the same man who had then looked askance at Major Abbott's report, vowing to take care of those "red devils" once and for all.

It had been so easy.

Chapter Eleven

"We're ready, sir."

Charles turned toward Corporal Bell. The stable was unnaturally silent in the semi-light of early morning as he scrutinized the men of his detachment. Corporals Hodge, Bell, Whittier, and Knoll were staunchly loyal soldiers who had not let him down. They had supported him during his illness. Had it not been for their allegiance, he would not have survived the trek to Fort Larned. They knew the risk their small brigade took as they prepared to start for the Cheyenne camp. They had not spoken a single word in protest.

Charles unconsciously squared his shoulders. The fever that had so completely incapacitated him had disappeared as quickly as it had come.

With two days of recuperation behind him, he was well again—almost his old self. With those same two days behind him, he also knew that Cotter's force could arrive at any time. It was essential that he depart before that happened.

He had taken his leave of Penelope Dolan a few minutes earlier, expressing sincere appreciation for her aid, and genuine remorse for careless remarks that might have offended her. It did not miss his notice that she had kept the secret of his approaching departure. She was a good woman.

He had taken care of the final details of his departure only minutes earlier, a short letter to be delivered to Major Abbott at mid-morning, specifying his intention to follow Major Bullen's orders to provide for Mallory Tompkins's safety. He was uncertain of the reaction the letter would receive, but he cared little. He would face the consequences later, when Mallory was safe.

Charles spoke softly in command. "All right, men. Mount up."

At the gate minutes later, he greeted the sentry's surprise with a brief order.

"Open up, Corporal."

"Sir, you're leaving before Major General Cotter arrives?"

"I'm returning to Major Bullen's command with my detachment as I was originally ordered. I want to get an early start." When the sentry hesitated, Charles snapped, "Open the gates, Corporal!"

Charles restrained the urge to glance around as the sentry hesitated a moment longer. Relief surged through him when the sentry slipped the bolt and swung the gates open.

Sensing a similar relief in the men behind him, Charles dug his heels into his mount's sides. They were moving steadily forward when the gates slammed shut behind them.

The gray clouds had disappeared as afternoon arrived and now the sun shone brightly. Seated beside Singing Spirit's fire, Mallory looked at the small woman, who filled cups from a steaming pot as she welcomed Gold Eagle and her to her lodge. With her customary smile, Singing Spirit placed the first cup in Gold Eagle's hands, the second in Mallory's. Mallory did not take offense at the reversal of courtesy to which she was accustomed, knowing that Singing Spirit acted in deference to Gold Eagle's support of her household since the death of her husband.

Accepting the light gruel, Mallory drank slowly as Gold Eagle and Singing Spirit spoke softly in their native tongue. The past few days had seen a slow awakening within her. She had walked the village with Gold Eagle, noting with surprise the extended size of the winter camp where constant work hummed within several hundred neatly spaced lodges during the warmer hours of each day. She had seen children playing, women working, men caring for horses. She had seen a contentment in their daily lives despite the obvious hardships that winter had wrought, and a strong thread of peace and tranquility that lay undisturbed despite the impending threat. She had witnessed in the eyes of all a respect for Gold Eagle that had been hard won, and she had been proud.

She had also begun to see smiles gradually turned her way. She had returned the smiles in kind. She had even managed a friendly salute for Two Horns when he passed them earlier, greeting them with a quip that had raised Gold Eagle's brows.

She had waited only until Two Horns walked out of sight to demand, "What did he say?"

When Gold Eagle did not immediately respond, she'd insisted, "Tell me!"

"Two Horns said that you look more like one of our people every day . . . that he waits for you to wear an eagle feather in your hair so the camp might know us as Gold Eagle and Fire Eagle."

Despite herself, Mallory had almost laughed. She had countered, "If Two Horns could understand me, I'd tell him that I often wore feathers in my hair for adornment before coming here, and that an eagle feather would suit me just fine."

Gold Eagle's reply had been offhanded. "Two Horns speaks your language."

"What?"

"He learned the white man's tongue when he was confined for many moons in the soldiers' jail."

"He understands everything I say?"

Mallory gasped, her face reddening. Twice, she had accompanied the group scouting for Cotter's approach. She had spoken freely during the course of the second day, with occasional intimate comments to Gold Eagle that she believed none of the others understood. Another thought struck her.

"Do Yellow Fox, Many Horses, and Burnt Antelope understand, too?"

At Gold Eagle's nod, Mallory had groaned aloud.

"Why didn't you tell me?"

Gold Eagle's response had been simple. "There was no reason."

She had pressed, "Does Singing Spirit speak my language, too?"

"No, she does not."

She had been disappointed. Once her momentary jealousy had been put aside, she had found Gold Eagle's sister to be a sweet, gentle person. She wished language was not a barrier between them.

Mallory placed her empty cup beside the fire now and glanced at the child who busied herself in the corner of the lodge. Language was not a barrier with Little Bird. No more than three years of age, Singing Spirit's daughter was a beautiful child who had taken to Mallory immediately. The gentleness with which Indian parents handled their children amazed her. Brought up in an authoritarian atmosphere, she was surprised to see that little scolding appeared to be necessary. The boys amused themselves most of the day, and the girls worked busily beside their mothers. That last fact had not missed her notice and she—

Gasping when a small body dropped unexpectedly down onto her lap, Mallory laughed aloud. Rambling on unintelligibly, the child giggled as she grasped a handful of Mallory's hair and squeezed it.

"Ouch!"

Singing Spirit reached for the child, but Mallory waved her off. The girl giggled again, repeating her disjointed statement. Mallory turned toward Gold Eagle to see amusement twisting his lips.

Mallory asked, "What did she say?"

"Little Bird is trying to see if she can squeeze the color of your hair onto her hands."

Mallory laughed. "Tell her she can't."

Gold Eagle spoke softly to the child, who replied with sudden earnestness. Mallory looked at him for explanation.

"The child says she has a secret wish. She wishes she, too, had hair like the color of fire, because it is beautiful."

Gold Eagle's eyes held hers in that moment, his gaze saying more than his lips dared, and Mallory's heart began a familiar hammering. She had a secret wish, too.

A sudden commotion in the camp interrupted the moment, bringing Gold Eagle to his feet. Placing Little Bird in her mother's outstretched arms, Mallory followed Gold Eagle outside to see people gathering around the scouting party which had returned with much excitement. Mallory watched as Two Bears walked into their midst and the head scout started to speak. The conversation was beyond her, but the effect was obvious. Men stepped forward aggressively while women and children fell back. A few glanced at her, speaking belligerently, at which Yellow Fox halted them with unexpected fierceness. Through it all, Gold Eagle remained silent.

Uncertain what was occurring, Mallory turned to him expectantly when the crowd abruptly dispersed.

"What's happening?"

His expression as hard as stone, Gold Eagle responded, "The great force approaches. It nears Fort Larned. It will not be much longer before it marches toward us. Two Bears has told the people to prepare."

"Prepare? How?"

"Go back to the lodge."

"Tell me, Gold Eagle! I need to know!"

Gold Eagle strode away without responding.

"You're not giving them enough time!"

Major Abbott glanced at Captain Tierney, his jaw tight when the expected confirmation of his statement was not forthcoming. The great contingent, with Major General Cotter and a triumphant Captain Tierney in the lead, had arrived at the fort an hour earlier. The tenor of the situation was immediately obvious, as was the grave error he had made in sending Tierney ahead with his report. Despite the report's clarity, Tierney had somehow primed Cotter for battle. Still struggling to overcome his blunder, Abbott again addressed the general.

"Sir, I explained to you in my report that the Cheyenne don't want to fight. They want peace."

"Is that the reason they continue to conduct raids on settlers along the Republican and Arkansas Rivers?"

"It's not a proven fact that the Cheyenne made those raids."

"I suppose it hasn't been proved that it was the Cheyenne who've been raiding the Santa Fe Road, either."

"No, sir."

"What about the hostages they refuse to return?"

"The Kiowa took those hostages. The Cheyenne know nothing about them."

Cotter's thin lips twisted with contempt. "I can see that we aren't in agreement. We'll just have to let the chief come here and speak for himself, won't we?"

"I'm sure Two Bears will come to the fort willingly. He's in no position to do anything else. It's been a hard winter. Cheyenne food stocks are low and their horses have been weakened by the shortage of grazing—but your deadline is too tight. You're not giving them enough time to make the journey."

Cotter's small eyes narrowed. "Captain Tierney tells me that we should be able to get a messenger there and back within two days."

"Possibly . . . if it were summer, when Cheyenne horses are at full strength and weather conditions facilitate travel. Under present circumstances, you're asking the impossible. And even if it were possible, you'd be taking too great a risk by setting such a narrow time frame."

"Let me make my thoughts clear on this matter, Major." Drawing his wiry frame up to its full height, Cotter said flatly, "Whether or not war will result from this expedition depends entirely on the Cheyenne. I will base my response on their behavior and the respect that is shown to me as an officer of the United States government. I tell you now that I am prepared for war and that I will tolerate no insolence. I intend to show these people that the whole tribe will be punished if they act in a hostile manner."

"Sir, you are eliminating any possibility of establishing a peaceful accord. I entreat you to reconsider."

"A detachment will be sent to the Cheyenne camp with the message as I have stated it. It will leave at dawn with instructions to return immediately, escorting Two Bears back to Fort Larned."

"Sir—"

"That will be all, Major."

Utterly frustrated, Abbott turned toward the door with a brief salute. He drew the door closed behind him, but not before he heard Cotter remark in a tone of disgust, "You were right, Arthur. He's an Indian-lover."

*   *   *

Day had come to an end. The camp was quiet. Mallory noted with growing apprehension that the arrival of the scouts had precipitated a marked change in the attitude of the Cheyenne village. Smiles had turned into frowns of anxiety, and all manner of casual activity had ceased. Women who had busied themselves outside during the sunny hours were now sequestered in their lodges. After a general council with Two Bears, the men had dispersed silently to their given tasks.

Mallory anxiously awaited Gold Eagle's return. Angry and uncertain, she turned toward the door as Gold Eagle entered. His expression was grim, and Mallory's blood ran cold.

Mallory demanded stiffly, "Tell me what's happening."

Facing her, Gold Eagle replied, "Two Bears prepares for all eventualities."

"Please explain what you mean."

"Much depends on the next few days. We must wait and see."

"I don't understand."

Gold Eagle reached out unexpectedly to grasp her shoulders. He held her fast. "Two Bears maintains a course of peace. He says he has expressed his thoughts clearly and the great general will not advance against him. He says he will talk to the great general and the great general will believe him."

Gold Eagle's hands bit into her shoulders as

Mallory took a shuddering breath. "You don't think that'll happen."

"No."

"Why?"

"Because I have seen the faces of those at Fort Larned. There is no love for my people there."

"That isn't true!"

"Would you put my people's fate in the hands of men such as Captain Tierney?"

"Major General Cotter isn't like him! He—"

"—is Captain Tierney's good friend."

"That's what he claimed, but I don't believe him!"

"The course of these next days will not be determined by what we believe. It will be determined by what is. My people prepare for that which they hope will not come."

"Gold Eagle . . ." Unable to control her sudden trembling, Mallory whispered, "You're frightening me."

"A warrior's heart knows no fear."

Fighting to control the quaking of her voice, Mallory rasped, "My only fear is that I'll lose you."

Drawing her suddenly tight against him, his lips only inches from hers, Gold Eagle rasped in return, "Then let us assuage that fear together, so we may be strong for the days ahead."

Gold Eagle's mouth touched hers, and Mallory accepted it willingly. His loving heat soothed her fear as she separated her lips under his. Seeking to memorize the taste of him, she slipped her arms around his neck to draw him closer, to press his kiss deeper, to end all thoughts but those of each other.

The fire's warmth heated their naked flesh as they shared their bodies joyfully. His powerful arms tense, Gold Eagle raised himself above her at last. He thrust himself inside her and she clutched him close as they reached mutual culmination in a burst of exquisite pleasure.

In the silence that followed, while Gold Eagle's muscled length lay slick against hers, Mallory felt a flash of true foreboding as he whispered against her lips, "We have this night to keep, ours forever."

Charles turned to glance at the men riding at his rear. Their detachment had ridden hard after leaving the fort the previous day, halting only when the darkness allowed them to go no farther. They had risen at the first light of dawn and had been traveling for hours. He had ordered his men to eat in the saddle, so great was his haste to reach the Cheyenne village. Through it all, they had voiced no complaints.

In his brief glance, Charles saw a determination not unlike his own on his men's faces, and he felt pride in their unyielding courage. He would speak to Major Bullen about them when he returned. He would see that they were commended for their dedication to duty, and he would—

"Sir! Riders in the distance!"

Squinting into the horizon, Charles strained to identify the horsemen rapidly approaching.

Indians.

His hand moving to his gun, Charles snapped, "Get ready."

His jaw locked tight, Charles led his men steadily forward.

"You think you've won, don't you?"

His expression unrevealing as he faced Major Abbott across the desk of the older man's office, Captain Tierney did not choose to respond. The situation was progressing exactly as he had planned. He had been cautious, making himself unavailable to Abbott the previous evening after General Cotter's pronouncements. It had not been difficult. Cotter had occupied him long into the night, pressing for information on the size of the Cheyenne camp, on the terrain surrounding it—picking his mind for every detail that might be of aid—not *if* Cotter ordered the attack against the Cheyenne, but *when* he did.

Obviously frustrated, Major Abbott had summoned him to his office that morning, but he had delayed in responding, citing a previous order from Cotter. Waiting until Cotter's message to Two Bears' village was an hour onto the trail, he had then made his way to Abbott's office. He had entered to find the man furiously angry.

Tierney responded carefully to Abbott's tight accusation.

"I don't know what you mean, sir."

"You know what I mean, all right!" Abbott advanced toward him, fists clenched. "I sent you to meet Cotter with strict instructions as to the manner in which you were to handle the con-tact!"

"Which I followed precisely, sir."

"You did—"

"I delivered your report to him as ordered."

"And you then proceeded to contradict every-thing I had written in it!"

His feigned sincerity masterful, Tierney re-plied, "Major General Cotter read your report, and he then asked me my opinion of the situa-tion. He insisted that I be truthful."

Abbott laughed aloud. "It's becoming more obvious to me by the minute, Captain, that you haven't spent a truthful day in your life!"

"Sir . . ."

"So, you believe the Cheyenne are planning an attack on the frontier."

"Yes, sir, I believe they are planning an at-tack, and it's my belief that we should make sure they don't have the advantage."

Abbott nodded. "You believe they're strong enough to make such a move."

"I have no way of estimating their strength."

"You don't. Of course, you wouldn't consider employing common sense . . ."

Tierney remained silent.

"You also believe two days will be sufficient time for the messenger to reach Two Bears with Cotter's message, and for Two Bears to return with him."

"It's not impossible."

"No, only nearly so."

"I can't attest to that, sir."

"What about the distortion of facts you presented with regard to Miss Tompkins?"

Tierney felt heat rising to his face.

"Oh, I've hit a nerve there, have I? You bastard, you made improper advances toward her—threatened her. You all but forced her to leave with Gold Eagle."

"Only a fool would have chosen to trust that savage!"

"Or a woman who felt she had no other choice!" Abbott paused. "That was the reason Gold Eagle took your ear, wasn't it . . . to teach you a lesson."

"The only lesson taught will be the one I'm going to teach him when I—"

Tierney halted abruptly.

"You almost revealed yourself, didn't you, Captain?" Approaching in broad strides that brought him close enough for Tierney to feel the older man's breath on his face, Major Abbott faced him squarely. "I want you to know that I intend to pursue your corruption of my report, and your dishonoring of this post and dereliction of duty in pursuit of personal concerns during my absence. In addition, if the next few days result in the debacle I expect, I intend to send my report directly to Washington to be read by the president himself."

"That's your prerogative, sir."

"I'm sure Miss Tompkins will be glad to corroborate the facts."

Tierney maintained his silence.

"As will Lieutenant Moore—who, by the way,

did not return to Major Bullen's command as is commonly believed, but who is making his way toward the Cheyenne camp at this moment, with the intention of bringing Miss Tompkins back with him. So enjoy the moment, Captain"—Abbott's expression was grim—"because I promise you, I will see to it that the moment is all you have left to enjoy. You're excused!"

Tierney turned with a sharp salute. Outside the office, he pulled the door closed behind him with a tight smile. He was a bastard and a liar, was he? And his future was dim.

Tierney's smile became a sneer. Abbott was too much of a fool to see that it was too late to halt the progress of what would soon be a glorious victory over the savage Cheyenne tribe— that Major General Cotter would be the newest hero of the American people once that triumph was established, and that he, Captain Arthur Tierney, would share liberally in the glory because he had ridden at Cotter's side every step of the way.

Yes, *Captain* Tierney today . . . *Major* Tierney tomorrow.

He had no doubt how the rest would be resolved.

Major Abbott was finished. He'd see to that.

The flame-haired witch, Mallory Tompkins, had signed her own death warrant. Lieutenant Moore didn't stand a chance of getting her out of that camp. When Cotter's forces attacked, she'd be killed in the crossfire. He'd see to that, too.

Gold Eagle was a dead man.

They had all sealed their own fates.

Even Cotter was a fool, for that matter. As for himself—well, they'd all see what he was made of.

Charles rode resolutely toward the Cheyenne camp.

The Indians they had encountered were a small scouting party numbering four Cheyenne. His detachment could easily have overcome them, but he had chosen to raise his hand in peace instead. He had exchanged a few words with the leader, telling him he had come for the white woman, Mallory Tompkins.

If he didn't know better, he'd believe the sober-faced Cheyenne had been tempted to smile. Instead, the fellow had led them back to the camp.

Riding beside the silent warriors as they approached, Charles felt his heart begin a slow hammering. It was a large camp—larger than he'd expected. He estimated there were several hundred lodges.

Subduing an urge to rest his hand on the gun at his side, Charles scrutinized the crowd gradually assembling. He saw the whispering that stopped as they neared. He saw the grim expressions. They were not welcome.

And then he saw *her*.

The blazing color of Mallory's hair was a beacon, setting her apart from the dark heads milling around her as she walked. With tousled hair and wearing the outrageous traveling clothes she had purchased for the journey to Fort Larned, she was somehow even more beautiful than he remembered.

Charles's gaze stopped short at the sight of the warrior who walked at Mallory's side. An eagle feather hung in the pale hair touching the fellow's broad, buckskin-clad shoulders, and undisguised enmity burned in his familiar light eyes. It was the savage, Gold Eagle. He wondered how he could have believed this man was anyone else.

Mallory halted as their party neared. There was something proprietary about the way Gold Eagle positioned himself beside her.

Charles's blood ran hot.

If the bastard had touched her, he'd kill him.

Mallory stared with disbelief at the approaching riders. It was Charles and his detachment!

Spontaneous warmth choked her throat. As soon as he dismounted, she ran up to him and hugged him tightly. She closed her eyes as his arms closed briefly around her.

Drawing back, Mallory greeted the other men in Charles's detachment, tears forming when she looked up again at Charles. She saw the same handsome face and honest dark eyes, the same endearing smile, but he appeared tired . . . thinner. Her voice was hoarse with emotion when she questioned, "What are you doing here, Charles? Don't you know it's dangerous for you to be here right now?"

"Yes, I know." Charles's smile faded. "It's dangerous for you, too. That's why I came to take you back with me."

Mallory glanced at Gold Eagle, who stood silently behind her, and Charles bristled. "Don't look at him. You don't need his permission to leave."

Choosing not to respond to Charles's obvious animosity, Mallory looked again at Gold Eagle. His gaze was narrow, his lips tight. She urged, "Gold Eagle, tell Two Bears who Charles is. Tell him Charles comes here in peace."

"That's right, he can speak, can't he?" Charles addressed Gold Eagle with open rancor. "You're not the mute, Matthew Bower. That poor fellow's dead. You killed him, didn't you?"

Mallory responded spontaneously. "No, he didn't!"

Not deigning to reply to Charles's accusation, Gold Eagle addressed Two Bears. They conversed in soft, guttural tones.

"What did Two Bears say?" Uncertain how to ease the renewed enmity between Gold Eagle and Charles, Mallory pressed, "Did you explain why Charles came?"

"I told Two Bears that this man came to take you back with him. Two Bears asked if I would let him. I told him that the choice was yours."

Mallory stared at Gold Eagle, speechless at his reply.

"You heard him, Mallory." Charles's tone was gruff. "He doesn't care if you leave. He won't stop you."

Mallory remained motionless and Charles took her arm.

"Let's go."

Gold Eagle took a warning step toward him. "Release her."

"Mallory's going back with me!"

"Release her."

Charles's hands balled into tight fists as they dropped to his sides. "Tell him you want to leave, Mallory."

Mallory stared at Gold Eagle, hardly recognizing the menacing man who looked back at her. What was wrong with him? Where was the gentle lover who had held her in his arms, who had warmed her flesh with his, speaking of forever?

She whispered to him, "Surely you don't doubt what I want to do."

No reply.

"Let's go, Mallory." Charles again took her arm.

With a silent blur of movement, Gold Eagle grasped Charles in a choking grip. Holding him helpless, he pressed his knife to Charles's throat.

Charles's men were immediately surrounded, but Mallory saw only the glinting blade at Charles's throat as she rasped, "Let him go! Please!"

Gold Eagle's blade did not relent and Mallory appealed more softly, "Please, don't do this, Gold Eagle! Charles is my friend. I don't want him hurt."

Gold Eagle's gaze met hers and Mallory entreated further, "Charles doesn't understand. I need to talk to him alone . . . to explain."

"No."

"Gold Eagle . . ." Mallory whispered, "You know I won't leave with him. I couldn't. But I have to make him understand why."

Mallory sensed the war that raged inside Gold Eagle before he released Charles abruptly. Speaking a brief Cheyenne command that dispersed the crowd, he walked away just as suddenly, without glancing in her direction.

Quivering with barely restrained wrath, Charles addressed his men. "Mount up. We're leaving and we're taking Miss Tompkins with us."

"No, I won't go."

Charles looked back at Mallory. "That savage doesn't frighten me, and I'm not going to let him scare you into staying with him."

"We have to talk, Charles."

Mallory took his hand.

"You can't stay! I won't let you!"

"You can't stop me, Charles."

They had walked a distance from the village. They stood on a rise of land warmed by the afternoon sun as Charles looked at Mallory incredulously.

"Do you know what you're saying? Do you realize that General Cotter has reached Fort Larned by now with a force strong enough to annihilate this whole village?"

"He won't attack, will he, Charles?"

Charles paused in reply, his gaze wandering the exquisite face turned up so anxiously to his. She *was* more beautiful than he remembered.

"Charles?"

Charles struggled against the need to take Mallory into his arms and hold her close—to assure himself that this wasn't another dream, that she was truly standing in front of him at last.

"Charles . . ."

"We need to leave here as quickly as possible, Mallory. I don't want you to be in the middle of things if they go bad."

"They won't. The Cheyenne don't want to fight. They only want to be left alone to lead their lives the way they always have."

"Mallory . . ." Charles glanced around them. The sun was already descending toward the horizon. They needed to start back immediately, so they could put enough distance between them and the village to guarantee their safety. It was time for brutal honesty.

"That won't happen, Mallory."

"What do you mean?"

"General Cotter wasn't sent all this way with a force the size of the one he's commanding to negotiate peace."

Mallory's face paled as she repeated, "What do you mean?"

"Cotter will make demands. Whatever they are, Two Bears will have to agree to them."

"And if they aren't reasonable?"

"You know that answer as well as I do."

"No . . ."

Mallory's breast was heaving under the heavy coat she wore. Her lips quivered as she struggled against emotion. The devastation in her expression tore at his heart as Charles urged, "Get your things together, Mallory. We have to leave as quickly as possible."

Unprepared for the reaction his words evoked, Charles watched as Mallory's chin rose. "I'm not going to leave."

"You must!"

"I'm going to tell Gold Eagle what you said about Major General Cotter. He'll know what to do."

"Think of what you're saying, Mallory! You're saying you're going to warn the enemy!"

"Gold Eagle's not my enemy!"

"Stop—stop right there!" Charles was suddenly angry. "Gold Eagle went to Fort Larned under false pretenses, pretending to be a man he killed."

"He didn't kill Matthew Bower!"

"How do you know he didn't?"

"How do you know he did?"

Charles abandoned that tack.

"He went to the fort to spy on the people there."

"Because he wanted to know if the rumors about Cotter were true."

"He attacked Captain Tierney before he left! Only a savage would've cut off the man's ear!"

Mallory's face again paled. She closed her

eyes briefly. "And now he knows Captain Tierney attacked me."

"Tierney *attacked* you?" Charles struggled to control his rage. "I'll make sure he pays for that." He shook his head. "Whatever you're thinking, I want you to remember—you're not one of these people. What do you expect will happen to you when Cotter shows up with his artillery? Even if you manage to escape the barrage, these people will turn on you when the blood starts flowing."

"Gold Eagle won't let that happen!"

"The man's a savage! How can you trust him?"

"Because he loves me!"

"Mallory!"

The pain of the moment almost more than he could bear, Charles was momentarily speechless as Mallory whispered, "And I love him, Charles."

"You don't know what you're saying."

"I do! Charles, please listen and try to understand." Her hand on his arm, Mallory moved closer to him. Her gaze was fervent. "You see Gold Eagle as a savage and your enemy. You refuse to see past his physical appearance to the man beneath. It isn't that way with me. I sensed the man beneath his exterior the first moment I met him. In him, I recognized a part of myself that I hadn't even realized I'd been searching for. But now that I've found him, I've found myself. He's a part of me. I can't leave him."

"No." Charles shook his head again. "No! I

don't know what he did to you, but you're confused."

"I was never more clear about anything in my life." Mallory's eyes filled. "Try to understand. I can't leave him."

"Mallory . . ."

"Please, Charles, go back and tell General Cotter that the Cheyenne want peace. Stop him from attacking any way you can."

"You know I'd do anything for you, Mallory, but that would be a waste of time."

"Please."

Oh, God . . . how he loved her.

Desperation touched Charles's mind. He would *do* anything, *say* anything, to convince her to come back with him. It was her only chance of survival.

"Charles?"

"All right, come back with me and we'll both speak to Cotter. You can tell him what you've seen here, and together we'll convince him to tread with caution."

"I . . . I can't."

Noting Mallory's hesitation, Charles pressed, "I can't question your love for Gold Eagle." His stomach twisting at the words, he continued more earnestly, "But I can question your judgment in staying here. Don't you realize that the only thing you can accomplish by staying is to watch the slaughter—while if you come back with me and talk to Cotter, you can prevent it?"

"I can't leave!"

"If you really love Gold Eagle, if you want to

help these people, if you want to stop the bloodshed that'll be inevitable if Cotter advances, there's only one thing you can do."

Mallory was wavering. He saw her tears welling. He saw her brave chin wobble . . . and when she stepped into his arms at last, he closed them tightly around her.

A distance away, Gold Eagle watched their earnest exchange. He saw the lieutenant pleading with Mallory, and he saw Mallory's ardent responses. The conversation was intense.

Mallory moved closer to the lieutenant. She placed her hand on his arm. A fierce, blinding emotion brought Gold Eagle a step forward as she raised her face to the other man's. The sunlight glinted on her hair, and Gold Eagle closed his eyes against the pain ripping through him as another man indulged himself in her beauty.

But he knew the danger Mallory faced if she remained at his side. He had suffered at the thought of it. When the lieutenant appeared, he knew the true test of his love was at hand.

He had told Mallory she was free to go. He had forced himself to put a distance between them, wanting the decision to be hers alone—but despite all that he had said and done, he had not believed she would leave him.

Gold Eagle opened his eyes to see Mallory step forward into the lieutenant's arms.

Fearing the consequences of the sudden rage that flared to life inside him, Gold Eagle turned to his horse. He mounted, leaving the scene of his despair behind him.

He had ridden until his mount could run no more. He had then dismounted, leading the wheezing animal behind him as he walked on. The sun dropped below the horizon and the land went dark, but he had no desire to return to the village. Seated with his robe around him, he passed the night hours battling the cold and the image of Mallory in another man's arms.

But the sun rose and the weight of a familiar burden pressed anew. Time was growing short. The destiny revealed in the sunlight of a sacred hilltop called out to him.

His heart heavy, Gold Eagle responded to its call.

The morning was unnaturally still when he arrived back at the camp. His duties would be many in the dangerous days ahead. They would occupy his time, driving the image of fiery hair and glowing eyes from his mind. They would fill the empty hours, and he would welcome their burden.

Dismounting at his lodge, Gold Eagle paused, dreading the silence within.

Gathering his courage, Gold Eagle pushed aside the flap and went inside.

His stood stock still, his joy profound when Mallory walked into his arms.

Chapter Twelve

Major General Cotter rode his horse with rigid military bearing as his contingent moved steadily forward. Livid, he was unaffected by the midday chill that continued despite the bright sunshine beating down on the prairie.

He had waited two days at Fort Larned for a response to his communication to the Cheyenne, only to find that it had been a total waste of time! He was tired of the endless delays encountered in his extended trek across this frozen, desolate wasteland which was fit only for the likes of the savages who inhabited it. He was filled with contempt for the military personnel stationed there who were incapable of accomplishing even the simplest assignment. And he was sick to death of the total lack of military professionalism in this godforsaken wilderness!

Cotter seethed. A case in point was the courier detachment he had met en route as it returned from the Cheyenne village almost a full day after his force had left Fort Larned.

Cotter listed again in his mind the ludicrous excuses they had given for simple incompetence.

The journey had been impossible to accomplish in the time allotted.

Indeed!

Two Bears and his lesser chiefs were not averse to returning with the detachment as demanded, but their horses were too weak to make the return journey to the fort.

Rot!

They could not force Two Bears to return to the fort because the detachment was vastly outnumbered.

Cowards!

It galled him even further that the detachment had left the Cheyenne without receiving a clear answer as to when the chief intended to comply with his demand.

Not that he had intended to wait.

Cotter glanced at Captain Tierney, riding beside him. Arthur was the only officer he had met on the frontier who was truly worth a damn! His grasp of the Cheyenne situation was clear and complete, and he conveyed it with conviction. He had not allowed his extended assignment among lax military personnel to contaminate his attitude. He knew who his country's enemies were, and he wasn't afraid to do what needed to be done.

Cotter suppressed a sneer. Major Bernard Abbott was another story. He was an Indian-lover and an officer who had forgotten a simple military precept—that there was no substitute for victory.

And then there was Lieutenant Charles Moore. Arthur had filled him in on the background there. Jealousy had affected the fellow adversely, severely damaging the potential for a bright military career. Moore was obsessed with Mallory Tompkins. Against Major Abbott's orders, he had gone to the Cheyenne village to bring her back. When he failed to do that, he had been so fearful that she might be injured, he had actually returned to make a personal appeal to him, claiming the Indians were peaceful.

But Lieutenant Moore wasn't a coward, of that he was sure. He wasn't an Indian-lover, either. That fact had been evident when one of his aides inadvertently mentioned the man called Gold Eagle. For that reason, Cotter had consented to Moore's request to join his force.

A cold wind gusted, and Cotter cursed the contingent's ponderous pace. He turned to the only man he could fully trust for accurate information on the area.

"How much longer do you expect it will be before we reach the Cheyenne village, Arthur?"

"We should reach the village in a few hours, sir."

Turning to a nearby aide, Cotter snapped,

"Send out another scout. I don't want any surprises."

"I'll be happy to ride ahead to reconnoiter, sir."

Cotter turned toward Arthur with surprise. "I don't think that'll be necessary. I have several scouts whom I can trust to do the job."

Arthur's brow furrowed. "They aren't as familiar with the territory as I am, sir, and in light of the threat they're likely to encounter—"

"They're good men. They can handle it. You're more valuable to me here. You'll get your chance to face the Cheyenne."

"Yes, sir."

Cotter couldn't help smiling. Arthur was disappointed. Arthur was as sick of waiting as he was. He couldn't wait to get into the fray. Brave fellow. Well, it wouldn't be long now.

Cotter turned again to his aide. "Let's move a little faster. I don't want to reach the village at sundown."

Overlooking the Cheyenne camp from a nearby rise, Gold Eagle sat his horse in silence. The sun had passed the midday mark and activity below him continued at a leisurely pace. Cooking fires burned in every lodge, sending narrow streams of smoke into the clear air. A few women could be seen between the lodges, their heads bent over their tasks. Several horses grazed on the sparse pickings a short distance from camp while men busied themselves nearby. The scene was peaceful, not unlike many Gold Eagle had observed over the years, but he gained little comfort from it as he scanned the horizon with apprehension.

The past several days had been anything but peaceful. Lieutenant Moore's arrival had stirred his people, drawing into clearer focus the threat of the great military force that had been reported marching toward them. Many had reasoned that the lieutenant knew the white woman was under Gold Eagle's protection, that he would not have risked coming to take her back to the fort if he did not believe she was in peril if she remained at the camp.

The arrival of Major General Cotter's messenger had added to the feeling of panic. The demands the great general had made, demands that could not possibly be met, had caused still more fear.

The councils had then begun. Two Bears had maintained his position, claiming that he had signed the paper that promised peace. He cited the general's unfamiliarity with the area, saying the great man did not understand the difficulties which made it impossible to meet his demands. He had been sure the great general would not attack them.

Walking Buffalo had then spoken. His gaunt figure contrasting sharply with Two Bears' thick frame, he had described the visions he had seen in the smoke, visions of blazing flames which far surpassed the small fire in which they appeared, and of screams that would echo long after the actual sound had ceased.

Others had then stepped forward—White Otter, Yellow Hawk, Tall Bull, and himself—and the council had worn on.

His thoughts interrupted by the sound of a horse's approach, Gold Eagle frowned. Flaming strands of hair flaring out on the crisp breeze, Mallory halted her mount beside his. "Why are you here?" he asked. "Where are Singing Spirit and Little Bird?"

"They're where they should be."

"Why are you not with them?"

"Because I'm where I should be, too."

He knew that look. A line had settled between Mallory's fine brows. Her gaze was so unyielding that she hardly blinked, and her lips were stubbornly set. No words had been necessary the morning he returned to the village, expecting that she would be gone. Their joining had been passionate, all the more precious because they had both known what would soon follow.

In an arduous discussion following the decision of the village council, Mallory's warrior heart had locked with his. The loving battle had not yet ceased.

His jaw firm, Gold Eagle pressed, "You know the danger in what I am soon to do."

Mallory's gaze held his. "Yes."

"I do not want you with me now."

"Yes, you do."

"I do not."

Mallory's lips parted. They stirred in his mind the memory of a sweet taste that ever lingered, of ecstatic gasps in the darkness and rasping words of love that he had sealed within his heart. He saw her lips tremble. "Truth, Gold Eagle."

Truth.

No further words needed to be spoken.

"You bastard!"

The great contingent had briefly halted. Tierney had moved apart from the others to follow nature's call when a hissed voice from behind turned him to see Lieutenant Moore standing a few feet away. Glancing up toward the position where he had last seen General Cotter, he heard the lieutenant grate, "Cotter's not looking this way. He can't save you now."

Tierney straightened up sharply. "I don't need Cotter to save me from you!"

"Yes, you do." The lieutenant walked closer. A hard smile flashed as he looked at the bandage Tierney still wore on his ear. "You can't wait to get at Gold Eagle, can you, so you can even the score for what he did to you? And you don't care how many innocent people get killed along the way."

"Major General Cotter asked me my opinion about the Cheyenne and I gave it to him. They're savages! They're a blight on the frontier, and there's not a man, woman, or child coming into this country who'll be safe until they've been disposed of!"

"You are a bastard!"

"And I'm telling you now, the first Indian I'm

going to take care of when I reach that village will be Gold Eagle."

Moore's eyes narrowed. "Does it surprise you to hear that I don't care what you do to him?" Moore took a menacing step toward him. "We're alone now, so I want to make something else clear, too. I know what you tried to do to Mallory."

"I didn't try to do anything."

"Don't lie!" The lieutenant took a rasping breath. "Just listen, because I'm only going to say this once. Whatever you do when you get to that village, stay away from Mallory."

"I don't want any part of her!"

"If you go anywhere near her, I'll kill you."

Tierney was shuddering with rage. "You're threatening a superior officer!"

Stunned into speechlessness when Lieutenant Moore turned away from him as if he had not spoken and started back in the direction from which he had come, Tierney stood stock still. The inescapable humor of the moment struck him abruptly, and he laughed aloud. The fool had actually threatened him—the fool who was already a dead man.

His impatience growing greater by the hour, Major General Cotter squinted at the horseman approaching. Minutes later, the scout drew his mount to a sliding halt a few feet from him, exclaiming breathlessly, "The Cheyenne village is no more than a few miles over the hill, sir!"

At his right, Arthur tensed as he asked, "Have they seen us, yet?"

"I don't think so, sir." The young cavalryman took a ragged breath. "Everything looks normal, with people walkin' around like nothin's happenin'."

"Good."

"Sir . . ." Cotter turned toward Major Abbott as the officer moved up to address him. "I'd like permission to go ahead to talk to Two Bears. Perhaps I can—"

"Don't waste your breath, Major! I'll do the talking with Two Bears, but not before he sees our might clearly."

"You're making a mistake, sir. If you approach the village with sabers drawn, the Cheyenne will believe they're about to be attacked. There'll be no way back then."

"We'll see who's making a mistake. Step back, Major!"

Turning to his aide, Cotter snapped, "Pass the word back for the cavalry to get ready. We'll ride up within a mile of the camp. We'll deploy the cavalry then, sabers drawn, to allow the artillery time to pull into position. The men at the rear will carry torches to allow the Cheyenne no misinterpretation of the cost should they defy us. The rest will be up to them."

"Don't do it, sir. You're inviting slaughter!"

"I told you to step back, Major Abbott!" Cotter snarled. "Another word and I'll have you taken into custody."

Turning to Arthur where he sat his horse with

anxious anticipation, Cotter addressed him directly. "I know you've been waiting for this, Arthur, just as I have. This will be your moment. I'm putting you in command of the cavalry's advance."

"Sir, you can't do that! Captain Sutter's in command of the cavalry."

Glancing harshly at his aide, Cotter snapped, "I can do it, and I will!" Looking back at Arthur, Cotter saw the eagerness in his eyes as he questioned, "Are you ready, Arthur?"

"Yes, sir!"

His chest heaving, Cotter ordered the contingent forward.

"They're coming!"

Trembling so hard that she could hardly speak, Mallory looked at Gold Eagle, who stood as still as stone, gazing down on the camp basking in the afternoon sun. He was angry with her because she had refused to leave him. She had tried desperately to explain that there was no need for him to be anxious about her safety, that as far as the soldiers were concerned, they had come to liberate her!

She had even tried to convince him to let her ride out and approach General Cotter so she might talk to him, but Gold Eagle had refused. He was concerned it would put her in too much danger, when the glaring truth was that *he* was the one really in danger.

"Gold Eagle, they're getting closer!"

Withdrawing his knife from the sheath at his

waist, Gold Eagle cautiously tilted the blade to flash a reflection of the bright rays of afternoon sun into the village below.

Many Horses looked up from where he worked beside the horses. Mallory watched as he signaled the man beside him, then called softly to others nearby and mounted to relay the news to those farther away.

Turning toward her, Gold Eagle directed, "Go, quickly. Ride toward the far hill and await me there."

Foreboding touched Mallory's mind. This was all happening too fast. She responded flatly, "I won't go without you."

"I will follow as soon as I make the final sweep of the camp."

"I'll wait for you here."

"Mallory . . ." Gold Eagle spoke with quiet urgency, "Your life is more precious to me than my own. With you nearby, I am distracted from my purpose by fear for your safety. Would you put me and those I am pledged to protect at risk because of my love for you?"

"No!"

"Then go, now."

Mallory's lips parted but no sound emerged. Abruptly aware that she had no choice, she turned her mount and started toward the distant hill.

Waiting until Mallory had disappeared from sight, Gold Eagle kicked his mount into motion. He rode a circuitous route around the village.

He saw Two Horns and Tall Bear slowly moving out of sight. He observed Yellow Fox and Burnt Antelope mounting at the far side of the camp where their horses were tied. He noted several others, all moving slowly, so as to arouse no notice—while before the lodges the women remained seated at their tasks.

A fleeting smile touched Gold Eagle's lips, knowing those same "women"—sacks carefully shaped and dressed—had maintained those positions since the day the decision of the council was reached. In the meanwhile, the people of the village had been gradually dispersing, scattering across the prairie in small groups with all they could carry. Most were already days into their journey, traveling in diverse directions that would confuse a force ill-trained in tracking on the Western frontier. A few warriors had remained to maintain the appearance of an active village, thereby granting time for the wind and sun to dull the trails further.

His carriage erect, his heart cold, Gold Eagle noted the success of a plan that would grant the Cheyenne time to gather again later, to grow strong again and eventually negotiate with the army from a position of strength, rather than weakness.

Gold Eagle held that thought in his mind as he continued to scour the camp with his gaze. Mallory awaited him on the hill. He would go to her soon, and together they would plan for a future where his people could hold their heads high, where peace would not be attained at the cost of dignity.

His attention acute, Gold Eagle watched the movement of the contingent. He saw the cavalry gather, then move forward at an echoing command. Drawn sabers glinted in the bright sunlight as they galloped toward the camp, halting to form a bold, intimidating line. Behind them, he saw the contingent stop its forward press as the great guns were rapidly moved into position.

The truth was suddenly clear, and he praised the collective wisdom that had allowed his people to withdraw to safety before the carnage could begin.

Scrutinizing the camp one last time, Gold Eagle saw that the last of the Cheyenne braves had withdrawn and were heading over a rise in the distance. The intended massacre of his people had been averted and he—

Gold Eagle's heart stopped cold at the sight of a familiar flash of red hair on a rise beside the camp.

Mallory.

She had been unwilling to leave the camp and Gold Eagle. She had ridden out of sight, remaining there until Gold Eagle became involved in his last check of the camp before she returned. But what she saw now chilled her.

Mounted on a rise beside the camp, Mallory watched with horror as drawn sabers flashed in the sunlight, as artillery drew into line in the distance, as commands echoing on the crisp air revealed the army's true intent with a clarity that could no longer be denied.

Major General Cotter stood poised to annihilate a peaceful village! The plan was suddenly clear. He only awaited the first shot that would ring out from the camp, the first war cry, the first arrow that might fall at the feet of the cavalry, before he would order the charge that would end forever this Cheyenne village's resistance!

Bitter laughter rose in Mallory's throat. Gold Eagle had been right all along! She had been too much of a fool to recognize the true reason for Cotter's advance. She was grateful that Gold Eagle had not allowed her to influence him. There would be no slaughter this day. The camp was cleared of all its people, and Gold Eagle, presently circling the rear of the camp, would soon be safe as well.

The sabers flashed, but there was no one to respond to their threat.

What . . . what was that?

Her gaze drawn to a flash of movement in the camp, Mallory caught her breath. A child. A boy of no more than ten years emerged from a lodge near the entrance to the camp with a rifle in his hands.

Red Hat stood proudly beside his father's lodge, his father's rifle in his hands. The other warriors of his camp had run away, fearing the soldiers' advance, but he was not afraid! The spirit of his dead father lived in him—the father who had been taken by the army to the soldiers' fort for stealing horses he had found wandering on Cheyenne land, the father who had been tried in the white man's court and who had been hanged with the white man's rope for all to see.

Red Hat raised his rifle. He would avenge his father's spirit! He would take the lives of the soldiers who had killed his father and who now threatened his village.

He was not afraid!

Mallory gasped aloud as Red Hat raised his rifle. She knew the boy. She had heard him speak of his father's death at the hands of the soldiers. He would kill someone and be killed in return— all to no avail! She could stop him if she got to him in time! The soldiers would listen to her. They weren't her enemy.

Her decision abruptly made, Mallory dug her heels into her mount's sides. She saw the heads of the cavalrymen turn toward her as she approached the village, riding recklessly. She saw Red Hat glance uncertainly at her as she neared him. She saw his rifle arm waver. She saw the child beneath the boy's angry exterior emerge in a split second of truth.

Captain Tierney's face flushed bright with rage as he sat his mount at the head of the cavalry. He watched as the red-haired witch appeared as if from nowhere and began racing her horse toward the Cheyenne camp. He knew what she was trying to do! She was trying to halt their advance with her presence, but he wouldn't let her. This was his moment of glory!

The Indian boy was the only Cheyenne who had shown himself, but his rifle was raised. That was all Tierney needed.

He drew his gun. Glancing at the officer beside him, he shouted, "Strike the torches, Lieutenant!"

"Sir?"

"Strike the torches and ready the advance!"

The red-haired witch had almost reached the boy! The smell of burning torches suddenly thick on the air, Tierney raised his gun.

Her horse was laboring, but she had almost reached Red Hat. The boy looked at her uncertainly. Mallory saw his indecision clearly.

Pressing her mount to the limit, Mallory did not see the gun aimed in her direction. Nor did she see the moment of triumph in Tierney's eyes as his finger twitched on the trigger, releasing a sudden bark of sound and a bullet that struck with blinding pain in her back.

Stunned into a moment of paralyzing realization, Mallory gasped, seeing the unexpected end to all that had been as the darkness closed around her.

Already racing toward Mallory, Gold Eagle heard the shot as it was fired. With a shout of tormented denial, he saw Mallory's body jerk with the impact of the bullet that struck her. He saw Red Hat fire back in response, then lower his gun in bewilderment as Mallory pitched to the ground a few feet from where he stood.

There was a sudden barrage of gunfire. Gold Eagle's rage knew no bounds when he saw the cavalry advancing on the camp with torches lit. He looked back to the spot where Mallory had fallen and saw Red Hat dragging her limp body into his lodge. He pressed his mount steadily forward.

Mallory, who was life. Mallory, who was the future. Mallory, who—

A bullet struck him, jolting him upright. His vision dimming, Gold Eagle denied the pain, continuing forward.

A second bullet struck.

The third bullet slumped him forward.

Sliding from his racing mount, hardly conscious of the impact as his body struck the ground, Gold Eagle called out to his thwarted destiny.

Darkness clouded Gold Eagle's mind, but he struggled against it. He heard hoofbeats pounding the ground around him. He smelled the choking smoke. Forcing his eyes open at last, he saw the peaceful Cheyenne village transformed into a scene of raging chaos.

He heard Mallory scream! The wail resounded in his mind as he struggled to see into the smoke-filled distance, as his anguished fears were confirmed. Red Hat's lodge was engulfed in flames.

Mallory screamed again and again as the flames licked at the sides of the lodge. But as a compassionate darkness closed around him, Gold Eagle heard the sounds no more.

Chapter Thirteen

Mallory's dying screams echoed again in his mind.

Lying on a narrow cot, Gold Eagle looked out through the barred window of the fort stockade. The sun shone in the yard beyond, its brightness in glaring contrast to the darkness that had enveloped his soul.

He had awakened in the same cell weeks earlier to find his wounds bandaged and tended by a silent physician who had been brought to the fort specifically to treat him. The doctor had looked at him coldly, had treated him roughly, and had spoken little, except to say that he would soon be well enough to hang.

The thought did not intimidate him.

Instead, his mind had been filled with images

he could not evade. Mallory raced her mount across his dreams nightly, just as she had across the snow-covered ground toward the lodge where Red Hat stood. The bullet that struck her rocked him with greater impact at each repetition, piercing him with a pain far greater than any his physical wounds caused. Her screams haunted him, allowing him no rest.

Denied any further information about that day, Gold Eagle had gleaned bits and pieces from his guards' conversations. In his rage at finding the village empty, the great general had burned it to the ground to ensure that the Cheyenne could not return. The guards' laughter at his people's homeless wanderings through the winter cold had raised a rage in Gold Eagle that was surpassed only by the thought of his own inability to help them.

During the silent hours as he fought to regain his strength, Gold Eagle had reviewed in his mind his failure to achieve his destiny. He had berated himself as he acknowledged that instead of achieving the ultimate victory he had sought for his people, he had allowed them to fall into a misfortune he had never foreseen.

But all had not yet ended.

Gold Eagle's powerful chest expanded as he drew a bracing breath into his lungs. He was well again, and his plans had been carefully formed. In the presence of others, he allowed his hands to tremble, although his arms were stable. He feigned a halting step, although his legs were strong. He spoke in an infirm tone, although the desire to roar his rage at the injustice that had been done grew almost uncontrollable.

He awaited the chance soon to come.

The sound of a familiar footstep outside the door of his cell raised a hard smile to Gold Eagle's lips. He had been allowed one visitor during his recuperation, and he awaited that person with great anticipation.

Gold Eagle pretended a half sleep as the door was pushed open and the expected, uniformed figure stepped into his view.

"You really are a malingerer, aren't you?" Meticulously groomed, his gaze triumphant, Captain Tierney looked down at him with contempt. "You're not fooling anyone, you know. Your wounds are almost healed. You're just pretending your weakness, and I know why. You know what's waiting for you, don't you?"

Tierney did not wait for his reply. "Just in case you aren't aware, a military entourage has already been dispatched. It's due to arrive here at any moment to transport you in chains to an undisclosed location, where you will then be tried for murder."

Captain Tierney laughed aloud. "You *are* a white man, you know. That fact hasn't escaped the notice of military authorities, although you try to deny it. Sentiment is running high against you on the frontier. A white man turning against his own—they're going to make you pay!"

Tierney's smile became a sneer. "I'm going to testify against you." Unconsciously raising his hand to the stub of his ear, he continued with growing heat, "You've provided me with excellent proof that you're a savage. A civilized jury will be repelled by the barbaric mutilation you performed. There will be no one to speak in your defense. It really is unfortunate that the fiery Miss Mallory Tompkins isn't here anymore."

Reacting to Tierney's provocation for the first time, Gold Eagle glared at him with a true rage that sparked Tierney's laughing shout. "So, you do have a spark of manhood left in you! That's good. I'd prefer to see you fight and squirm as the noose is tied around your neck, rather than see you plead for your life. It'll give me so much more pleasure that way."

Hatred churned inside Gold Eagle as Tierney continued his vocal abuse.

"Just in case you're wondering, Major Abbott won't be testifying in your defense, either. He's been reassigned at Major General Cotter's request, and a note's been put in his file stating that he's an Indian-lover. If you're wondering what happened to Lieutenant Moore—unfortunately, he was shot during the melee at the camp and General Cotter saw to it that he was shipped directly back to Major Bullen's command to recover. He's been barred from testifying in your case because of prejudice. Oh, yes . . . General Cotter has pushed on deeper into the frontier. He'll only remain a month longer before returning to Washington, but he's made a statement to be read at your trial that's sure to tighten the rope around your neck. As for me, you know that Cotter put me in charge here at Fort Larned until someone else can be assigned to take over. He's also written me up for a promotion for my performance at the Cheyenne camp."

Widening his stance, Tierney looked down at Gold Eagle with a smile of pure malice. "You bastard, you're going to pay for what you did to me. And if I can arrange it, I'll personally tie that rope around your neck!"

Glowering a moment longer, Tierney whispered, "Before I go, I want to tell you something else, so you may fully appreciate the extent of my reprisal. You see, I fired the bullet that brought Miss Mallory Tompkins down."

His rage held barely in check, Gold Eagle watched as Tierney smiled, then turned abruptly, instructing the guards as he departed, "Watch him closely. The bastard's a coward, but he's desperate. He might try something."

The bars slammed shut behind Tierney.

Shuddering with fury, Gold Eagle closed his eyes. It wouldn't be long now.

Gold Eagle heard the military entourage when it arrived to transport him. The excitement generated in the courtyard could not be mistaken, and Gold Eagle frowned. He hadn't expected that it would arrive so soon. He had hoped for another few days so he might ensure the success of his plan, but he could put it off no longer.

Slowly, unsteadily, aware that his every move was watched, Gold Eagle drew on his buckskin leggings. He did not turn as the guard taunted, "What're you doin', Gold Eagle? Gettin' ready for company?"

Not deigning to reply, Gold Eagle walked to the bucket in the corner to relieve himself. His weak step faltered. He reached out to steady himself on the wall, but his hand slipped. Falling heavily to the floor, he lay flat on his stomach, breathing heavily.

"Get up!"

Gold Eagle attempted to raise himself, only to collapse more heavily than before.

"Get up, I said!"

Gold Eagle did not move.

"What in hell's the matter with him?" Mumbling under his breath, the guard called out to the soldier at the end of the corridor, "Walters, get down here! I have to go into the cell. It won't look too good if them fellas come all this way and find this white Injun lyin' on the floor the way he is."

Motionless as the cell door creaked open, Gold Eagle heard the guard's approaching step.

"Get up!"

He did not move.

"Get up, I said!"

Springing to his feet in a flash of movement, Gold Eagle retrieved a gun from behind the bucket and snaked his arm around the guard's neck. He held the man helpless as he hissed to the sentry outside the door, "If you make a sound, I'll shoot!"

Both men were unconscious on the floor behind him when Gold Eagle moved slowly down the corridor.

They had finally come for the savage bastard!

Captain Tierney drew a mirror from the desk drawer and checked his appearance. He looked well. He looked *impressive*.

Slamming the drawer shut, Tierney waited. He had heard the sentry at the gate announce the arrival of the military entourage. It had been a long several weeks while he had watched Gold Eagle's slow recuperation from his wounds. Three wounds—one that had narrowly missed his heart—yet the barbarian had hung on! He had cursed that last bullet for its near miss, but he had later told himself the best was yet to come.

Actually, he had come to enjoy Gold Eagle's confinement. Those weekly visits when he had tormented the self-proclaimed Cheyenne with what he told him—and with what he neglected to tell him—had helped to soothe the rage he felt each time he looked in the mirror and the horror of his mutilation was renewed. But it wouldn't be long now.

Gold Eagle would be removed from the fort in chains. He would be paraded through the streets of every town he passed so all might witness his humiliation. Only the moment when

Gold Eagle's body dangled from the end of a rope could surpass the pleasure those sights would evoke!

What was taking the entourage so long to reach his office? He had decided against going out into the fort yard to greet them, preferring instead to remain in his office where they might be formally presented *to him*.

Tierney fidgeted, curiosity finally raising him to his feet to approach the door. Damn it all, where were they?

No longer able to control his impatience, Tierney jerked open the door. He gasped aloud at the unexpected sight of Gold Eagle standing there, gun in hand.

Thrust suddenly backward, Tierney stumbled, finally striking the floor with a harsh jolt. Wheezing with fear when Gold Eagle drew a blade against his throat, he looked up into the pale eyes of death.

"Do you recognize this blade?" Not waiting for Tierney's reply, Gold Eagle rasped, "It was returned to me by a friend. I prefer it to the gun that allowed me to escape my cell, because this blade knows your flesh well."

"Bastard!" Tierney raged. "You'll never get out of this fort alive!"

Gold Eagle hissed, "You care for your life as I do not. I care only to see you cringe as I draw your blood. I seek only to feel your fear when I bury my blade in your heart. I aspire only to speak the name of the woman whose life you ended, at the same moment when I end yours!"

"No—that isn't true!"

"You deny your fear even as it quakes through you."

"You don't understand! I didn't kill Mallory!"

"Liar!"

"No, I—"

The sound of pounding footsteps outside the door raised Gold Eagle's head. Prolonging the moment before pressing his blade home, Gold Eagle looked up as the door swung open.

Mallory!

Motionless, Gold Eagle stared at the apparition in the doorway. Fiery hair bright, clear eyes moist, she whispered, "Don't kill him, Gold Eagle."

Gold Eagle's heart pounded as he held his knife firm.

"Please . . ." Mallory entered the room and approached him slowly, "I'm all right. I was shot. My head hit the ground when I fell from my horse, and the next thing I remember, I was at home in Chicago. It took me a while to recall what had happened—to put it all together—but when I did and I found out they intended to make an example out of you by trying you in the white man's court for murder, I tried to contact you. All my letters and wires were returned."

Tierney . . .

Gold Eagle's knife moved against Tierney's neck.

"No! Please!" Her plea was meant as well for the uniformed soldiers behind her. Mallory turned to indicate the older man at her side as she whispered to Gold Eagle, "This is my father. I explained everything to him and we went to the authorities together. These soldiers have come to take Captain Tierney into custody!"

No. Gold Eagle's blade twitched at Tierney's throat. There was no justice for the Cheyenne.

"Don't, Gold Eagle." Close to tears, Mallory moved closer still. He could see that she was thinner, her skin pale, but her beauty was undiminished as she pleaded tensely, "If you use that blade now, it'll forever brand you and all Cheyennes as savage. It'll sever any chance of understanding for your people, and it'll bring new waves of soldiers into this country to hunt your people down. Gold Eagle, please . . ."

Her chest heaving with the zeal of her words, she whispered, "By shedding Captain Tierney's blood, you'll shed your own, and the pain of that would be more than I could bear."

Mallory's anguish shuddered through Gold Eagle. He ached to hold her, to assure her that he would never be separated from her again, but reality held him fast. He would never be judged fairly in courts run by men such as Captain Tierney. He would not allow those courts to imprison him, or end his life at the end of a rope like those of many trusting Cheyenne before him.

Mallory was standing so close that he saw the shimmering trail of the tear that marked her cheek as she implored him, "Don't sacrifice our life together for a vengeance that will only bring tragedy."

Those words lingered as Mallory whispered, "Truth, Gold Eagle—to lose you now would be to lose my heart." Her glittering gaze held his. "What is your truth?"

Her final plea was one he could not deny. The wall of doubt within him shattered, and Gold Eagle whispered in return, "There is only one truth."

Releasing Captain Tierney to fall into a shaken heap upon the floor, Gold Eagle stood up. Love in his eyes and in his heart, in the touch of his hands and of his lips, he took Mallory into his arms.

Epilogue

The train bumped and swayed along the track. The clatter of the rails was a familiar cacophony of sound as Mallory looked out through the soot-streaked pane toward a vast prairie that glowed in the summer sun.

The train whistle blasted shrilly, sending another dense cloud of smoke up into the warm afternoon air.

Glancing at the man seated silently beside her, Mallory saw a fellow whose appearance was not unlike the Matthew Bower she had once known. But there was a difference. His pale hair unbound against well-tailored shoulders, he wore the clothing of a white man with no pretense that he was one. The eagle feather worn proudly in his hair proclaimed that he

387

was Gold Eagle, a man of the Cheyenne people, as he would always be.

Mallory indulged herself in the sight of him. The legal proceedings against Gold Eagle had been dismissed. They were returning from Washington, where they had been invited to confer at a meeting held in the highest office of the land. Gold Eagle had spoken eloquently of his people's love for the land of their fathers, of their need to remain close to it, and their desire for peace. She had affirmed all that he had said and made a plea of her own, but when it was through, she and Gold Eagle both knew that there was much more to be done before his people's future would be secure.

Other matters had been brought to a conclusion at that meeting also. Major General Cotter had been recalled from the frontier. They had been assured that he would not be allowed to return. Captain Tierney was facing charges that would bring his career and perhaps even his life to a bitter end. Major Abbott had been reinstated at his post. He had been appointed agent for the Cheyenne and his record had been cleared.

Stunned when Charles had appeared unexpectedly at the meeting, Mallory had hugged him tightly, her affection for him never more sincere. She and Gold Eagle had listened as he clearly and earnestly stated the facts of the incidents he had witnessed, and it was revealed for the first time that it was Charles who had pulled her from the burning lodge before he himself was wounded.

Mallory remembered with genuine warmth the moments after the meeting when Gold Eagle and Charles stood together, no longer enemies. She had suppressed a tear at the flash of longing in Charles's eyes when they said their farewells. Her heart had lifted when he mentioned a woman named Jewel and his intention to visit her. She hoped that woman recognized the true value in Charles's honest dark eyes and earnest smile. She surely did.

Before leaving Washington, Gold Eagle and she had visited the home of Matthew Bower. They had put into his widow's trembling hands the journals in which her husband had so faithfully recorded the cures that had helped so many. She knew the dear woman would put the journals to good use, while keeping Gold Eagle's words in her heart.

They were returning to Gold Eagle's people, who had lost much, but who approached each day with new hope. She was filled with hope as well that the articles which she would continue to forward to her father's newspaper, *under her own byline*, would bring new understanding to all who read them.

They would stop briefly at Fort Larned to visit Corporal Walker and Penelope Dolan, who had joined forces in Gold Eagle's hour of need to slip a gun into his cell so he might escape. She knew that Gold Eagle would never forget their act of friendship.

Then, they would go *home*.

Mallory looked up into Gold Eagle's eyes as he regarded her silently. She recalled that she had once considered those eyes cold, but they were cold no more.

The train drew to a halt. They disembarked in silence.

Riding across the welcoming prairie at last, Gold Eagle was again dressed in buckskins. The white man's civilization was far behind them when he drew his mount to an unexpected halt and turned to Mallory.

Silent for long moments, Gold Eagle whispered, "I would have you tell me now if you are truly happy."

Mallory released a relieved breath. Touching the ring Gold Eagle had placed on her finger when he repeated the white man's vows for her benefit, she responded, "I am. I am very happy."

Suddenly uncertain, she inquired in return, "Are you happy, Gold Eagle?"

Gold Eagle swept her from her saddle unexpectedly. Settling her in front of him, he drew her back intimately against him as he had done once before. His strong arms tight around her, his lips against her ear, he replied in a voice that throbbed with emotion, "You are my love. You are my life. You are *mine*."

Truth.

Yes, she was his—always and forever.

ELAINE BARBIERI

Dangerous Virtues

Purity

Purity, Honesty, Chastity—They were all admirable traits, but when they came in the form of three headstrong, spirited, sinfully lovely sisters, they were...

Dangerous Virtues

From the moment Purity sees the stranger's magnificent body, she feels anything but what her name implies. Who is the mysterious half-breed who has bushwhacked the trail drive she is leading? And why does she find it impossible to forget his blazing, green-eyed gaze?

Though Pale Wolf attacks her, though he is as driven to discover his brother's killer as she is to find her long-lost sisters, Purity longs to make him a part of her life, just as her waiting softness longs to welcome his perfect masculine form. There may be nothing virtuous about her intentions toward Pale Wolf, but she knows that their ultimate joining will be pure paradise.

___4272-X $5.99 US/$6.99 CAN

Dorchester Publishing Co., Inc.
P.O. Box 6640
Wayne, PA 19087-8640

Please add $1.75 for shipping and handling for the first book and $.50 for each book thereafter. NY, NYC, and PA residents, please add appropriate sales tax. No cash, stamps, or C.O.D.s. All orders shipped within 6 weeks via postal service book rate. Canadian orders require $2.00 extra postage and must be paid in U.S. dollars through a U.S. banking facility.

Name_____
Address_____
City_____ State_____ Zip_____
I have enclosed $_____ in payment for the checked book(s).
Payment <u>must</u> accompany all orders. ❑ Please send a free catalog.

WINTER LOVE

NORAH HESS

"Norah Hess overwhelms you with characters who seem to be breathing right next to you!"
—*Romantic Times*

Winter Love. As fresh and enchanting as a new snowfall, Laura has always adored Fletcher Thomas. Yet she fears she will never win the trapper's heart—until one passion-filled night in his father's barn. Lost in his heated caresses, the innocent beauty succumbs to a desire as strong and unpredictable as a Michigan blizzard. But Laura barely clears her head of Fletch's musky scent and the sweet smell of hay before circumstances separate them and threaten to end their winter love.

_3864-1 $5.99 US/$7.99 CAN

MONTANA Angel

THERESA SCOTT

Amberson Hawley can't bring herself to tell the man she loves that she is carrying his child. She has heard stories of women abandoned by men who never really loved them. But one day Justin Harbinger rides into the Triple R Ranch, and Amberson has to pretend that their one night together never happened. Soon, the two find themselves fighting an all-too-familiar attraction. And she wonders if she has been given a second chance at love.

___4392-0 $5.99 US/$6.99 CAN

Theresa Scott

Savage Revenge

"Theresa Scott's romances are tender, exciting, enjoyable, and satisfying!"
—*Romantic Times*

A fiery Indian beauty, Haina will accept no man as her master, not even the virile warrior who has made her his captive. For years their families have been fierce enemies, and now Chance finds a way to exact revenge. He will hold the lovely Haina for ransom, humble her proud spirit, and take his fill of her supple young body. But Haina refuses to submit to his branding kisses and burning caresses. Only exquisite tenderness and everlasting love will bring her to the point of surrender.

___4255-X $5.99 US/$6.99 CAN

Dorchester Publishing Co., Inc.
P.O. Box 6640
Wayne, PA 19087-8640

Determined to ruin those who kept him from his heart's only desire, handsome Guy DeYoung becomes a reckless marauder who rampages the isles intent on revenge. But when he finds his lost love, and takes her as his captive, he will not let her go until she freely gives him her body and soul.

__4456-0 $5.99 US/$6.99 CAN

Dorchester Publishing Co., Inc.
P.O. Box 6640
Wayne, PA 19087-8640

Please add $1.75 for shipping and handling for the first book and $.50 for each book thereafter. NY, NYC, and PA residents, please add appropriate sales tax. No cash, stamps, or C.O.D.s. All orders shipped within 6 weeks via postal service book rate. Canadian orders require $2.00 extra postage and must be paid in U.S. dollars through a U.S. banking facility.

Name_____
Address_____
City_____ State_____ Zip_____
I have enclosed $_____ in payment for the checked book(s).
Payment <u>must</u> accompany all orders. ☐ Please send a free catalog.

Flames of Rapture
Lark Eden

"Great reading!"—*Romantic Times*

When Lyric Solei flees the bustling city for her summer retreat in Salem, Massachusetts, it is a chance for the lovely young psychic to escape the pain so often associated with her special sight. Investigating a mysterious seaside house whose ancient secrets have long beckoned to her, Lyric stumbles upon David Langston, the house's virile new owner, whose strong arms offer her an irresistible temptation. And it is there that Lyric discovers a dusty red coat, which from the time she first lays her gifted hands on it unravels to her its tragic history—and lets her relive the timeless passion that brought it into being.

_52078-8 $4.99 US/$6.99 CAN